EVENING STAR

DEA TRIER MØRCH

EVENING STAR

**TRANSLATED BY
JOAN TATE**

**ILLUSTRATED BY
THE AUTHOR**

SERPENT'S
TAIL

BRITISH LIBRARY CATALOGUING IN PUBLICATION DATA

Mørch, Dea Trier
Evening Star.
I. Title   II. Aftenstjernen. *English*
839.8'1374 [F]   PT 8175.M7/

ISBN 1-85242-118-5

First published as *Aftenstjernen*, by Vindrose, Copenhagen
1982
© 1982 by Dea Trier Mørch. Translation © 1988 by Joan Tate

This edition first published 1988 by
Serpent's Tail, 27 Montpelier Grove, London NW5

Typeset by Theatretexts, London

Printed on acid-free paper by
Nørhaven A/S, Viborg, Denmark.

EVENING STAR

It is said that a long time ago, out of pure curiosity, the earth asked the sun for an explanation of the great riddle of life and death.

The following conversation ensued between the earth and her ancestress:

"What does living mean?"

"Asking."

"What does dying mean?"

"Receiving answers."

"So I'm really quite wise," said the earth.

"Yes, you are," replied the sun.

But the earth said nothing and thought to herself: maybe even she doesn't know any more, either.

[from Troels-Lund: *Daily Life in Scandinavia*]

CHARACTERS

Bett (69): *retired headmistress*
her children:
1. Niels Peter (38): *arts graduate and translator*
his children: Jacob (9) *and* Zigzag (7)
2. Mette (34): *teacher*
married to Hans (35): *doctor*
their child: Milla (5)
3. Simon (33): *artist*

Elin: *Bett's sister*
Viggo: *Bett's brother*
Gertrud: *a friend of Bett*
Isia: *Niels Peter's girlfriend*
Ditlev: *Niels Peter's friend and landlord*
Karin: *previously married to Niels Peter*
Bjarne: *Karin's friend*
Lajla: *one of Niels Peter's neighbours*

PLACES

Forest House: *Bett's house in the country*
Marstrand Street: *Niels Peter's apartment in Copenhagen*

TIME

The autumn holiday, 1980
with some flashbacks, particularly over the previous six months

FRIDAY 17 OCTOBER 1980

The evening star is not yet visible — nothing but the half moon in the pale daytime sky.

The rear lights of a taxi disappear down the avenue of half-grown birch trees.

They unlock the door and step into the entrance hall, into the smell of wood and mice. They see their wellington boots, their wooden-soled shoes and their indoor shoes on the floor, neatly in line. Her thin overcoat hanging on the wall. And the mirror.

He puts his backpack down on the kitchen table under the white hanging light shade and starts unpacking the food.

The older of the two boys goes into the living-room, kneels down and strikes a match. Moments later a fire is blazing in the grate.

"Some crates have come," says the younger boy.

"Where are they?"

"Out in the barn. They're those sort of folding packing-cases."

They're sitting in a semi-circle on the coconut matting in front of the fireplace, poking at the fire. Lighted candles in the windows.

He thinks about many previous evenings he'd arrived here. Alone or with the boys. And how she had waited for him. He savours this intense feeling of homecoming.

Despite everything, Forest House has never been so lovely as it is tonight. The fire flickers, throwing shimmering shadows on to the ceiling. The candlelight reflected in the window panes shows twelve candles, not six.

They bring cold bedclothes down from the attic rooms. Tonight all three of them want to sleep in the big low bed in the living-room.

The fire falls in on itself in the fireplace, the embers glowing red and gold.

The boys fall asleep. Zigzag face down. Jacob with an apple in his hand.

Niels Peter lies flat on his back, his hands behind his head and his eyes open.

Then an owl starts hooting, and his sense of unease increases.

In nine months, his life has been completely changed.

The earth circles the sun in a year. The outer planets take longer. The stars in the Milky Way appear to stand still.

None the less, they too are changing — only that change cannot take place within any individual's lifetime, because we don't live long enough.

Everything is change upon change, in one great swirling movement.

In February, he was sitting in his study in Copenhagen translating a book from the Serbo-Croat.

Outside his window — a city humming in the sunlight, a sky containing more white than blue.

"I've translated all my stamps," said Jacob.

He was nine years old. In class three.

"What do you mean, translated?"

"I've translated them from my tatty old album into the new one, silly!"

The boys took turns in hauling each other along on the toboggan.

Came in and brought the cold with them. Both talking excitedly at once:

"Dad, we saw a swan frozen into the lake today."

"And somebody phoned for help. Then a frogman came and went out on the ice."

"The swan was scared. It flapped all over the place. It looked

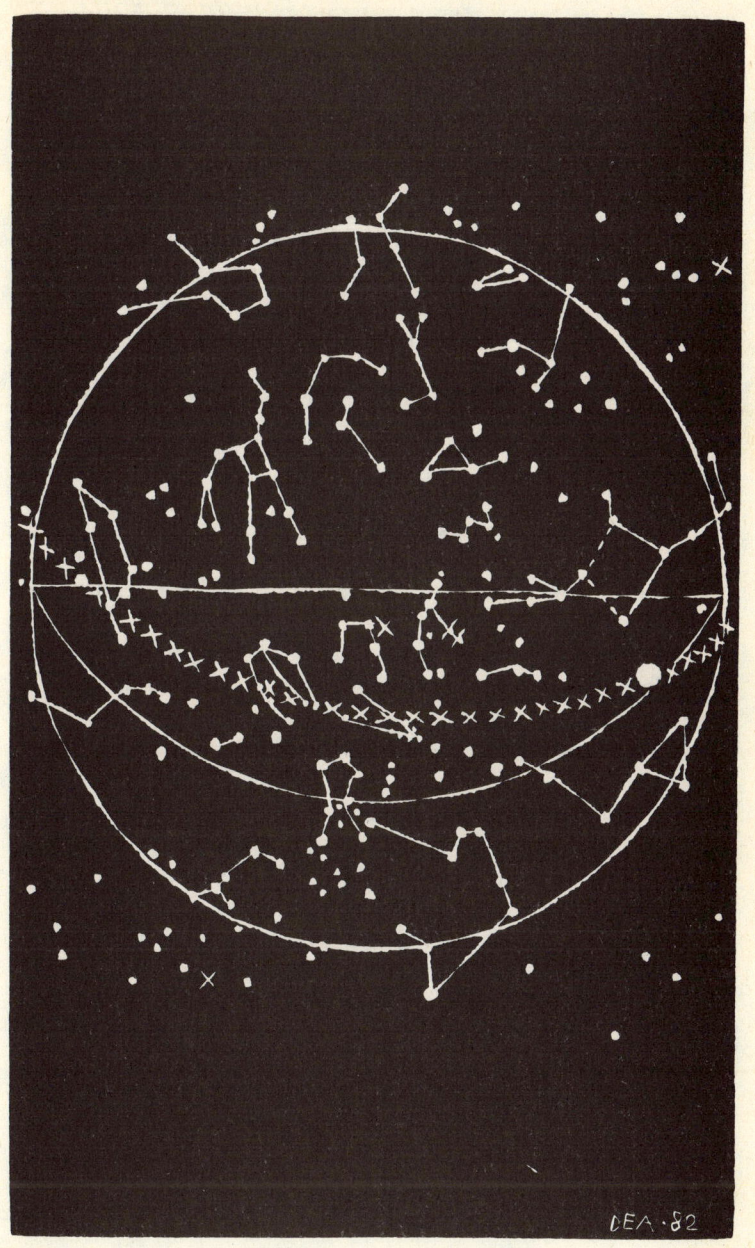

as if it was going to break its wings."

"Then he felt all round it to see if he could get it free."

"Then he pulled out his diver's knife! And shouted at all the children on the bank to turn their heads and look the other way."

"Then it went clonk! Clonk!"

He got them started on their homework.

Zigzag was seven and in class one. He was very keen on learning to read. His older brother helped him.

"T-h-e-r-e-'-s-, it says, a, a k-n-o-c-k-, say 'knock', o-n-, say 'on', t-h-e-, say 'the', 'door', 'there's a knock on the door'."

Karin came to fetch the boys. Their backpacks and green wellies were all ready.

"Look, Mum," cried Zigzag. "My other front tooth's come out."

Karin nodded as she gathered up their belongings.

She never seemed to get further than the hall. She had lived here for so many years, and yet Niels Peter couldn't get her to come into the living-room.

Another one of those long , free weekends — one of the great bonuses that comes with being divorced.

He read the paper. President Tito had had a leg amputated. He strummed on his guitar for a while. Then, taking the thermos with him, he went up to work.

He tuned himself like a violin, planning how many pages he was going to translate each day. What he didn't get done during the course of the week would be finished at the weekend.

He was translating from one minor European language to another, from Serbo-Croat into Danish.

Translating is like playing music from a score. The notes are there and can't be changed. But the interpretation — that's up to the translator.

Was he going to keep it literal, or not? As usual, it depended on the character of the book. The strength of some books lay in the narrative, others more in the language.

The book he was working on at the moment was a novel by a Bosnian author named Selimović.

The publisher had set a May deadline for the translation.

Niels Peter lived in a two-storey rented apartment in Marstrand Street.

His study — books all over the place — was on the top floor, and he slept there in a large double bed. The boys shared a bedroom, and there was a third room, which had been Karin's.

Next to Karin's room was the bathroom and w.c., the electric water-heater and a shower.

On the ground floor was the kitchen-dining area with its various robots — the washing machine, the dishwasher and the coffee maker. From there you went into a simple living-room, containing a cupboard, a sofa, a low table, two folding chairs, a globe of the world, his guitar and the television.

Since he had been alone with the boys, his life had been very simple and spartan.

No pictures on the walls.
No flowers.
No superfluous objects.

The only person he spoke to that weekend was Ditlev.

Ditlev owned the house and lived on the top floor.

They met on the stairs, Ditlev with a French loaf and a newspaper under his arm.

Living in a fog-bound country. Thick, greyish-white mist pouring in like cold clouds from the harbour. A dampness settling on the skin.

After Shrove Tuesday the weather changed. Icy winds pounding the roofs, the window-panes steaming up and dripping. Everything soaking wet. Østerfarimag Street black. Shiny. Dangerous.

Sickening Danish weather.
Infuriating Danish weather!
One should live in a Mediterranean country — five months every year, from November to April. And settle for spending the spring, summer and early autumn in Denmark.

It poured with rain all day. It was incredible that the sky could contain so much water.

In fact it was not bad weather for Niels Peter to work in.

He sent off an article commissioned by a newspaper. Apart from that, he sat in his room with his papers, his books and his typewriter.

After he had been translating for several hours, he could sometimes hardly speak.

The boys talked and talked and asked one question after another. He looked at them. Absent-mindedly. Without really understanding. Unable to find words. Or getting them muddled.

"Have you remembered to put the refrigerator in the milk?" he once asked them.

The boys laughed. He laughed too. But he still couldn't find the right words.

The novel he was translating was called *Death and the Dervish*.

The book was set in Turkish-occupied Bosnia and was about a dervish — a holy man living peacefully in his retreat.

But the dervish's younger brother was being persecuted by the country's tyrannical rulers.

In his desire to prove his brother's innocence, the dervish is forced to become more and more involved in the world outside his monastery.

One day Niels Peter had been teaching at the university. He caught the bus home. Stood behind the driver. It was raining, the windscreen-wipers whirring.

Suddenly he caught sight of his mother on the street and felt a warmth spreading through his body.

But then he caught a glimpse of her face, and it scared him. Her eyes were dark and fixed on the pavement. She was walking slowly, searchingly.

The evening star was in the west when he phoned her to find out if she was all right.

"Everything's fine," said Bett. "Is there anything I can do for you?"

"There's a parents' meeting at the school, the same night as my Slavonic Society meeting."

"Shall I go to the parents' meeting for you?"

Bett had shared in bringing up her grandchildren ever since they were little — Niels Peter's two boys and his sister Mette's daughter.

"I'd love to look after the children. Whenever I can," Bett had said. "I've been studying to be a grandmother for years."

She put a lot into the time she spent with her grandchildren.

If they were ill they stayed with her in Havne Street. They played football in her apartment there. She would sew or play picture-puzzles with them. She pampered them and gave them Danish caviar and cream on toast.

When the children were not in nursery or at the kindergarten, she took them round the city visiting the family, friends or art exhibitions.

Or she took them to Forest House, where they slept late and then told one another their dreams. Went swimming. Climbed trees. Had visitors.

The children slept in the big bed in front of the fireplace and had books read aloud to them which you would think they wouldn't have been able to understand.

Magical years for the children. The years when their personalities were established.

Jacob and Zigzag enjoyed being in this area between their parents and their grandmother, and were no real problem.

So Karin and Niels Peter were able to hand over two relatively well-adjusted boys to the primary school.

On the other hand, Karin and Niels Peter's marriage had not been so well adjusted. They had divorced, and Niels Peter — in accordance with both their wishes — had taken custody of the children.

Thinking back now, he realizes that something had happened

early last March.

The boys had woken him, shouting:

"Dad, Dad, birds do whistle. It's true!"

"And Gran's down in the kitchen with the carpenter."

Bett had apparently arranged for a workman to come round.

That didn't surprise Niels Peter. He was no good at carpentry, and after Karin had moved out, his mother had helped out on the practical side.

But it did surprise him that the carpenter was making a bed in the little room next to the boys, the room that had been Karin's.

It turned out to be a kind of bunk stretching from wall to wall. Too short — unless you lay on it diagonally.

What this room was going to be used for was not quite clear to Niels Peter.

He saw it as though through a pane of glass.

Perhaps he didn't *want* to understand.

There were crocuses and aconites on the southern slopes of Østre Anlæg. A thin purple patterning drawn with a thin brush on the white crocus petals surrounding the orange stamens. The aconites raised spherical yellow heads on their green collars of leaves.

The flowers unfolded and opened their mouths.

A couple of lovers sat kissing on a bench.

Trains rumbled along below to Østerport, gulls shrieking between tall birches. Tree trunks flickering. Black and white. The thin profile of twigs against an illuminated sky, a little piece of Siberia here in the middle of Copenhagen.

Yellow buses glided past the wire fence.

Niels Peter and a dark-haired girl walking hand in hand, their faces turned to the sun.

When he came back, Bett was there.

Zigzag was standing in front of her giving some elaborate explanation about something. The boy was gesticulating, waving, talking and talking. He was not yet at the stage where he could summarize.

Jacob was sitting on the sofa beside Bett, leaning against her. Her arm was round his shoulder.

Bett's hands looked frail as they stroked the children's hair. She no longer had the energy to take the boys on to her lap.

With a fairly definite movement, she pressed her hand to her breast.

"Does it hurt?" said Niels Peter.

She shook her head.

"Won't you come up to my room," he said. "Then I can put a record on for you."

She obviously found it difficult going up the short staircase. She stopped twice, out of breath.

He shuddered. How on earth is she getting around? How does she manage the stairs up to the second floor in Havne Street?

As they sat listening to a record of Serbian folk-music, Niels Peter grew increasingly tense.

He was concerned to show his mother how fond he was of her. By now he had no doubt. Life was about to leave this pale figure who sat opposite him, listening intently, her hands clasped round her knee.

He thought back. When had he seen her at her happiest?

Many years ago they had been on a visit to Greece. Bett and her three children.

They had rented whitewashed rooms and woken to crystal-clear mornings, to the dry clanging of sheep-bells and goat-bells and the baaing of lambs and kids.

Simon had painted. Mette took photographs. Niels Peter read, while Bett drew, wrote and went round speaking in sign-language with the Greek children.

Bett was absorbed by it all, delighting in the slightest detail.

The three children noticed and were moved by it. Their affection for her grew.

All his life, he had missed her enormously whenever they had been separated. And then, when they had met again, he had been able to draw her into himself, enjoy her.

Thinking about it now, Niels Peter realizes he had enjoyed

not just her humour and firm convictions — but also her physical presence. His mother was a small, fit woman, her dark hair pinned up, her skin fair. She had dry, slightly furrowed palms.

She smelt so clean. He remembers that from way back in childhood; that soapy smell of hers was something quite special.

Later, when he was away travelling, he often found himself thinking: Bett should have been here! She should have seen this.

He wondered whether he was capable of living through it all without her also being involved in his experiences.

He looked at his mother now.

"What about you and me and the boys going to Greece in the spring?" he said.

"That'd be marvellous. But how could we afford it?"

"I'm sure I can manage the money. It's not that expensive out of season. I can take the boys out of school for two weeks in May."

"But weren't you going to Italy with... "

Bett had still not met his girlfriend.

"With Isia, yes, in April."

"What exactly is it Isia does?"

"She lectures at the Institute."

"So how would you be able to afford two trips?"

"The trip with Isia will be a working holiday."

"This one could be, too. I could look after the boys while you work... "

"Remember those wells where the water was so good?"

"And the blue and white-washed houses and the pink rowing-boat. And the children waving and shouting hello."

"Can you get hold of a brochure?" he said. "Maybe you could organize the trip."

A week later, Niels Peter went to the Tivoli concert hall for the first time. Ditlev had invited Isia and him to see Dario Fo and Franca Rame.

It was Franca's night. Most of the evening was taken up with her one-woman show.

Together with hundreds of others, Isia, Ditlev and Niels Peter stood side by side, clapping in time, stamping their feet and cheering.

It was a good boost. They met a lot of people they knew.

"Let's go for a beer, shall we?" said Ditlev, blinking at them from behind thick glasses.

"Bett's looking after the boys," said Niels Peter.

"So what?"

"Things aren't too good with her. I must get back and relieve her."

The boys were asleep when they came creeping in. Bett was reading, her glasses on the end of her nose.

"Did you enjoy yourselves?"

She got up to greet Isia. They smiled and were immediately on first name terms.

Bett put a hand on Ditlev's arm.

"How are things with you, my dear?"

"Fine," said Ditlev. "But I think I'll go straight up to bed."

"I must be going too," replied Bett.

Niels Peter and Isia stood in the doorway, waving to Bett as she disappeared into the distance.

"Your mother's very sweet," said Isia. "A wise and discreet woman."

"I know."

He closed the door.

"You know," he said, "I'm very fond of you."

"Why do you say it in that tone of voice?"

He wondered whether he had not sounded convincing. He threw his arms round Isia and kissed her hair. He was below average height, so he felt gratifyingly tall beside her.

"Do your mother and Ditlev know each other well?"

"Oh yes. Ditlev's a former pupil of hers. He often used to come back to our house in Havne Street. He and my sister Mette were rather attracted to each other once, despite the fifteen year gap."

"How old is he?"

"Must be getting on for fifty."

The next day Bett had fixed the trip to Greece. Niels Peter cycled down to the Vandkunsten travel agency and paid the deposit. Two adults and two children for fourteen days in May.

He was feeling depressed. Things had not gone as well as he'd hoped the day before, with Isia.

Spring came on Thursday, 20th March — according to the calendar, at least.

Bett came to Marstrand Street holding Mette's little five-year-old daughter, Milla, by one hand and carrying two boxes of eggs in the other. Jacob and Zigzag came rushing up.

"I've got a surprise for you," said Bett. "They say that when it's the spring equinox, ordinary eggs can stand on end. I mean really stand on end. The pointed end."

"Why?"

"Because night and day are the same length. Shall we try?"

Jacob knelt down and carefully held one of the eggs upright on the floor — for a long time — then let it go. It fell over.

Zigzag and Niels Peter tried. With no success.

Suddenly the boys' little cousin cried out:

"Look, look! I told you so!"

Triumphantly she pointed at an egg standing on end in front of her.

A kind of shiver went through them all. Milla threw herself into Bett's arms and the egg fell over.

A moment later, Zigzag also managed it.

"It seemed to sort of draw itself firm!"

"You see!" said Bett contentedly.

They tried it on smooth surfaces. On wood. On material. They found the floors in Marstrand Street were very uneven.

They telephoned Mette and Simon.

"Let's phone Gertrud too, shall we?" said Bett.

Gertrud was a physics teacher and one of Bett's former colleagues at school.

"Gertrud, do you think a raw egg can stand upright?" Bett asked.

There was a pause, then Bett turned to the others in the room and said: "Gertrud says that theoretically a raw egg can't stand upright."

Then she returned to the phone.

"Try for yourself, Gertrud," she said. "Today they can, really!"

The children leapt round the floor and got twelve eggs in a row to stand, breaking two in the process.

Niels Peter went across to the dairy to get some milk.

"We've just got twelve of your eggs to stand on end."

"Nothing extraordinary about that," said the man.

"It's because it's the spring equinox."

"No it isn't. Eggs can stand on end any day of the year."

"How do you know?"

"I just know."

Jacob continued all evening trying to get eggs to stand up. As soon as an egg fell over, he stood it up again.

"You're very determined," said Niels Peter.

"It's not me that's determined," said the boy. "It's the eggs."

Gertrud rang back.

"You're right," she said. "They do stand on end!"

There was something touching about the eggs just standing there, defying the laws of physics.

The remarkable thing was that the eggs stood on end for a certain length of time. Then they would topple over. Maybe after two minutes. Maybe after ten. First one would go, then a moment later the next one to it would follow.

The way they fell over was as if all their energy had been drained.

Milla's father came to pick her up.

"I've done a swap with Milla," said Jacob.

"What have you swapped?"

"I've swapped my Phantom comic for her Daisy doll."

"I hate Daisy dolls! And what are you going to use the Daisy doll for, anyhow?"

"To go with my Action Man, of course."

"Swap, swap, merchant man, never swap it back again," the children said when a swap was decided on.

"Fullstop, fullstop, fullstop," they added.

Then it couldn't be reversed.

"Aren't you going to stay here tonight, Gran?" said Jacob.

Bett was looking pale. She looked at her watch.

"Well, as it's so late... "

The boys were put to bed. Bett and Niels Peter again started dreaming about being on a balcony on a Greek island.

Day-dreaming. That was their speciality.

Greece rose before their eyes. They saw olive trees and tamarisk bushes against the red soil. They heard the quiet rustling of brooms as women in black swept the whitewashed streets. The gentle rattle of komboloi beads gliding through the men's hands.

They heard the screech of the peacocks.

They didn't think about Forest House. Nor about how they would be able to afford to keep up a large summer house and at the same time travel south. Nor about his examination class, nor his students.

Night fell and the constellations of the spring sky slowly appeared. The Great Bear hung just above Marstrand Street.

A single egg remained upright all through the night.

The egg remained upright until Saturday morning, when Bett wanted to go to the Central Library to change some books for Niels Peter. He protested.

"It's good for me to keep on the move," she said. "And then I can bring the boys' comic books back with me."

She leant against the doorpost for support as she felt carefully for the step with her foot, a white carrier bag with the books in her hand.

Slowly and hesitantly, she made her way into town.

And was away for a long time! Too long.

When she came back, she looked as if all the blood had drained out of her. Transparent. She sank down on to a chair, the carrier bag of new library books slipping down between her feet.

Niels Peter's heart thumped.

"What's happened?"

"Nothing," she said breathlessly. "Maybe I was just overdoing things a bit."

Perhaps she had fallen? Or fainted?

She closed her eyes and pressed her lips together, clearly trying to say something.

"Yes?" said Niels Peter, putting his hand on her shoulder.

"I think I have to admit it — the stairs at Havne Street are getting a bit difficult for me."

"You can't manage them any longer?"

"No."

"Then move in with us," he said simply.

Karin had once told him: "Now that I'm no longer living here, don't you go moving in with your mother!"

Niels Peter had been evasive in his reply: "No, only in the holidays at Forest House, as we've always done."

"Because you need your head seeing to, if you do."

"Yes, I'd like to live here," Bett said again. "In the little room next to the children's."

She looked calmly at Niels Peter.

"It's no good at Mette's — on the third floor. And Hans working there on his thesis and... "

"And it wouldn't work in Simon's collective, would it?" added Niels Peter.

"Oh, heaven help us! But at least I hope I can be some use to you, helping out with the boys."

The dishwasher rumbled and the wind blew. The candles in their brass candlesticks flickered uneasily, reflected in the window-pane and on the television screen. As if there were six, not just two.

Niels Peter fetched bedclothes, her alarm clock, a couple of blouses and some trousers from Havne Street. Bett was given her own cupboard space at his place. Her own towel and tooth-mug in the bathroom.

Jacob and Zigzag were delighted.

"Now we're a real family!"

"Now we're a real family," they had said.

But they aren't any more.

Niels Peter is lying with his hands clasped behind his head on the big bed at Forest House. The boys asleep on either side of him. An owl is hooting.

It's the autumn holiday.

Tomorrow Mette and Simon are coming, and then they're to go through every single room and every single object in the house.

This house, which has been the stuff of their dreams.

What is the difference between dream and reality? Between vision and illusion?

He opens a bottle of wine, pours himself a glass and lies down on the bed again.

We could live quite a different life. To some extent we already do.

SATURDAY 18 OCTOBER

How can we possibly change anything in this world — socially and politically — if we don't dare change things in our own lives? If we don't risk breaking bonds?

That's what is on Niels Peter's mind this morning as he wakes up at Forest House.

Time probably heals all wounds, or so they say.

It would probably take a year or two — and then they'd get over it.

The three of them are lying on the big bed in a jumble of pillows and quilts. It is light in the room — white. The fire has gone out. It is cold.

"Can you get your own breakfast, Zigzag?"

"Yep."

"And can you make me a cup of coffee, Jacob?"

"They're coming, they're coming," shouts Zigzag. "Mette and Simon, and they've got Milla with them."

Mette's little Citroën is in the yard outside.

Simon is the first to get out. Thin. Fair. Dishevelled as usual. In jeans, a thick Icelandic sweater and white training shoes. He stands a head taller than Niels Peter.

One of Simon's front teeth glints silver as he calls: "Hello everyone!"

Then he helps Milla out of the car.

"God, the traffic!" says Mette, opening the back hatch of the car. "You can tell the holiday has started."

She embraces Niels Peter. Slightly taller than he is. He's the smallest of the three.

Mette has fair hair down to her shoulders and three thin gold bangles round her wrist. Both she and Milla are wearing blue boiler suits and black wooden-soled shoes.

Suddenly the house is swarming with life.

"Where's Hans?" says Jacob.

"He's not coming until Saturday. He's got to work."

"Where on earth are we going to begin?" asks Simon.

They walk round the house, stopping now and then to look each other in the eye.

"How long have we had this house?" says Jacob.

"Since 1965."

"Was that when there were cowboys?" asks Zigzag.

Jacob claps one hand to his forehead and rolls his eyes. Then he digs his younger brother in the side.

"Let's go down to the woods, eh?"

"I want to come too," says Milla.

"Yes. Let's go down to where the foxes are."

The three children put on their wellingtons and race off across the fields.

"I think that's where we made the mistake."

"What are you talking about?"

"I'm not sure I know myself," says Niels Peter. "Yes, I think it was a mistake buying the house. I mean, when Bett bought the house, it was at the time when the three of us were ready to fly and should have been pushed out of the nest. I must have been twenty-three then."

"Yes, and I was nineteen," says Mette. And Simon eighteen — but you can't call that a mistake! When you think of the fantastic years we've had here... "

"Hmm." Niels Peter frowns. "Well?"

"Wasn't it the first year when we started planting the avenue of birches?"

"I think it was the second," says Simon.

"It was raining the first time we came... "

The rain trickled and gurgled everywhere, the first time they were at Forest House.

They came to love the sound of rain — on the roof, in the trees, on the gravel and the grass. Wet summer days enveloped in dark leaves.

It was an old farmhouse with two wings. Isolated and set in a lovely location. They got it at a decent price.

They had soon started on clearing up, pulling down walls, repairing and decorating. They felled trees and planted new ones. Bought old furniture at the flea market and stripped it down to bare wood.

They lit bonfires and sat up at night, talking or playing the guitar. They worked in the daytime. And studied. Or lazed about.

There were fields all round the house, a forest, and a fjord gleaming in the distance.

They spent all their holidays there and filled the house with friends. Danish and foreign. Just as Bett had always done at Havne Street.

They were sure that Forest House would stay in the family for ever and ever.

It was so lovely.

So unusual.

They had great visions.

When Bett retired, she moved most of her things there.

But she managed to hang on to the apartment in Havne Street, where she still spent the winter.

She loved the activity in the house and was always asking: "What are you going to do? What do you feel like doing today?"

Did she live through her children, perhaps? Were they the purpose of her life?

Niels Peter felt uneasy with that. She ought to be living her own life, too, he thought.

But that wasn't the whole truth, either!

She had a great many friends of her own.

If her friends came too close, the three children used to take her back for themselves. They had always made sure they kept a rein on their mother for their own purposes. Monopolizing her.

Sometimes he wondered whether in fact it was the other way round — whether they perhaps lived through her.

The family grew and Forest House grew with it.
Niels Peter came with Karin and they had Jacob and Zigzag.
Mette came with Hans and they had Milla.
Simon came with various friends. No one ever knew quite where they stood with him.

Their great wish had now been fulfilled. They were a three-generation family. A family collective. But also a collective which gradually had to limit the number of visitors, now that the grandchildren were taking up so much time.

The children spent part of their time in the trees, part in their favourite hiding places.

It seemed that in the course of their early childhood, they were to live through the whole development of mankind: from the Stone Age to digital watches.

Mette and Hans were inseparable. Neither could survive without the other.

It was different with Niels Peter and Karin. They each needed time on their own.

Niels Peter used to sit working in the attic, at peace with himself. A green tapestry of leaves half-covering the window-pane, the sunlight filtering through it. He loved being there.

Karin was the opposite. She was restless and preferred busy

streets. She would take herself off into town, while Niels Peter and the boys stayed behind at Forest House with Bett.

They'd begun to discuss whether it would be possible to divide Forest House into smaller lots, so that Niels Peter, Mette and Simon could each have a plot and build a house on it.

"Like some kind of strip-farming," as Simon put it.

But then they probably wouldn't get planning permission.

And anyway, none of them could afford to build a summer house. They had their student debts to pay off, and there were the everyday costs of living in the city.

They shared the costs of Forest House roughly between them, although their outlay was forever rising because they kept taking out loans for extensions and improvements.

Simon, for instance, had a studio in the cowshed. They put a new roof on the main house and had all the windows replaced.

There's something about society being built up in this way. You borrow. You go into debt. You live partly on credit. In that way the wheels keep turning.

But the question is, can you afford the repayments when they fall due?

Bett held the whole thing together. She was the focal point.

She went along with just about everything. Only one thing was beyond question: her sovereign ownership of Forest House.

Then it became obvious her health was deteriorating.

Her illness began to develop at about the same time as Karin and Niels Peter were deciding to separate, shortly after Niels Peter had been given a grant for post-graduate studies at the Slavonic Institute.

All at once — this was in the spring of 1979 — they noticed that Bett had begun to fade. Noticeably. Her skin turned white. She was tense and irritable in a way they had never known her before.

Reluctantly, she allowed herself to be examined by a doctor, and with even greater reluctance she went into hospital in Lindebjerg.

The day she was to go in was Bastille Day. She had her hair cut short — before, she had always worn it up, with a bun at the back of her neck.

Bett underwent one examination after another.

It turned out that she had stomach ulcers, was anaemic, had a slight temperature and a high blood sedimentation, which was almost constantly at 120–130. Normally it should have been at 5–10.

Niels Peter looked at his mother in the way you look at a watch and think — it can't be right! And you look round for other watches to compare it with.

Suddenly he saw what was happening. She had cancer!

It was like a bullet in the chest.

He spoke to his brother and sister.

"Look, I think Bett has cancer."

"Don't say that word!" cried Mette.

"What do you mean?"

"Well, it's as if you wanted her dead here and now."

"I don't, and you know it," said Niels Peter. "So shut up."

"Cancer's what people die of," said Mette in a low voice. "I won't allow her to die! Don't you understand? I can't do without her. I don't know what I'd do if anything happened to Bett."

"She won't survive on our pious wishes."

"Do you have to be so cynical?" said Mette.

Simon tapped his silver tooth with his thumbnail.

"You don't necessarily die of it."

Niels Peter raised his voice.

"If Bett is as ill as I think she is, then she's going to need treatment. For God's sake, Mette, your husband's a doctor. We can discuss it with him, can't we?"

It was easier for Niels Peter to talk to his brother-in-law than to his brother or sister, It always had been.

"Mette's very unhappy about you thinking Bett is so ill," said Hans.

"I know."

"I feel very sorry for Mette," sighed Hans.

"But what do you really think yourself?"

Hans gazed at him with his blue eyes.

"I think you're right," he said.

"But what do you think we should do?"

"I think you should try to talk to Bett."

Since it was no easy thing to broach the subject with Bett, Niels Peter went on his own one day to see the consultant.

"Could you tell me what you know about my mother?"

"Yes. We have examined your mother. She is in good condition for her age. But we have found a stomach ulcer. Also a slight swelling in the liver. And then this high blood-pressure, which we can't explain."

"High blood sedimentation can be a sign of cancer, can't it?"

The consultant looked up sharply.

"Perhaps. Or perhaps just an inflammation somewhere."

"She looks as if she has cancer."

"That's definitely not true. We haven't found the slightest trace of cancer."

He underestimates us, thought Niels Peter. This man isn't telling the truth.

"I've brought her will with me."

The consultant looked surprised.

Niels Peter took a document out of his shoulder-bag. He knew the contents almost off by heart. It was a printed form. Bett had given it to him several years previously and she also had a copy of it herself.

In the will it said: in the event of an incurable illness, in which she looked likely to be deprived of the possibility of living life on her own conditions, she wished to be spared artificial life-prolonging intervention, whether mechanical, surgical or chemical.

She agreed to being treated with powerful pain-killing medicaments, even if they led to a curtailment of her remaining life.

Finally, she expressed the wish to remain in her home and to die there, in so far as this was practically possible, and not to be a burden on those around her.

The will was signed by Bett, with Hans and Niels Peter as witnesses to her signature.

"Would you like to keep this?" said Niels Peter. "In case it becomes relevant."

"Of course," said the consultant, putting the document into a drawer.

"You've been talking to them at the hospital," said Bett, frowning.

She always knew everything.

"Yes."

"I don't like that at all. I don't like your going behind my back."

Niels Peter nodded. He couldn't lie. He had never been able to. It was more than just a principle — it actually made him feel bad if he said anything that did not accord with the truth or with his convictions.

In particular he could not lie to his mother. That would have been inconceivable. He would, but also should and could, only tell Bett the truth.

But he needn't necessarily tell her the whole truth.

He could keep quiet about certain things. Avoid questions. In fact he was never quite sure if Bett really knew what his conversation with the consultant had been about.

The doctors recommended immediate surgery.

But Bett didn't wish to be operated on under any circumstances.

"They saw right through your breast-bone," she said. "I'm frightened I'd never get up again. Now that's enough talk about illness! I don't want to hear any more. I'll manage, I'm sure."

Bett cancelled the rest of her appointments with the hospital and went on living as if nothing had happened.

Going to exhibitions with Mette. To parties with her friend Gertrud. Looking after her grandchildren. Living partly in the country and partly in the city. Growing thinner and thinner. And all the time in astonishingly good humour.

Certainly, they felt, they had to let her decide for herself.

She was a fully grown adult, after all.

What else could they do, except approve the stand she was taking.

But from that moment on, a strange reserve had settled on the family.

Niels Peter worked on as before. Every day was there to be lived to the full. He had learnt that as a child. Don't waste time. Always have a purpose.

He was the kind of man who couldn't sit still for two minutes. Always walking around, finding things to do.

The opposite of this restlessness was a form of apathy. Niels Peter drooped. Came to a full stop. Paralyzed, especially during the first half of the day.

They were all in a state of uncertainty. Searching. A job lay ahead of them — and they didn't want to face it.

For the first time ever, Niels Peter, Mette and Simon are all together at Forest House without Bett.

Mette seems to be the one most prepared to face up to it all. She starts taking pictures down from the walls in an unsystematic way. That's the first thing that people usually do. The pictures leave patches. The walls looked pleasant before, but now they're disfigured.

She stacks the pictures against a wall.

Most of them are by Simon.

How desolate everything looks after a couple of hours' clearing up.

Mette goes into Bett's little bedroom behind the bathroom and starts emptying the cupboard, while her brothers carry the pictures out to the barn.

Shortly afterwards, Mette re-appears holding a number of small jars.

"I found them in with her clothes — various painkillers."

That evening, the yard outside Forest House is suddenly full of sparrows and a single titmouse. Jacob fetches some white bread and puts it on the step.

The birds fight over the bread. When they get a piece, they fly off to the pergola to eat it.

The little titmouse is the quickest of all.

"How many birds are there in Denmark?" says Zigzag.

"A few million, I expect. Maybe more."

"Do they know?" Milla asks.

"Do you mean do they know they're birds?"

"Yes."

"I don't know what birds think," says Simon.

SUNDAY 19 OCTOBER

So here he is again in his same old bed in the attic room at Forest House.
   Where he's lain a thousand times and more.
   Lying gazing up at the cobwebs in the corners.
   His heart tight and tense.
   Listening to sounds in the house — Mette moving round the kitchen with the children, and Simon whistling out in the yard.

During March, Niels Peter had woken every morning in Marstrand Street with a sense of guilt. My students, my translation, my children, my mother (living with me and me responsible for her), my girlfriend, my finances, the two trips I've agreed on. I don't think I can handle it! He'd lie there for a full quarter of an hour before getting up, worrying.

Once his class was over, he'd cycle to the chemist's to fetch calcium tablets, skin-cream and toothpaste. And several pink Doloxene for Bett. He'd also take her letters to the post office, calling in at the greengrocer's on the way.

Jacob and Zigzag and two of their friends came in from the street, panting.
   "We'll tell you something if you promise not to tell us off."
   The boys were beaming happily at each other, then at Bett and Niels Peter.
   "What's this all about?"
   "Promise you won't get mad, Dad? Nor you, Gran?"
   "We promise."
   Pause.

"Come on, out with it!"

"We've put a dog turd through grumpy old Sørensen's letter box. It was great."

"*What* have you done?" exclaimed Bett in horror.

"It's all right, calm down," said Jacob. "We used a plastic bag to hold it."

"No, no, no!" Niels Peter shouted at him.

Zigzag looked alarmed.

"You promised you wouldn't tell us off."

"Oh — how could you do anything so disgusting!"

"Well, he shouts and yells at us just because our ball goes into his front garden."

"You should be polite and friendly to the neighbours," said Niels Peter. "Regardless!"

"Shan't," said Jacob.

Zigzag turned his back on his father and said to Jacob: "Come on — let's go."

Bett was sitting at the table, wrapped in a fringed blanket.

Zigzag and Niels Peter were emptying the dishwasher. Back and forth between the machine and the cupboards.

Zigzag dropped an enamel plate. Niels Peter was sensitive to noise, and irritable, and the acoustics in the kitchen echoed loudly.

"Why did you drop that, silly! You're a clumsy idiot!" he shouted.

The boy ducked to pick up the plate.

Bett glanced darkly at Niels Peter.

"Why do you shout at him like that? It's nice of him to help you out."

Niels Peter felt like a piece of paper that's been set on fire. His shame speading — the shame which was to engulf him in the months to come.

"I think I'll go up now," said Bett.

"Shall I give you a hand?"

"There's no need. I can manage."

She didn't sound very convincing.

Last thing that night he heard the end-of-transmission tone of the television, still on after the epilogue.

Found the boys on the sofa. Got Jacob to his feet. Carried the sleeping Zigzag upstairs.

Went back down to the ground floor.

Went through the boys' school-bags. Tipped out crumpled pieces of paper, empty plastic bags and small bits of string. Turned the bags upside down and found a letter in his elder son's lunchbox: *Deer Jacod if you lyk me then say so I lyk you. Love from Sofie*.

He went through their school books and fixed the occasional torn page with sticky tape. Rubbed out the rude drawings in the margins.

Looked into the contact-books and found a message from Zigzag's gym teacher:

> Zigzag was an hour late today. He has not had his gym kit with him for the last three lessons. If it happens again, I must ask you for a doctor's note, or I shall have to report it to the inspector, as this situation is unacceptable and is also demoralizing.

Niels Peter hunted all through the house for the gym bag and found it in the dirty laundry basket. Put it — together with its unwashed contents — into the boy's backpack.

Opened the pencil box.

Sharpened the pencils.

Cut Jacob's eraser in two so that Zigzag could have one half.

Turned out the light.

Crept back up to his room.

Closed his books and ring-folders and went to bed.

On Wednesday, 26th March, Bett went to Lindebjerg Hospital. By train. On her own. Hans had persuaded her to have herself admitted. This was her first visit since she had refused the operation the previous autumn.

She was to have a blood transfusion and treatment with a drug called Tagamet.

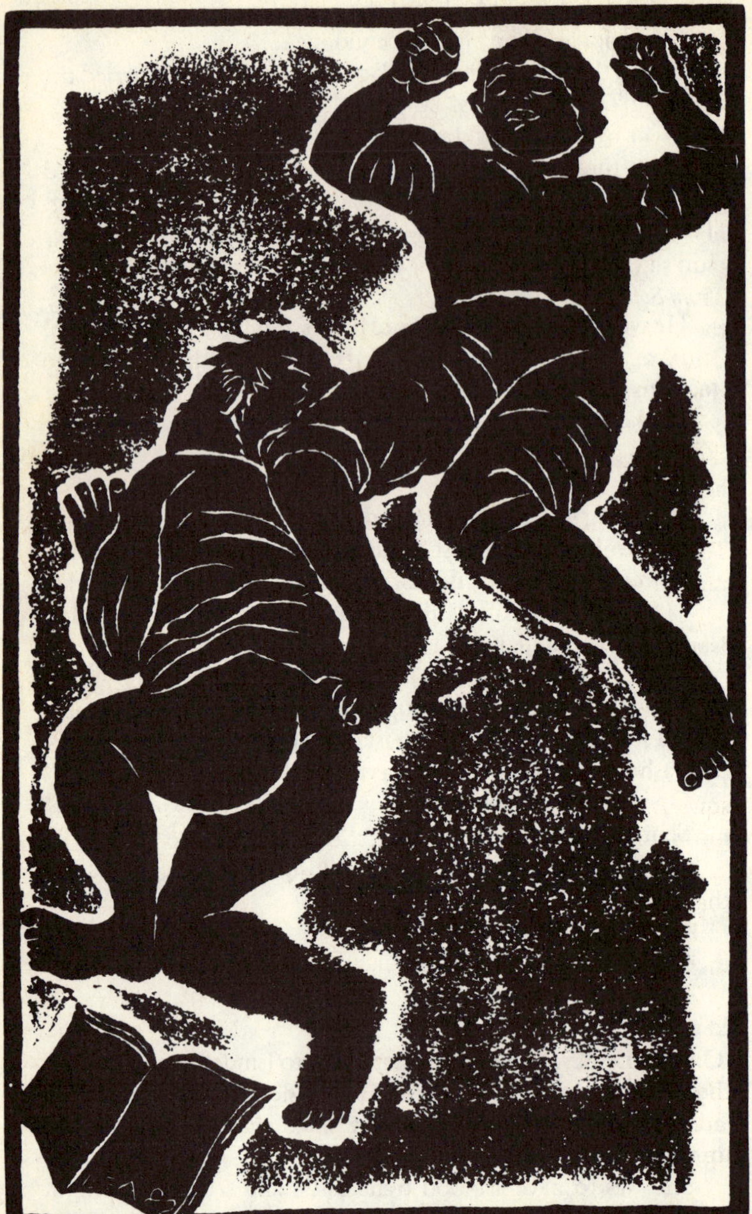

Is she going to manage this trip? thought Niels Peter. What if she falls at the station?

A March evening in Copenhagen. Hazy blue. Twittering birds hiding in the shadows of the park. Whistling and chirping. Through people's windows, television screens with the latest news about Afghanistan, El Salvador and the American hostages in Teheran.

The boys started a club called The Blue Sock. This entailed all the children in the street, every Wednesday, wearing blue all over and walking up and down the street going through various rituals.

Jacob and Zigzag had also drawn a strip cartoon for Bett. To thank her for the Valentine she'd sent. They posted it to the hospital.

The swans had begun butting each other's beaks. At dusk, ducks came flying in and landed in a rush.

Isia came with a bunch of red tulips.

"They're for your mother when she comes out of hospital."

Talked about their trip to Italy, and what they needed to take with them. Niels Peter's mind was elsewhere.

"Try listening to this," said Isia, grasping the tulip stems and squeezing them slightly. "Can you hear them creaking? Isn't it a nice sound?"

"Isia," said Niels Peter, "I've come to a very difficult part in this translation. I need to work today... "

He sat looking at Selimović's portrait, as if trying to fathom the man's true meaning.

Then Karin phoned. They agreed on when she should come to pick up the boys.

After their conversation, he found it difficult to get back into the translation.

Anyway, he had to go out and do some shopping. And pick up the travellers' cheques from the bank.

On Maundy Thursday, Bett came back to Marstrand Street in an ambulance.

Pale. Tottering through the hall, supported by two ambulancemen.

Sat down on the sofa and hid her face in her thin hands. Wept.

Jacob knelt down in front of her and took her hands away.

"What is it, Gran?"

"Oh, God, I feel so bad," she whispered. "I don't think I've ever felt so bad."

Niels Peter helped to settle her on the sofa, with pillows and blankets.

"What's that?" he exclaimed, pointing at the bandage on her thin forearm.

"They took a tissue sample."

Jacob busied himself fetching iced water and supporting Bett so that she could drink.

"I have to go back in," she said. "On Monday."

Outside, it is fine spring weather. White and purple crocuses opening to the sun, orange mouths between green leaves. As if trying to kiss.

Sparrows hopping about, chirping.

Niels Peter sat down on the sofa beside his mother.

"I can't bear the thought of leaving you. I think I'd rather cancel my trip to Italy."

"You mustn't," she said firmly. "It's important to you. And to Isia. You both need it. You need peace for your work. I should be able to manage. Don't think about it... "

On Good Friday, Niels Peter opened the refrigerator, took one final look to check that it contained everything she might need: eggs, cream, bouillon, ice cubes. Bett certainly looked in no state to go shopping.

Checked his passport and tickets again. Started packing some books.

He was to leave the next morning. Karin would pick the boys up just before he went.

But what about his mother? She was to stay in Marstrand Street — alone — over the weekend. On Monday she would be taken by ambulance for a new series of tests at the hospital.

"Don't say anything to Mette and Hans. It'll only worry them," said Bett. "Let them have their little holiday at Forest House in peace."

Simon was in Poland. He had a girlfriend in Krakow.

Ditlev was away.

There were not many people in Marstrand Street. Everyone was away because of Easter. This was what was tormenting Niels Peter — the thought that something would happen to Bett during the two days she would be alone in the house.

"Don't you want anyone to visit you over the weekend?"

"Definitely not. All I need is some rest."

Fixed a bit of food for dinner. Bett almost seemed to choke on a raw egg.

"Is it a free egg or a torture egg?" asked Zigzag.

"What does he mean?" she asked curiously.

"He means is it free-range or battery-farm." He turned to the boy. "It's a torture egg. You only get free eggs at Forest House."

Bett was back on the sofa again. Zigzag snuggled up to her.

"Careful, dear. I'm feeling a bit fragile."

Went for an evening walk with the boys. Told them once again what was going to happen while they were away. Who was to be with whom, and where. Tried to assure himself that the children had grasped it fully.

Behind a low metal fence in one of the small front gardens in Marstrand Street, a small tree was in bloom. Otherwise everything was in bud. Hedges with green shoots in green mantles. The roses all pruned.

The sun was throwing an unreal copper-coloured light on to the high windows of Østerfarimag Street. They were shining. Dark. Heavy. As if not made of glass, but metal. As if no one was behind them.

The sky above the lakes and over North Bridge was turning a darker and darker shade of red. Higher up — brilliant blue. Still. Steely.

The evening star was low in the sky. Shining unusually brightly.

"You must have a bath, Zigzag, and your nails need cutting."
"But I'm as clean as a little duckling."
"Between your toes too?"
"I've got webbed feet, Dad."

The windows in Marstrand Street caught the parallel rays of light and changed to a mild pink. He locked the bicycles in the front garden and opened the front door for the boys.

He said goodnight to his mother. She was lying in the little room, her hands together under her cheek, her legs slightly bent. In the foetal position.

Finished his packing. Phoned for an alarm call and got a crackling line...

The alarm call rang at seven on Saturday morning. He had a shower. Woke the boys. Helped Bett down the stairs. Made some herbal tea and sat on the sofa with her for a while.

She ran a slim cool hand through his hair. Oh, God, that feeling...

Karin came at the agreed time to fetch the boys. She stood in the doorway. One hand raised in greeting. But she didn't go in to talk to Bett. Karin's fear of illness showed in her green eyes.

Jacob and Zigzag kissed their mother good morning. And their grandmother goodbye.

When Niels Peter went out with them, a burly fair-haired man was waiting outside.

"This is Bjarne," said Karin.
"Good Lord — I remember you..."

It was the carpenter Bett had asked to work on the house.

"We're going up to Bjarne's summer house for Easter," said Karin.

Niels Peter carried his suitcase and backpack down to the living-room. He knew he had to leave, but could scarcely bring himself to go when he saw his mother sitting there, looking so incredibly small in her white nightgown. With the telephone on its extension lead. With the cold, grey screen of the television in front of her.

"I can't bear the thought of leaving you here!"

"You *must*! I'm not that ill."

"But... "

"You can phone me from Italy, can't you."

He stared at her angrily. Bett and her striped toilet bag. Hurriedly, he kissed her. Still angry. And left.

She had pushed him away!

Now he could no longer protect his mother.

He would have to live his own life.

It was unbearable.

He met Isia at Kastrup Airport.

On the flight, he paid scant attention to her. He was thinking... supposing Bett commits suicide this weekend? This is her opportunity. She's alone for two days in Marstrand Street. The ambulance to take her to hospital isn't coming till Monday. Her toilet bag is full of sleeping pills.

Simon is in Poland.

But Mette would certainly phone. And if Bett didn't answer, then Mette could phone Bett's sister, Elin. Or Mette might decide to come back from the country straight away.

What if Bett falls down the stairs?

Can she actually get up from the sofa if she wants something to drink?

How long can a person live off a glass of water?

As they flew above the layers of clouds, in his mind's eye he saw Bett in her white nightgown — the one Mette had got her to make last summer.

It was possible that at this very moment Bett had taken a taxi and was driving out to a wood somewhere in order to disappear for ever. But then they would start searching for her. The driver would remember where he had dropped her off. She would soon be found. And stomach-pumped. And her suffering would be even greater.

Or she might hang herself. But would she have the strength? And could she bear the thought of us finding her?

It's so difficult to take your own life.

But on the other hand, a person can die so easily — that's a possibility that you have to bear in mind every single day.

"What are you thinking about?" said Isia, nudging his arm.

"What if my mother dies while I'm away?"

"There's nothing you can do about it. You can't be with her day and night. Supposing she lives much longer than you think? You'll end up completely drained."

They landed at Rome airport. Took a southbound train, then on by bus and taxi. Towards evening they were at a small hotel that Isia knew of.

The first thing they did was to push the two single beds together to make a double bed. They took the religious picture down from the wall and put it in the cupboard. Then they unpacked, hung their clothes on hangers, and set up their typewriters on two rickety garden tables.

Isia arranged her little pipes alongside her tobacco on the table.

He was lying naked over her, propped up on his elbows.

"I can't," he whispered.

"Don't think about it," whispered Isia, and kissed him.

He put his mouth to her ear: "Help me forget what we've left behind."

In the morning they had cappuccino coffees and were given white bread and red-cherry jam.

No mail, nothing to disturb them, nothing but themselves and the Italian countryside — which climbed the mountainside in front of their balcony like a toy landscape of small villages, churches and trees in bloom.

They sat in their room, each with work to do — she with her articles, he with his translation. Wrote and read for several hours each morning. Went into the village to fetch food for lunch — ham, sardines and black olives.

Worked again until about five. Perhaps until six if it was going well. Had their evening meal in the hotel. Sat and watched the passers-by or strolled up and down the streets in the darkness with their arms around each other.

Last thing at night, a zinc counter in a brightly lit bar and a grappa.

Niels Peter looked at himself in the mirror behind the bottles.

Felt Isia's eyes on him. Looked away from his reflection and stared at his shoes.

The door of the bar stood open on to a dark empty street.

A white plastic bag blew by. Moving — rustling faintly — to and fro in the doorway.

Isia's eyes sought Niels Peter's and caught them. Held them. They gazed at each other without blinking. A sign of love. A faint electric shock. It became too much.

51

In the middle of the night, he whispered:

"I'm scared I won't be able to love you when we get back to Denmark."

"Why not?"

"There's so much in the way."

"Just wait and see."

"You're so persistent," he said, as if surprised.

"Yes, because it's not good to isolate yourself as much as you do."

"Isolate myself?"

"Yes, you can be very distant. Sometimes I can't even make out what you're feeling, Niels Peter."

"I'm not sure I can myself, either."

"Don't you ever think that other people — me, for instance — might also have problems?"

The church bells rang and a brass band played. A warmth glowed from her clothing. A warmth glowed down from the sun, through the cool April air, and found his body.

The camelia had burst into flower, its blossoms wine-red and pink.

Green lizards scuttled across the stones and disappeared into dark holes.

Scraps of silver paper lay scattered like mirrors.

There were days when sky and sea were more or less the same colour — as if there were no transition between the elements.

Yet he still felt a pang in his heart — even in these idyllic surroundings. He saw his mother lying in hospital in an endlessly grey room.

I've left her in the lurch! Yet she means so much to me! And I love her so dearly!

He phoned the Lindebjerg Hospital from Italy. After much difficulty, he managed to get through to Bett. So she's still alive. She had to be taken from her room to the office where the telephone was.

He could hear how much she was suffering. He asked how things were going. Received a meaningless explanation.

Regretted having phoned at all. But she had asked him to call!

Always the same. Don't forget to phone!

Yes, from wherever he had been in the world, he had always phoned home.

It cost him a lot of money to phone from Italy.

It never occurred to him to phone his children. They were not going to be brought up that way.

As he went through life, he had often been surprised by people's lack of family ties. They took decisions without first having to consult their parents. Even without their parents expecting to be asked.

But Bett's three children were used to showing and receiving affection. Used to being in constant contact with one another.

"Phone home," their mother used to say.

"Why?" they would ask.

"To see if anything's happened."

"Like what?"

"You never know... "

Niels Peter sat gazing at the pattern on the tiled floor. Trying to break it up and see it in another way. Creating symmetry where there was none. Disorder where there was order.

It was morning. The phone call to Denmark had left him feeling restless.

"If you don't like phoning home, why do you do it?" said Isia. She was at her work table — in light-brown corduroy trousers and a red blouse with narrow white stripes.

"Because my mother's ill."

"But it just seems to irritate you."

"That's right. Because I'm always expected to phone home, regardless."

"What would happen if you didn't?"

"Hm," said Niels Peter, bending his fingers and cracking the joints. "I suppose I'd be worried about — losing her love."

Isia pulled the paper sharply out of her typewriter. Her dark hair was curlier than usual.

"I have to tell you," said Niels Peter, "that my relationship with my mother is incredibly close and dependent. You have to remember that my father died when Simon was born. I'm the eldest. As children, the other two were a little group on their own."

"What was your father like?"

"I never really knew him. He was never at home."

"Where was he, then?"

"At work."

"What impression do you have of him?"

"Only my mother's."

"And what was that?"

"She worshipped him."

"Did she have any reason to?"

"I don't know. Only that he had been the love of her life — or so she said. No one could match him. We children had to respect that."

Niels Peter wrinkled his nose and shrugged his shoulders.

"Has your mother always had to manage alone with the three of you?"

"Yes, but she comes from a big family. They helped out."

"So you became very tied to her because you were the eldest."

"Yes, she always talked to me a lot. About how she missed my father, about her work at school, about her problems in making ends meet. She and I also talked a lot about the other two, and how things might work out. She was particularly concerned about Simon, because he was having problems at school."

"Did you feel that you had a responsibility?"

"Of course I did."

"Can I ask you something? Do you think that your childhood was — how can I put it — cut short?"

The question startled Niels Peter. He looked sharply at Isia. She was calmly cleaning out her pipe.

"Cut short? In a way — perhaps. I stopped playing very early on."

"Weren't you very good at playing?"

"Yes and no — it just didn't interest me much."

Isia got up and went out on to the balcony. She stood by the railing, silhouetted against the brilliant backdrop of the mountain.

"Anyway," he said to the silhouette, "I was terribly fond of my mother. She's wonderful. She's so... alive. She's always had so many interests. And I'm not the only one to think that. I felt slightly... "

"Dominated by her?"

"Oh, come now!" He started back in his chair. "I didn't mean that. More as if... as if I had been chosen."

"What would your brother and sister say if they heard this?"

"I suppose one hopes that they've also felt chosen in their way. Mette's probably the one who's felt the pressure most."

"But you're the one who's really responsible for your mother?"

"That's right."

"Is that a burden on you sometimes?"

He tugged at one of his sideburns.

"Occasionally I get desperate about the way that she and I are so dependent on each other. I've often thought about where the responsibility for that dependency lies. With her or with me. Or maybe somewhere quite different? I suppose it lies with both of us. Which came first, the chicken or the egg?"

"When did this idea of dependency first strike you?"

"In puberty. That was why I was so keen to travel when I grew older."

"I think," said the silhouette, turning in profile against the mountain, "that what puberty means is that the child has to free itself."

Niels Peter rose and poured some wine into two small glasses.

"I don't know, really. I think the idea of children freeing themselves from their parents is more or less an illusion. How can they free themselves?"

"By distancing themselves from their parents."

He straightened his books.

"But how?"

The silhouette came in from the balcony and turned back into a human being.

"Through independence. If you can't free yourself at puberty, then the parents become even more demanding later on. Parents go as far as they're allowed to!"

Niels Peter laughed.

"Well, I'm damned..." he exclaimed. "I'll have to think about that."

Isia wanted to go on, but he interrupted her.

"I thought I'd got free when I lived in Yugoslavia for all that time. But when I got home, Bett's interest in me was even greater. Then I married and had children while I was still a student. So Bett stepped in and helped us look after the children."

"What did your wife say about it?"

"On the one hand, it was a great help. But on the other hand, Karin often felt pushed aside by my mother. I know she did."

Isia nodded, trying to light her pipe with one of those curious little Italian wax matches. Niels Peter found a Danish match and struck it for her.

"How on earth do you free yourself from parents you love?"

"Clearly you've not found out yet."

"No. You see, I don't even really know whether it's such a good idea."

Then, a moment later:

"Anyway, I've never been given a chance to free myself."

There was a new glint in Isia's dark eyes — almost menacing — as she went on:

"Now it's too late. Because she's so ill. But isn't it possible your mother has often tried to free herself? From you... from all of you? But you and your brother and sister have prevented her."

He had never thought of it that way.

"Tell me now... " said Niels Peter. To his surprise he found his voice changing. "Do you believe that parents and children *have* to leave each other?"

"Yes," said Isia calmly. "I'm convinced of it. They need to make the break — in order to be able to approach each other again, on a different basis."

"Oh," said Niels Peter with a groan. "There's something in all this that I find perplexing."

He stared into Isia's brown eyes.

"Do you think," she asked, "it might have been a relief to the three of you if your mother had married again?"

"To be honest — I don't really know," he said hesitantly. "Maybe we would have felt something had been taken from us."

"You might have been jealous?"

"Yes, maybe. But as things are now, it seems to me that my mother has given and given — and it's quite impossible that I'll ever be able to pay her back."

He got up and went across to look in the mirror above the basin.

"My debt's too great — I can't even pay the interest."

"That's crazy!" exclaimed Isia. "It makes no sense! People can't invest in each other as if they were bank accounts. Wouldn't you say that you're carrying round a huge great burden of guilt about your mother?"

Niels Peter nodded at his reflection. Then he caught sight of her in the mirror. A clear mirror-image, but slightly distorted, as everyone is in a mirror.

He saw her open her mouth and say:

"Guilt is particularly strong when you're young. But I think it fades with the years and becomes... "

"What?"

"A sense of responsibility, I would say."

The mirror image started putting on its jacket.

"I'd like to go for a walk before lunch."

He nodded, left the mirror and took his own jacket from the hook.

"Tell me something — what do you think a sense of guilt is?"

"I don't know if I can answer that," said Isia. "I imagine it's something universal. I assume it exists in all societies. Yes, I think guilt is a person's way of expressing their desire for close ties. Through feelings of guilt, you want to be tied to your mother. That stops you living independently. By the way, do you think that she feels guilty over you?"

"I sincerely hope not!"

"When parents have guilt feelings over their children, it's much worse than the other way round."

"I don't think I'm satisfied with that answer," said Niels Peter.

"All right. Let me put it another way," said Isia. "Inducing guilt in a child is one of the strongest weapons parents have in bringing up children. You can make a child who feels guilty comply."

They went down the steps of the hotel.

Isia asked: "And what about me? Where am I in all these discussions?"

"Right next to me."

"No, that's not what I mean."

Niels Peter stopped and said: "Do you want a straight answer?"

She nodded. "Yes."

"I love you so much, Isia. You know I'm doing what I can to keep our relationship together under all these pressures."

Pause.

"But at the same time, I feel compelled to keep what we have between us somewhere in the background."

"But I'm not sure that I want to be kept in the background," said Isia.

Sunlight fell on the white sheets, on their bodies in close embrace.

The still of morning was not yet at an end. The world not yet awakened. However, Niels Peter was fully awake. Awakened by her kisses.

"Let me tell you what I've just been dreaming of," said Isia. "A park with small, thin trees. The trees had been cut back to just above head height — so you could just walk beneath them. They were elegant and so close together they formed a sort of wall that continued upwards."

She lay in his arms. He held her closer. She seemed enchanted as she continued: "The park was very blue. The tree trunks rose with a grey luminescence. I could see small fountains, too. They imposed themselves on the picture. They were round, and the water rose high into the air. It sparkled like silver. The park reminded me of a park I'd seen once in Samarkand. But there weren't any fountains there."

A cock crowed. Then a cart came rattling down the winding road. The village was waking up from its afternoon siesta.

They heard children shouting in the playground.

Isia was in the bathroom singing — out of tune.

He encouraged her to sing.

"I like it when you sing."

Now she was whistling "Oh Susannah".

And letting the tap run! She used huge amounts of water. Niels Peter thought they should be more careful with it.

"No," said Isia. "Water should be kept moving. Otherwise everything comes to a stop. No one should ever be afraid of using water."

They walked down the narrow steps in the mountainside, Isia in front. There was an obituary stuck to the stone wall. A woman by the name of Filomena had died.

"Bittibittibitti," sang a bird.

"Isia?"

She stopped on the step below him.

"Yes?"

"Isn't it also true that separating children from their parents can be very tragic? Separation can bring great bitterness with it. All love or joy suddenly goes from the relationship. That's sad, isn't it?"

"Yes," said Isia, returning to her theme. "But in a case like that, I don't think there's really any love to start with. It's more likely to have been a need to possess."

They passed a ravine full of rubbish, blue plastic bags, cans, broken china — all simply thrown over a stone balustrade. The village rubbish-tip.

Isia appeared to ignore it. She looked at a priest walking past and laughed.

"He's just like Dario Fo, isn't he?"

"Yes."

Then she continued.

"Surely, one separates oneself in order to be oneself? That's what I believe, anyway. It's natural. Then you know that your children will separate from you one day too."

"Yes, indeed," said Niels Peter, noticing the pulse racing in his throat. "But then why are you still seeking such a change in me?"

Isia stood for a moment and frowned.

"Have I said that?"

"Yes, you have. Not once, but several times."

"I didn't mean it that way! What I feel for you... it's as if we had an agreement. We are different in many respects. But we have a need for each other. There has to be equality between men and women... "

"Just look at those," he said, pointing at clusters of large yellow lemons hanging between smooth green leaves. "Look at those nets."

Black nets were spread out over the lemon grove, terrace after terrace.

"You know," he went on. "I've always been afraid of getting too close to people."

"Why?"

Isia flung her arms round him and kissed him. He put his hands on her shoulders.

"In case they make demands on me that I can't honour."

Locked arm in arm they walked down the stone steps and across the metal grids that spanned the water bubbling below them. At home, he found it hard to touch a woman when other people were around.

"Have you noticed how difficult it is going down?" he said.

"Yes, almost more difficult than going up."

"Your father's dead, and you told me you'd freed yourself from your mother. I find that right. But all the same — your mother's alone somewhere and you visit her now and again."

"Yes, I do. I'm very fond of her."

"If you want me to be really honest, I think there's something impoverished in your relationship."

"Yes, but it's not my fault," said Isia calmly.

"Your mother must have done a great deal for you?"

"Yes, some of the time. At other times, nothing."

"Then don't you feel any need for her to do more?"

"No. My childhood was good on the whole. But you can't expect your parents to go on and on giving."

Niels Peter's eyebrows rose.

"How can you bear it that she's so lonely?"

"I wouldn't be able to bear living with her," said Isia. "And if I'm to be rather cynical... "

Niels Peter smiled cheerfully.

"Be cynical — feel free!" he said.

"If I'm to be rather cynical," Isia went on, "I would say that my mother is responsible for her own life. It's not up to me. But now and again it really does worry me that she is so passive. That she can't take on new things. Her old friends are dead, and she doesn't seem to make any new ones."

"What would you do if your mother got cancer and couldn't manage on her own?"

"Well, I suppose she'd end up going into hospital."

"But what would she say to that?"

"I think she'd accept it..."

They passed terraces, delicate blue trellises with green vine shoots curling up round them.

"What do you think about me feeling responsible for my mother?" he asked.

"You can't do any more than you already are. You can't start trying to free yourself from a person when they're terminally ill. But in other circumstances I would probably have challenged you to do so."

"Why?"

"Because parents are a child's first decisive meeting with authority. The way that children relate to their parents will affect their later relations with authority. I've noticed it at the university. In one way or another you believe in authority, Niels Peter."

The next day, Isia started reading Niels Peter's translation of Selimović's novel *Death and the Dervish*.

Now and again she checked it against the original, *Derviš i Smrt*, or with the French translation Niels Peter had brought with him.

"It's good," she said. "You've got it just right, just the right tone."

And a little later: "But isn't it a little difficult, with all this Muslim religious vocabulary?"

"Yes," said Niels Peter, laughing. "That's why I've brought *A Thousand and One Nights* with me! To see what words they use..."

"I see."

In fact he had a whole list of words that he didn't know — dialect expressions and strange names he couldn't find in the dictionary.

He would write to the author — directly from here in Italy — asking his advice.

They celebrated Isia's fortieth birthday at the hotel. Niels Peter felt like writing her a letter on her salty skin. To wish her happiness.

Next to his glasses on the bedside table there were conch shells and small votive offerings, relief pictures in tin.

They walked up steps and along mountain paths, side by side, striding along and wrapped in the same raincoat. The wind blew on the two figures, each with an arm round the other's shoulder and each supporting the other on the tiny narrow paths.

The mist gathered closer round the mountain peaks.

He had to tell her how happy he was. Happiness was not too strong a word.

They didn't say a lot: "You first... ". "After you... "

Wandering round in the drizzle until their path brought them back to the same place again.

As their double bed was made up of two narrow, creaking beds, they had to lie close to each other on one half so as not to fall down the crack.

Niels Peter lay behind her, close, with one arm round her waist.

He tossed and turned throughout the night, and she responded to every movement. She pulled the quilt up round his shoulder, made sure he didn't get too near the edge of the bed, or lifted his head and pushed a pillow under it.

Her pulse beat in her groin. Early in the morning she opened her eyes and smiled; a smile that was to stay with her all day.

Between the balcony and the mountain, an airy spring light, a smoke-coloured cloud drifted by.

Niels Peter wished he'd never have to get up. He wanted to stay in this wonderful bed.

He was hoping some natural disaster might block the way back to Denmark.

No such disaster blocked the way.
 They returned.

That was all seven months ago.
 And here he is with his brother and sister in front of the large bookcase in the living-room at Forest House.
 They are going through the books in the house. Sharing them out between them. Putting them in different piles.

From time to time one of his books would suddenly disappear from Marstrand Street.
 Then Bett would have it re-bound and make him a surprise present of it.

Mette is most interested in the old illustrated children's books. Simon goes for the art books. Niels Peter picks through some of the poetry anthologies and the novels, among them some he had given to Bett himself.

"Can't we sell the rest to a second-hand bookshop?" says Simon.

"Yes, but I doubt they'll fetch much," says Mette.

"How much?"

"A thousand kroner at most," says Niels Peter.

He is standing there with *The Book of Forgotten Things* in his hand. When he opens it, faded pressed violets fall to the floor.

"Can I read you the last lines of a poem? It's by Mayakovsky. It's called "To Sergey Yesenin".

> Our planet is not prepared
> for our joy.
> From our future
> we must wrench it avidly.
> Here in life
> it is hard not to die,
> creating life
> in exchange is highly troublesome.

Misty October. Friendly October. The apples have fallen, but the roses are still there.

The moon rose an hour before the sun disappeared.

Towards nightfall, Niels Peter carried the two sleeping children up to their room. He had slept in this room with Karin and Jacob when the boy was born.

When they had just come back from the hospital.

They had slept here, with the baby in a basket between them. Those small sounds from the basket.

That light sleep.

The kisses they exchanged.

So he misses Isia tonight.
    He arranges one of the quilts in a definite shape.
    As if she were lying there.
    But only for a moment.
    Or his longing will be too great.

MONDAY 20 OCTOBER

"We never did get that willow pollarded," says Simon. He is in the kitchen, a saw in his hand.

Niels Peter is sitting reading *The Book of Forgotten Things*.

Mette is cleaning plastic bags and empty bottles out of the larder. Bags of flour and barley. Plaited baskets and the dust left by woodworm.

She brings preserving jars of wild blackberries and raspberries and lines them up on the kitchen table in front of Niels Peter.

"What shall we do with all these?"

"Can't we give them to the children while we're here?"

"Do you remember going blackberrying with Grandmother?" says Jacob. "Down there on the slope."

The blackberries ripened in September. And the elderberries. And the hazel nuts, which Bett used to keep in damp sand until Christmas.

The blackberry brambles were all in a tangle, with their firm triangular thorns, their jagged heart-shaped leaves covered with small brown spots, the light shining through them.

The berries were of every colour imaginable — from pinkish pale green to greenish-red and madder red, soft ripe berries hanging alongside hard unripe ones, the ripe ones indolent and seemingly weightless, so bloated that they fell into your hand of their own accord.

Large fat clouds floated by in the September sky.

All afternoon a soft thudding noise could be heard as the cherry plums fell to the ground. Trodden and half-rotting, they lay in the grass. The wasps settled on them and buzzed furiously whenever anyone approached.

When Niels Peter came back from Italy, Bett was lying on the sofa in her nightgown and a blue woollen jersey, just a white quilt-cover over her.

It was Thursday, and all four of them were back in Marstrand Street.

The boys were prancing about. He had given them a large conch shell and a card-game each.

"I can't hear the sea in my shell, Dad!"

"Take it out on the street. It'll work better outside."

There was too much commotion in the house.

Niels Peter took Bett's hand in his.

"When did you get back from the hospital?"

"An hour or two ago. The boys came shortly after. Karin and the man with her didn't stay long."

She looked up.

"What kind of time did you have?"

"I've brought an olive branch back for you."

As she hadn't taken her own life — with Simon in Poland, Mette at Forest House and me in Italy — she won't ever, Niels Peter concluded as he finished unpacking.

Bett was not a candidate for suicide.

She simply wasn't that kind of person.

"What did they do at the hospital, apart from giving you a blood transfusion?"

"They took a sample of my liver."

"And what did that show?"

Pause.

"It showed cell changes."

"Cell changes?"

"Yes. They've sent it to be analyzed at the Finsen Institute. I have to go to the hospital on Wednesday morning to hear the results."

Bett and the boys sat at the table while Niels Peter moved back and forth with plates and cutlery.

"Wouldn't you like the living-room as your room? It's on the ground floor, and besides we can easily do without it."

"Wouldn't hear of it," she replied. "I love my little room next to the children. And anyway, I would still have to cope with the stairs, wouldn't I, because the shower and the bathroom are on the first floor."

"Have you seen my bow and arrow, Gran?"

"Yes. How did you get on with Karin's friend, by the way?"

"Bjarne? He's great!"

"Yes, and we fired our bows and arrows too!"

"And you know what? He took us to the pictures!"

"And he's great at cooking. Real food, I mean!"

A while later Zigzag whispered to his father:

"You know what I think Karin and Bjarne did?"

"Sleep together, you mean?"

"Yes, I heard her going 'YES!' with lots of little squeals and eeehs and ooohs!"

"That's good."

"Dad," Jacob broke in. "Would you buy me a bottle of nitric acid?"

"No. I'm having nothing like that in the house!"

"But I want to know what it's like!"

"No!"

On Wednesday morning at half past eight Bett had an appointment with the consultant at Lindebjerg Hospital to hear his diagnosis.

Niels Peter insisted on going with her.

In the train on the way, he read the papers. There was fighting in Teheran between Muslim fundamentalists and left-wing students.

The consultant sat leafing through the file on his desk. Bett and Niels Peter were sitting side by side, watching him expectantly.

"We've now had the results of the liver sample we sent for analysis."

Bett looked lost in the chair.

"And what was the result?"

"Not good."

"Is it cancer?"

The consultant looked at his patient for a long time — without blinking — and finally replied:

"Yes, as near certain as it's possible to be."

Niels Peter wanted to take his mother's hand, but she drew it closer to her.

"Well, it's better to know it, anyway."

"We've thought of giving you chemo-therapy," the consultant went on — with slightly more enthusiasm. "In co-operation with the Finsen Institute in Copenhagen."

"How does that work?" said Niels Peter.

"Chemo-therapy can reduce the pain and unpleasantness and stop the cell growth. What do you think?"

"Certainly!" said Bett without hesitation.

"Can my mother be an out-patient? She can live either with me in the city, or in her own house in the country."

"Yes, that's no problem," said the consultant, clearing his throat and leafing through his papers. "So I'd like you to come in soon — for a couple of days — so that we can plan a course of treatment."

Niels Peter put his hand on his mother's shoulder and looked questioningly at this arbiter of life and death.

"We'd thought of taking a fortnight in Greece in May. We've booked a holiday with a travel agency. We'll be flying. Will that be all right?"

He regretted the question as soon as he asked it. We should just have gone without asking anyone!

"I would strongly recommend that you don't!" said the consultant.

Bett sank another inch or two further into her chair.

"Your mother might take a turn for the worse — and it could be very difficult, perhaps impossible, to get the right help in Greece."

"Do you mean we should cancel the trip?"

"Yes. I can give you a doctor's note," said the consultant, getting up. "Would you discuss the admission details with my secretary before you go?"

The consultant was very tall. They shook hands and thanked him. Thank you very much. That was that!

The countryside slid unsympathetically past the thick windows of the carriage, a bush here and there bursting out in acid green.

Out of the corner of his eye he could see his mother clasping her thin hands, then unclasping them and clasping them again. She tried to put one leg over the other and clasp her hand round her knee.

Reality retreated — retreated and retreated. The landscape began to disintegrate, shattering behind the glass of the window.

Their bodies did not belong to them.

Like fish in a net, they were being drawn towards death.

As a child, Niels Peter had once asked his mother:
 "What would you do if I died?"
 The answer came promptly.
 "I'd lie down and die beside you."

Bett had often said: "One shouldn't really live past seventy."
And she had quoted Grundtvig:

> Seventy are the years of mortal clay,
> the proudest struggle and toil.
> If eighty years a giant achieves,
> the more he must endure.

"No, I don't think one should live too long. It's no fun being old. If there were some of those little pills — then I'd take one when I got to seventy, while I could still decide for myself."

Niels Peter constantly had those little pills in his mind's eye.

If the conversation came round to funerals, Bett would say things like: "Oh, I hate funerals. The worst thing in the world. When I die I want to be cremated. And I don't want a burial place, either. You mustn't feel you're duty-bound to hold some kind of ceremony. They're a tremendous torment and strain. And they're expensive... I joined the Cremation Society a long time ago. They arrange it all... "

He often thought about what she'd said.

Back at Marstrand Street, Bett lay on the sofa and closed her eyes.

The boys came back from school.

"Why are you looking so peculiar, Dad?"

"Am I?"

"Yes," said Jacob, frowning and pulling down the corners of his mouth. "Like that!"

"It's just that I've got a headache."

"Dad, I wish I had a bottle of nitro-glycerine."

"What for?"

"Just to see what it is."

"Oh, you and your chemistry!" cried Niels Peter. "I've had enough of it... !"

Mette and Hans and Milla came to visit. Milla ran over to Bett.

"I haven't seen you for ages, Gran!"

She kissed Bett and wanted to sit on her lap.

"Careful, dear."

Niels Peter left the flask of coffee on the low table and took the three children upstairs with him so that the others could be on their own.

When he came back down to the kitchen, he heard Bett's voice: "I'm agreeing to the treatment they've suggested. I've complete confidence in the hospital."

"Don't you think it'd be better if the Finsen Institute took on the treatment?" said Hans. "After all, it's the main centre for cancer treatment in Denmark and it's quite near here. You could get there and back in a taxi, which would save you that long and difficult journey to Lindebjerg."

"No," said Bett. "Under no circumstances do I wish to be treated at the Finsen. They say you never see the same doctor twice there."

"But wouldn't it be easier?" whispered Mette.

"No," said Bett. "I know that everything will be done properly for me at Lindebjerg."

She turned to Hans.

"Simon's coming back from Poland tomorrow," she said. "Would you explain the situation to him. You're probably the best person to do it. You're a doctor... "

They were alone again. Niels Peter moved the candles and fetched another glass of iced water for his mother. She was lying on the sofa with her hands over her eyes.

He sat down beside her.

"All through my childhood, you always said you didn't want to live longer than seventy. And you'll be that in a couple of months."

"Yes."

"Things like that used to frighten me when I was a kid."

Bett nodded. Ran the back of her hand over her eyes. Pressed her lips together to keep back the tears.

Niels Peter placed one hand on either side of her body and looked steadily into her eyes.

"You've always put seventy as a kind of deadline," he said.

She returned his gaze, steady but somehow different.

"Yes, but now I've changed my mind."

Then she began to cry.

"I do so want to see the children grow up. I've promised Jacob I'll be here for his eighteenth birthday."

The tears were pouring down her cheeks.

Niels Peter handed her a table-napkin.

"Are you afraid of dying?"

"No, but I feel sad about saying goodbye."

Now it was Niels Peter's turn to cry. He took off his glasses, then poured himself a grappa.

"I don't believe you die when you die," he said. He got up and moved around the room.

"I think we're part of something greater," he went on. "The thing that distinguishes our planet from all the other planets in the universe is that there is life here! Every individual human life is part of this greater life. Our bodies disappear, but the actual spirit of life remains."

He drew a dotted line in the air.

"Not as a clearly defined personality, but an individual memory and consciousness, a part of the living mass that goes on existing. Don't you think so?"

"No," said Bett. "I don't believe in any kind of life after death. Death is and always will be the end of everything."

"But life goes on... "

"Not for me!"

She was a genuine atheist, in the proper sense of the term. He got no further in his attempts to persuade his mother of a more spiritual universe. This had been a constant topic of conversation between them ever since he was thirteen or fourteen.

"You're too earth-bound," he exclaimed.

"No! Life stops and disappears with the mortal frame," said Bett, almost cheerfully, as if the discussion had given her heart.

"You mean life disappears with you?"

She thought for a moment, then nodded.

He shook his head.

"But it doesn't! Life goes on. Neither of us is the centre of the universe."

"Yes," said Bett quietly. "That's what I believe, and I think each and every one of us thinks the same."

He sat down on one of the camp-chairs and thought about it.

"If we regard ourselves as the absolute centre — if the world dies when we die — that must imply a huge fear of death, surely?"

"I've never been afraid of dying," said Bett.

"But aren't you now?"

"I've no *desire* to die. My life is not over yet."

They sat in silence for a while.

Bett's voice was trembling.

"If it gets really bad, I want to be here or at Forest House. I definitely don't want to be in hospital."

"Of course," he replied. "Have you given any thought to what might happen? I know it could be a long time yet, but... "

"Yes, it'll be really quiet and peaceful, just the four of us."

"You mean the boys and you and me?"

"Yes."

Niels Peter felt the floor vanishing beneath him.

At about eleven o'clock, he helped her up the stairs. For a long time she'd found the fourteen stairs difficult, but this evening it was even slower than usual. Up till now, he had gone up a couple of stairs ahead of her and pulled her up with one hand.

Now, for the first time, he was having to put his arm round his mother's waist in order to support her.

On more than one occasion, Niels Peter had wished to die himself. To find out about death. To see it face to face. To have his curiosity satisfied, to get it over and done with.

Late the following evening, Hans appeared. Unannounced. Niels Peter was in his study.

"I've told Simon," said Hans. "He knows everything now. And Mette sends her love."

"Shall we go downstairs," whispered Niels Peter. "We can talk more freely there."

He nodded in the direction of the little room where Bett was asleep.

They crept downstairs and put the lights on in the living-room. Zigzag was asleep on the sofa, wrapped in a crumpled quilt-cover.

Hans took off his jacket. Niels Peter fetched two glasses and a square bottle.

"Niels, we really need to talk. I'm worried about what's going on in this house," said Hans. "You'll have to open up a bit. Whenever anyone comes here, you say that everything is fine. But I can see with my own eyes that it's not."

Niels Peter raised his glass and nodded.

"I think Bett believes that any sign of weakness means giving up."

"Do you really think that you can handle it, looking after her on your own here at home?"

"Yes. It's the only natural way to do it. Bett has a real fear of hospital — of a mechanized death in alien surroundings. She feels it would leave her no human dignity."

Hans ran a hand through his fair hair.

"Which is entirely possible..."

"That's why she got us to sign that will... I've given it to the hospital, by the way."

"When was that?"

"Last autumn, when she refused to be operated on."

Hans gave him a sharp look.

"I see... "

"The very idea of sending her permanently to hospital or a nursing home is ridiculous," said Niels Peter. "She's helped us so much all her life — I'd really like to have her here with me... "

"She's our mother too," interrupted Hans. "You mustn't take her away from us completely."

"Is that what I'm doing?" said Niels Peter in astonishment.

"Yes, you... how can I put it... you underestimate the rest of us. Or perhaps Bett does..."

"Yes, I suppose she and I are as bad as each other," murmured Niels Peter, softening a little.

"You mustn't try to be so self-sufficient, you and Bett," said Hans. "You're too inclined to push the rest of us aside. Think about what that means to Mette."

Niels Peter looked at his brother-in-law in bewilderment.

"The rest of us," said Hans, "Mette, Simon and I — we've also got some claim to be involved."

"For Christ's sake, I'm also trying to protect you and Mette, protect your marriage!"

"What on earth do you mean?"

Niels Peter's eyes flickered.

"I mean — I mean that Bett has always been delighted to have you as a son-in-law. She always thought that Mette was very lucky to have found you."

"Oh, I see what you mean," said Hans, calming down.

But Niels Peter was angry now. He got up.

"If Bett moved in with you and Mette now," he said, "I think you would find it quite a strain on your marriage. Especially as you're in the middle of writing your thesis. It really is more sensible for Bett to stay here..."

There was a long pause.

Then Hans spoke:

"What about your financial situation?"

"As long as I've got my grant, then..."

"How long does your grant run for?"

"Until the end of the year. Eight more months."

"And what will you do when it runs out?"

"I'll try to get it extended for another six months. And I'll carry on translating — from Serbo-Croat, English or German. Otherwise I'll teach evening classes, which I've done before. Or try to get a job with a publisher..."

"If things don't work out, could you get social security?"

"Yes. I'm not keen on the idea, though."

Hans poured himself another drink.

"What's this we're drinking?"

"Grappa — from Italy."

"Niels, if you have any problems with money, you must tell us."

"Thanks," said Niels Peter.

"Well, that seems straightforward enough then. Bett will be here with you. And we'll help in whatever ways we can."

"If only I knew how it was going to work out," Niels Peter muttered as he lit his pipe. "If only we could wake up one morning and find that she'd died in her sleep. That would be so simple."

"Yes. But she's going to get weaker and weaker," said Hans. "Soon you'll find she won't be able to walk. How are you going to get her up and down the stairs? Well, I suppose we'll be able to get hold of a hospital bed."

"She's said that if things get really bad, then it's to be just her and me and the children, calm, peaceful..."

At that moment, Niels Peter felt like a traitor. A damned Judas. Before the cock had crowed for the third time...

Hans raised his eyebrows.

"It's highly unlikely that things are going to be calm and peaceful. She might haemorrhage. She might lose consciousness. I also think it'll be alarming for the children to be so close."

It occurred to Niels Peter that perhaps Hans was thinking about his own daughter. So she wouldn't be allowed to come here for a while.

Hans sat upright in his chair.

"You'll have to find out about all this," he said. "You'll need to have a proper talk with the hospital — about the way things are likely to turn out. You must get help from them. And here at home. You're a single parent with two children and a dying person in the house. That's more than most people can cope with."

"Yes," said Niels Peter. "But there's not much we can do about it. In one way or another, it'll probably... "

"In any case, you're going to have to be more open, you and Bett," said Hans. "I think you're probably too introspective."

"Am I?"

Niels Peter got up out of the chair. Crossed the room and stared at the globe. The light inside it was on. He gave it a gentle spin and poured himself another grappa. "I really am *not* afraid of death. Neither hers, nor my own, nor anyone else's. Death is a natural thing. It has to be accepted... "

"For the person about to die, it's a highly unusual event," Hans interrupted. "Death is the absolute end of the world. It's total disaster."

"No, now steady on." Niels Peter threw his hands up.

"Don't you ever feel that we're all part of something bigger? A greater human fellowship that makes the individual person's death slightly irrelevant? I've tried talking to Bett about this, but either she can't understand or she doesn't want to. We can imagine this fellowship including great qualities. Qualities that don't age — that are universal... "

"What, for instance? What qualities are you talking about?"

"Intelligence, loyalty, imagination, love — they exist everywhere. They're constant qualities that can't be simply dispensed with. They last — like a layer of ozone — even when one of us dies."

Hans clasped his hands behind his head and stretched.

"Well, I don't really know... "

"But it's the truth," said Niels Peter. He was standing in the middle of the floor, pointing his pipe at his brother-in-law. "And does the truth make us despair? It doesn't. The truth is the only thing we can live with. Will the world go on living when I die? Yes, it definitely will. So I can also live with the thought of my own death."

Hans couldn't help smiling. He got up and started putting on his jacket.

"That doesn't help you much in this particular situation."

"On the contrary, it most certainly does."

"You're full of religion, you know," cried Hans. "And you call yourself a socialist! Socialism is supposed to be based on scientific theory, not faith."

"Yes, that's true. But we have to preserve the world, and the human race has to develop. That's not going to happen just with theory and practice — there has to be faith too... "

Niels Peter followed Hans out into the hall.

Out on the street, Hans said:

"Do you think Bett has ever considered taking her own life?"

"Yes, I think she has. But at the same time, I also think she's not that kind of person. If she were, then she would have done it at Easter, when she was alone."

Hans unlocked his bicycle, switched on the lamp and said quietly:

"I'm firmly convinced that people who decide to commit suicide should do it two days at most after the diagnosis has been made."

"How are you to know the diagnosis is right?"

"You know it. You feel it."

"And why so quickly?"

"Because otherwise you're tempted to start on some treatment which is going to drag the whole thing out. Once you've taken the first step in the treatment, you're already into all that... well, what can you call it... that circus."

He tried to forget the situation he was in. Tried to force himself to sleep. Couldn't. Read. Put the light out. Woke to the sound of creaking doors — of cars accelerating.

He sat up in bed. How on earth was he going to get through all this? In a few days' time, he had to set the questions for his students' written examination. And at the same time finish the translation. He was still waiting for a letter from Selimović.

The translation was due to be handed to the publisher in two weeks' time.

Immediately after that, he had to set his students the assignments for their oral examination in June.

He'd had his post-graduate grant for about eighteen months now. It ran out in December. He had not done nearly enough. Partly because he had been translating, trying to earn some money, which he wasn't supposed to do. Partly because he had been teaching. And that meant a great deal of preparation, because he wasn't used to it.

It was all particularly painful because of his age. He hadn't completed his studies until he was thirty-four. Now he was thirty-eight. Many of his contemporaries had gone much further.

How would he ever find the time to cope with work, and the boys, and Bett? How would he ever find time to be with Isia?

He had to try to find someone to help him.

He shelved the problem of whom to look to for help, because they were all due to go to Forest House — Bett, the boys and himself — for a few days together. To enjoy the first days of spring, as they usually did.

At the top end of the avenue of birches, the poplars were singing and talking in the wind, waving their hands uneasily and bidding them all welcome.

Bett always used to say: "Shouldn't we have the poplars pollarded?"

It was good to be back at Forest House. They hadn't been there since the Christmas holidays.

Messy, muddy and wet.

Now, in the last days of April, spring was breaking out everywhere.

The boys climbed trees, then came in and dressed up for Bett, who was lying in the big bed in the living-room.

When Niels Peter told them to clear up before dinner, Zigzag started arguing: "Why should we... ? Children in China don't have to!"

"What do you know about children in China? They have to clear up ten times as much."

Zigzag cried back: "Why are you so horrible to me?"

So they comforted him.

Washing up. Happened to break the jug Bett used for iced water.

"It's not the end of the world," said Bett.

Things got broken. Far too many things in the house needed

mending. Bett was no longer able to keep everything together and nobody else was there to take on that role.

The morning of May Day found him sitting on the warm steps of Forest House, listening to the voices of the children as they moved around the garden, listening to that strange sound of sunlight, the satisfying, dense yet clear sound of sunlight. The day was only just starting. Brilliant, the grass slightly damp from the night dew. Gooseberry bushes and elders with green buds on them.

The others had gone to the May Day march in Fælled Park.
A lark soared in the sky.
A cup of coffee sat next to him; an old copy of a Yugoslavian newspaper, *Sovremenik*, lay at his feet.
Sitting on these steps in the sun. The best thing he knew.
As if he were in some Fra Angelico paradise.

Hesitantly, uncertainly, Bett moved round the house. Unable to do anything. But insisting on preparing her own food, which meant soft-boiling an egg and fetching cream from the refrigerator.

It took an infinitely long time. That morning, just as she had finished getting her breakfast ready, she tipped it over. She sat down and stared.

Jacob came running up.
"Don't worry, Gran. I'll do it."
"No, let me do it myself. I'll just boil another egg."

So the whole long slow process began again.
They watched the television news about the fighting at the adventure playground, the North Bridge playground the authorities were trying to close.
"It's horrible, Dad, isn't it... ?" cried Jacob. "Sending bulldozers and policemen to clear everything away!"

Bett sat in the entrance to the barn, out of the wind and wrapped in a rug. Looking out over the yard and garden which were bathed in sunlight. Niels Peter was up in the attic working on *Death and the Dervish*, but kept coming down to sit with her.

"Are you getting enough work done?" she asked gently.

"Don't worry. Another week and I'll be ready to hand it in. I've just had a letter from the author."

"What was it like?"

"Very friendly, and he answered all my queries."

The boys were flying a black plastic kite, a cheap Chinese one. They were up on the hill and waved at the two of them in the doorway.

The kite rose, flapping in the wind. Jacob ran with it, letting out more string as he ran. Up it went. He was dancing with it.

"I feel like the yolk of an egg," exclaimed Jacob breathlessly.

"That's good," said Niels Peter. "And how do you think I feel?"

The boy let out a loud laugh.

"You're like the eggshell!"

The sun shone. The door to the garden stood wide open. Niels Peter found his mother sitting on the big bed in the living-room, her face in her hands.

He knelt down, took her hands in his, and kissed away the tears on her cheeks.

"What are you thinking about?"

"I think it's hard on you, everything that you're going to have to do," she whispered.

"I'll be doing it with the greatest of pleasure."

"Yes, but I won't even be able to help you."

And she started crying again. Silently. She, who was so unused to crying.

"We love you," Niels Peter whispered. "You haven't forgotten that, have you? It's lovely for us to be with you. It's so important to us. Much more than perhaps you realize."

"I'm no use to anyone any more."

He was filled with tenderness.

"Yes you are! You're so warm. And beautiful. We learn so much from you."

Bett was truly beautiful. Light, transparent, with a fine sharp profile and clear grey eyes. Her slim hands. Her body so delicate in that white blouse. Her white hair.

There was something about her that reminded him of a

newborn child.

Niels Peter's words seemed to calm her.

He helped adjust the rug over her knees.

"Would you fetch me a sprig of lilac," she said.

Zigzag came creeping up.

"Will you play picture-puzzles with me, Gran?"

"No, treasure, I haven't the energy. But wouldn't you like to lie here with me for a while?"

Within minutes they were both asleep, the old and the young, side by side. The garden door still stood open, the curtains moving faintly.

As if the room were gilded.

Like gold leaf.

On Sunday, the day that President Tito died, they went back by train.

"What a drag, having to start the week with maths," Jacob grumbled. "Can't I stay in bed a bit longer?"

Got his two tired children up and off to school.

Went into the little room and saw to Bett.

"How did you sleep?"

"Isn't it amazing," she said. "The nights are so crystal clear. And every night I dream the same dream. I dream that all my things are packed into boxes. The contents are white and very beautiful. Every box has a number. But the dream floats above the boxes — like a lid unwilling to close."

"What time did you wake up?"

"At about three. I was trying to find the glass of water."

"Do you think I ought to sleep beside you?"

"No, I don't."

A little later he phoned Hans and told him that Bett was finding it hard to sleep.

"What does she take?"

"Pacisyn to get to sleep, 100mg of Doloxene for the pain, and 800mg of Mechloral."

"She should be taking Truxal," said Hans. "I'll phone a prescription through to you. Tell me, have you found anyone to help you in the house?"

"Yes. My neighbour's daughter, Lajla. She sometimes looks after the boys in the evening, and I've asked her if she could come in twice a week and help with the cleaning."

"What's she like?"

"She's really nice."

"If you ask me, you ought to have someone coming in every day."

After their stay in the country, Niels Peter had a lot to see to in the city.

First he cycled over to his publisher and handed in the translation. It was a relief to get it off his hands.

"We'll give you a ring when we've read it," they said.

Then he went for a haircut.

"Your hair's very long," said the hairdresser. "Must be a long time since you last had it cut."

At two o'clock, he pushed his bicycle across Gråbrøde Square. The square was crowded with people drinking beer and playing guitars in the sun.

At three, he met Isia at the Institute. They had exam assignments to discuss.

On his way home, he picked up Bett's new sleeping-pills at the chemist's. Truxal, 50mg, it said on the label. They were small and black and looked lethal.

When he got back home, Bett was sitting out at the back with Mette and Simon. Bett in the shade, the others in the sun. Simon had his arm round Bett's shoulders and was telling her about his new paintings.

The children were drawing a hopscotch grid in chalk on the asphalt. A blackbird was singing. The chestnuts along Østerfarimag Street were in flower. White blossoms. Red in front of the General Hospital.

The dishwasher was rumbling in the kitchen. Mette must have switched it on before she left.

Bett had come indoors and was sitting by the window.

He wondered whether the noise of the dishwasher disturbed her.

Maybe they ought to do the dishes by hand?

Bett coughed and clutched at her chest. She had difficulty swallowing and tears came to her eyes.

His throat contracted as he looked at his mother — with trembling hands, drinking water from a child's cup. The same little cup that first his own children had used, then their cousin Milla.

Mette must have brought it over with her.

Jacob and Zigzag were squabbling over their food. Bickering.

Niels Peter banged his fist on the table.

"Do you realize how horrible it is, sometimes, being a grown-up?" he shouted. "You're trying to get things worked out all the time, and the moment you turn your back, you fucking kids start squabbling."

Zigzag got down from the table and slammed the front door behind him. Jacob and Bett sat without looking up.

"But why is it like that?" said the boy.

Bett still had the strength to try and change the subject.

"Have you seen the hyacinths on the window-sill? The blue and white ones? Don't they smell lovely? Simon brought them."

That same evening he had three meetings to go to. One with Zigzag's teachers; one at the Slavonic Society; and one with the translators' section of the Society of Authors. He had to decide between them. Which was the most important?

He chose Zigzag.

At the parents' meeting, the teachers explained that there were problems with the class. The pupils were getting out of hand. And Zigzag wasn't doing particularly well.

He was capable of playing up for whole lessons at a time. Especially during music.

Niels Peter promised to have words with his seven-year-old.

He looked at his watch and left the meeting early, at half-past eight, knowing full well that there were still important questions on the agenda.

Cycled home with a feeling of having let down the young teacher.

The boys were in the living-room with Bett. The whole house was in a mess, even though Niels Peter had cleared up before he left. They had been cutting out. Glueing. And making paper darts.

"Bedtime," said Niels Peter. "And that means NOW!"

"Shall we go on up now?" he said, bending over his mother.

She turned her head away. Maybe he shouldn't have gone to the parents' meeting after all...

"You smell of tobacco," she said.

All of a sudden, for reasons that he couldn't define, something seemed to have gone wrong.

He ostentatiously lit his pipe.

"Did you want to say something?" he said.

"How do you mean?"

"I can see that you've got something on your mind."

She placed one hand on top of the other.

"I've been wondering about whether to give up the apartment in Havne Street... "

"I've been wondering about that, too," said Niels Peter coldly.

"...and move all my things to Forest House. Then I'd have everything together in one place. That'd be the most practical. If only Simon could take over the apartment."

"Isn't he quite happy where he is, in his collective?"

"Havne Street would be much better for him, though," said Bett.

What's it got to do with you? thought Niels Peter.

The tone between them had turned harsh.

An uncertain feeling had been dogging Niels Peter for several weeks now, and suddenly it broke through. An uneasy feeling that perhaps he was making a mistake. Maybe he should be saying and doing the opposite of what he was doing now? The thought made him react aggressivly.

Bett was looking straight at him and she repeated what she'd told him before.

"If things get really bad, I'd like to be here or at Forest House. With no doctors. Just peace and quiet... "

Niels Peter looked at his mother guardedly.

"Can you be sure that it'll be quiet and peaceful?"

"What do you mean?"

"Nobody can ever really know what it's going to be like to die."

Bett's mouth tensed and seemed to disappear.

"*I* will be with you all the time," he said. "That's only natural after the life that you and I have shared together. But I'm not sure that the children should be there the whole time."

Now, why had he said that?

Why was he being so harsh?

She gave him a dark look.

A shutter went down for Niels Peter as he heard himself saying: "This is a big responsibility for me. I'm the one who's looking after you. I may find myself in situations when I won't know what to do. I think we ought to talk to the consultant. Together. You and me... to find out what we're letting ourselves in for!"

Her eyes grew even darker.

"I really don't see why we have to see the consultant again. I've been told everything I need to know."

"No," said Niels Peter. He filled his glass and noted Bett's disapproval. "You mustn't try and evade things. We *haven't* been told everything. Neither you nor I know about how things might turn out."

He saw a bitterness rising in his mother. Or perhaps a deep disappointment.

He went on — although by now it was quite unnecessary.

"I don't know how long the children should be made to live with all this. We have no way of knowing whether it's going to go on for a long time. Or whether you'll be permanently bed-ridden... that sort of thing."

Bett gave her son an icy look, as if to say — *now* you're taking the children from me.

And behind the look he gave her lay the thought — yes, but don't forget that they're my children! I'm the one who has to go on living with them.

A long moment of looking at each other. Then Bett spoke.

"When I go in to start my chemo-therapy tomorrow, I don't want any visitors. I'd rather be alone."

"All right. But can't Mette and Simon and I take it in turns to visit you?"

"Yes, if you've got time. But only you three — and only when I say so. Under no circumstances do I want anyone else. And most of all, no unannounced visits."

"I'd very much like you to have other visitors too — Elin or Gertrud or... "

Bett cleared her throat.

"Why?"

"Because perhaps they can talk to you in a way that we can't."

"About *what*, though?"

"We-ell."

"It seems to me that everyone wants to talk *seriously* to me. As if you all think I've got something very important to say. But I haven't! Why can't you all leave me in PEACE!"

He paced the room, smoking nervously.

"Don't you think it'd be a good idea if we got a home-help to come in every morning? When you come out of hospital."

"And what would she do?"

"Help you to the bathroom, for instance."

"Thanks, but I think I can manage that myself."

"She could help clean up, too."

"But Lajla already comes twice a week. Isn't that enough? Does the place really need any more cleaning?"

Yes it does, he thought. What's more, I pay Lajla out of my own pocket. And we need a lot more help. And the social services would probably pay for a proper home-help.

After a while, Bett spoke again.

"On the other hand," she said, "I'd be really pleased if we could look into finding me an apartment in the street here. Maybe even opposite your house."

"Do you think that's a good idea?" said Niels Peter, his heart sinking.

"Yes. I can't go on living here, that's obvious. When we give up the apartment in Havne Street, I'd like a place of my own; the sort of place where the children could come and see me."

He helped her up the stairs. One step at a time.

Put his arm round her waist. Her body was astonishingly heavy.

"If it gets more difficult for you to get upstairs, then maybe I could ask Ditlev if he would give a hand. Then we could carry you up."

She stopped and looked at her son.

"I sincerely hope it won't come to that."

Fetched her iced water while she got herself ready in the little bedroom. Handed her her nightgown. Turned his back and fumbled with something in the cupboard while she sat — half-naked — behind him. Then she said quietly:

"Have you given the consultant my will?"

"Yes."

"Did you give it to him last year?"

"Yes!"

Niels Peter was seething with anger, his back turned to her.

"And I suppose I wasn't meant to, eh?"

No reply. Silence. He turned round.

"For Christ's sake," he hissed. "I just can't understand why you keep going on about that will! You made me sign it and keep it. What was I *supposed* to do with it?"

He left her without saying goodnight.

Perhaps for the first time in his life.

One of the family's cardinal rules had always been never to let the sun go down on your anger.

He switched off the light on the stairs and took a shower.

To wash the day out of his system.

Opened the window to let the steam out of the bathroom. Heard cats mating in the back yard. He hated that noise!

When cats mate they scream. Was it orgasm or pain? He'd often wondered.

Perhaps he'd been precipitate in giving the consultant her will...

Were the children aware of him bending over their bed in the dark? Looking at them.

Did they notice a shadow in their sleep?

The man in the dairy-shop looked at Niels Peter with obvious concern.

"What's the matter with you?" he exclaimed.

"My mother has cancer."

"Oh, I know all about that, Niels Peter. I've been through it myself. My father had cancer. He used to argue with the home-help all the time. Drove us all crazy."

"How long did it all take?"

"A year. And I'm telling you, we didn't see much of the rest of the family. They seemed to have forgotten where we lived... "

The man put his arm round Niels Peter's shoulders.

"I'm very sorry to hear it. Your mother's a really wonderful woman."

"Two litres of fresh milk, please. Two cartons of orange juice, one yoghurt... " Niels Peter read down his shopping list. " ...and a packet of oats."

"Do give her my regards, won't you?"

"Yes, I'm just going back now, to see her off to hospital."

This time Bett was to be admitted for a longer spell. Probably twelve or thirteen days. So that the chemo-therapy treatment could start.

Simon was going to pick her up in a car he'd borrowed from someone at the collective. Why wasn't she going in by ambulance? Because this admission really was a big moment for Bett.

Niels Peter went round the house and packed the few things she was to take with her. Toilet things, address book, writing paper, envelopes, stamps, ballpoint and notepad.

The whole of Bett's slight figure expressed her disapproval.

Niels Peter knew what she would have to go through. The endless waiting on stretchers in cold corridors outside examination rooms, X-ray rooms and laboratories. Long nights. Sleeping problems. Anxiety.

Simon phoned in desperation. The car wouldn't start, and he was trying to get hold of a mechanic.

After their clash the night before, Niels Peter couldn't send his mother off without saying something.

Now she was going to have to manage on her own. Who could she count on for support in a situation like this? Only the people closest to her. And that meant Niels Peter, as the eldest son and his mother's closest confidant...

Simon phoned again. The mechanic couldn't repair the car and it would have to go into the garage.

"Forget it!" said Niels Peter, furious. "I'll cope."

Bett's treatment was due to start in an hour's time. He phoned for a taxi.

The driver came. An old man, staring blankly ahead. Couldn't even be bothered to get out of the vehicle.

Niels Peter helped his mother into the front seat.

They kissed each other. A brief, dry kiss.

"Don't forget, I don't want any visitors," she repeated. "Apart from the people that you and I agreed on Saturday. I'll phone Mette and Simon myself and tell them."

He stood out in the street waving her goodbye.

He should have gone with her!

But what about his work at the university? He was supposed to be teaching.

He arrived home a few hours later. Somehow the whole day had gone wrong. He sat smoking in his study.

Got up and moved restlessly around the room. Put on a record. Lay down on the bed and folded his arms across his face.

Then he sat down at the table and wrote a letter:

> You've been gone for seven hours now. And I've been thinking about you all the time. I miss you and I can't bear the thought of you being so far away.
>
> Today, looking back, it seems to me that we talked too much yesterday. But I feel we'll need to talk a lot more in the future. You say you don't need so much talk. But I do. I need it. Even if I know perfectly well how tired you are.
>
> I hope that things are all right for you now. If only it was Saturday — so we could see each other...

They telephoned from his publisher to say that the translation was extremely good and that they were sending it immediately to be typeset. They sent him their best wishes.

Niels Peter asked if his brother, Simon, could design the jacket.

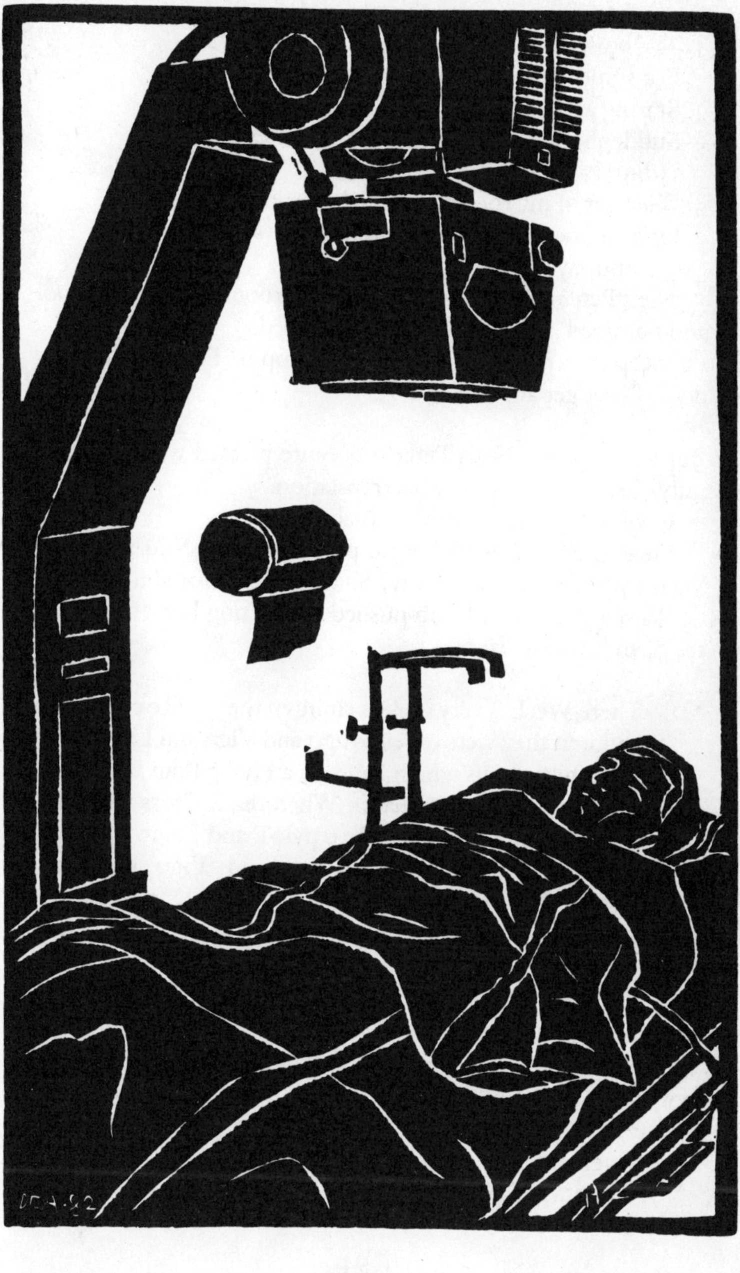

He ought to be pleased with things. He was.

The boys came home from school.

For some reason they were very irritable.

Staring at each other. Teasing each other.

Suddenly Zigzag shouted:

"Idiot!"

"Get out of my room," shouted the elder boy.

"It's my room just as much as it is yours!"

"Shut up, you pig!"

Niels Peter rushed into the children's room, picked up a stool and slammed it hard against the bunk-bed.

"Stop it, now!" he shouted. "Just stop it! For Christ's sake, don't I ever get any peace?"

But all the same, Niels Peter was quite pleased with what the publishers had said about his translation.

Cooked dinner and tried to make the peace.

Helped Zigzag with his simple arithmetic. Said to Jacob: "Have you written your story? Shall I check it for you?"

With a wry smile, Jacob pushed his writing book across the table. In it was written:

> There WerE 3 very cROss children they weRe crosspatch children they were called Hugo and Vigo and Littel Kurt. They bilt a hous which coud fly a Flying hous which had wings and a hooge jetenjin When the 3 Cross CHildren grew up littel Kurt became a pyloT and Hugo became a Milkman on the millKY waY and Vigo became a postMAN and Rored round on his mopED from plannet to plannet Throu Spaice.

"You've got all your capital letters and your small letters muddled up."

"My teacher says the most important thing is that it's a good story."

Niels Peter was lying on the sofa.

"It's nice when you're tired, Dad," said Zigzag.

"Why?"

"Well, when you're tired and lying on the sofa — and aren't at a meeting or at the university — then it's nice."

A moment later, Jacob appeared beside his younger brother and complained:

"Dad! You forgot to put that note in my bag! I should have taken it to school today."

"I put it on the dining-table. Didn't you take it?"

"I can't remember."

Niels Peter sat up abruptly.

"For God's sake, I can't go remembering everything for you! You have to learn to remember things for yourselves. I'm not here to... "

He was just about to say "mother you", but managed not to.

He stood for a long time in front of the mirror.

I'll probably go grey before the year's out. How long is all this going to take?

Does grief always involve a certain amount of anger? For he was certainly angry.

He had a recurring image in his mind: his mother in a high bed in a dismal grey hospital ward. At the head of the bed a lamp bracket and an emergency bell. She finds it difficult to turn over in bed. Now there's a fly buzzing around. She can't get rid of it. She's thirsty. Her water jug's empty. And she doesn't want to inconvenience the nurse for something so trivial.

He couldn't bear the thought of his mother's loneliness — surrounded as she was by this darkness of unknowing.

He set his wristwatch by the radio. His watch gained two or three minutes a day but he always reset it at midnight.

He listened to the radio news; then as the classical music programmes had finished, he tuned in to a mixed bag of folk and funk.

Two children were standing by his bed, crying and looking sheepish.

"I forgot to feed the cat," said the older of the two.

"What cat?"

"I promised to feed Lajla's cat."

"Never mind. It doesn't matter," said Niels Peter, taking the children back to their bunk-beds. "You can feed it early tomorrow morning."

"You won't tell, will you?"

Standing at the bedside, he comforted Jacob.

"Goodnight, Jacko. Sleep well, now."

Jacob closed his eyes and pulled the quilt up over his shoulders.

Niels Peter bent over the little profile in the lower bunk.

"And what's the matter with you?"

"I keep coughing."

"I'll get you some cough mixture."

"Good old Dad."

"Good old Zigzag."

As a child, Niels Peter often used to walk in his sleep.

He remembered his mother taking him back to bed. So gently that he'd hardly notice it.

At two o'clock, he looked out of the window to see which of his neighbours were still awake.

At three o'clock, the birds began to sing. Only four hours to breakfast.

Niels Peter roamed back and forth across the floor of his study, feeling profoundly uneasy.

The whole house was falling apart. Lajla wasn't coming until tomorrow. The boys were at school.

He couldn't get it out of his mind that his relationship with his mother was breaking down. In fact perhaps it had already come to an end.

He had to talk to someone. But who? It had to be a woman. He always found it easier to talk to women.

He rang Gertrud — a close friend of Bett's and a former colleague from school. Niels Peter had known her all his life.

Luckily she was at home.

"What is going on at your place?" asked Gertrud. "Why aren't any of us allowed to help you?"

"Aren't you?"

"No. We're always told that everything's all right and that you're managing on your own."

"But I'm phoning you now, aren't I?"

"So tell me, how are things going?"

"Fucking awful."

"Wouldn't it be better if I came over?" she said. "I could be there in twenty minutes."

Gertrud arrived. Tall and slender, wearing a light cotton coat. She folded it and put it on his bed.

He looked at her in surprise.

"You're two years older than Bett, but you look ten years younger."

Gertrud was wearing a pale brown sweater and light tan slacks, her glasses on a chain round her neck.

She helped herself to coffee.

"You've lost a lot of weight, my boy. Are you eating properly?"

"I've no appetite."

"And you've started smoking?"

"Yes, like a chimney."

"Try one of my roll-ups," said Gertrud, unpacking a miniature industry out of her bag.

"How are the children?" she enquired.

"Fine. So-so."

"So-so?"

"Well, I mean... Zigzag seems to be losing his way a bit. He's got problems at school."

Gertrud sat with her back to the window, so that the light fell on Niels Peter's face.

"Is it true that you're planning to give up the apartment in Havne Street? And move to Forest House?"

"Yes. But it looks... as if it'll be all too complicated now. There are so many things we have to decide beforehand."

"Can't it wait? Can't you postpone it?"

"Yes."

"Until sometime in the autumn, when... "

"Yes."

Niels Peter took off his glasses and hid his face in his hands.

"What is it?" said Gertrud quietly. "You'll have to take your hands away, Niels, otherwise I can't hear what you're saying."

"We had a big row the night before Bett was due to go into hospital. And now she's lying there, cutting herself off from everyone. And it's more than I can take."

"Why is she cutting herself off?"

"Because this is something that she's going to have to live through herself. I just think it's so harsh. And Mette and Simon and I have been given strict instructions as to when we can go and see her."

"When are you going to see her?"

"On Saturday."

Gertrud gave him a thoughtful look.

There was a long pause. Then she said:

"You never got away at sixteen like most youngsters, did you?"

"No, I thought I had, but I hadn't... obviously, after all, and..."

He came to a full stop.

"And what?" said Gertrud.

"And now I feel I need to make that break."

"How do you mean?"

"Well, Bett's been ill for almost two years now. It was already obvious last summer, when the hospital suggested an operation and she refused it. Since then things have gone steadily downhill, and the problems have simply got worse and worse. The worst of it is... "

To his horror, he found himself crying.

Sat there, one hand holding his glasses, the other covering his eyes.

It didn't seem to trouble Gertrud.

"The worst of it is that my feelings for her are so mixed... so contradictory. I can't get her out of my mind. *I think about her all the time*. And at the same time, in between, I resent the fact that she dominates my mind so completely!"

"I can understand that."

He raised his face, wet with tears.

"Can you really?" he exclaimed.

"Yes, that's very human."

"But how can I? I've loved my mother dearly. You know I

have. How can I now hate her? Because that's what's happening, isn't it? Maybe the hatred came the day she and her illness moved into this house? But then, where else could she have moved to?"

"Couldn't she move in with Mette?"

"No, I think they should be spared. Mette teaches full-time and Hans is working on his thesis. And Mette's more tied to Hans than... than I have ever been to a woman. I think they really do love each other."

"And you're afraid that it'll affect their relationship if Bett moves in with them?"

"Yes. No doubt at all. Bett's too strong a personality. Has been all her life. No, it would never work. Mette would be crushed."

"What about Simon?"

Niels Peter smiled as he replied.

"In an artists' collective in Christianshavn? That would go down well! Anyway, Simon's too immature and he's got more than enough problems just managing his own life as an artist."

"I've always liked Simon. He's the most spontaneous one among you. And he's got talent. But tell me, what about you? Would you be able to accept Bett living anywhere else but with you?"

"I suppose I wouldn't. It's just that it's all so incredibly difficult and expensive. Bett doesn't want us to get a home-help. She doesn't realize how difficult it is having to arrange all the transport to and from the hospital. Our family life is getting really messed up."

"You could hand over some of the work to the rest of us."

"She wouldn't want that. I'm the one who's taken the job on, but the trouble is, I can't cope with it. It's all too much for me. I feel so useless."

"No you're not, Niels Peter."

"Yes, I am."

"Not at love."

He wiped his eyes and put his glasses back on. A great sense of relief.

Leant over towards Gertrud and said:

"Do you have any ideas about how her illness will develop?"

"Oh, I've known several people who've had cancer. I also

know someone who has lived a reasonably good life with cancer for many years. I suppose Bett will get weaker and weaker. Soon she won't be able to walk. She'll have increasing problems with eating. And with her digestion, because she can't move. It's quite possible pneumonia or jaundice may set in. And then she'll slowly become more and more listless. That's probably the way it'll go. How are your relations with the hospital, by the way?"

"Bett wouldn't let me speak to the doctors, but I've managed to see them a couple of times already. It's hard to get anything out of the consultant, though. So far, he's been very evasive. Or perhaps I've not been asking the right questions. But we do have Hans..."

"Dad!" came a cry from downstairs.

Niels Peter went over to the door.

"I'm up here," he called. "Gertrud's here to see me. We'll be down in a minute."

"I'm going out to play."

"OK," said Niels Peter. He went back in and sat down.

"How long do you think it'll go on?"

"I can't answer that."

"It seems that nobody can. Not even Hans."

"No, because no one can say anything with certainty. It'll depend a great deal on how strong Bett's will to live is. And that's always been very strong."

"Yes. I think I'd feel very defeated if it wasn't."

"You see!"

"But I can't bear to see her cutting herself off like this. I can't accept it. For God's sake, surely we must be allowed to help her!"

"Haven't you got a girlfriend?" asked Gertrud, rolling herself another cigarette. "Don't you discuss things with her?"

"Yes. A lot. And she's very understanding and helpful. But she sometimes feels pushed aside, too. Anyway, she's in Dubrovnik at the moment. At a conference. You know, sometimes I just want to be rid of my love-life... there's no room for it..."

"I really don't think you should do that! You can't put your own needs wholly to one side in a situation like this."

"I just wonder whether it wouldn't make everything very

much easier."

"You have to take Bett's condition into consideration. It is a truly terrible thing for her to have to adjust to the loss — of everything — which death is. All her life, Bett's been a very giving person. You should have known her when she was young, Niels Peter! She was fantastic. She kept us all together. Such a sense of humour, such generosity. Can you imagine what she meant to the school! To the pupils. To her colleagues."

Gertrud's eyes glistened.

"Her feminine sense for the small things in life. Her letters and poems, the little gifts she gave. Her consideration for other people. And her interest in art. Yes, Niels Peter, your mother's a rare creature."

Gertrud got up and reached for her coat.

"Are you coming over to see us this weekend?"

"I'm in the middle of preparing exams. I haven't the time."

"But you must. Bring the children with you. They can play in the garden."

"That's a good idea."

"I think I'll drive over to see Bett now."

Niels Peter was momentarily alarmed.

"But she told me no unannounced visits, under any circumstances."

"What if I don't know anything about that! Maybe you and I haven't had this talk. Does she have to know?"

Gertrud telephoned a few hours later:

"I've been with Bett. She sat up in bed and she talked and talked. We had no difficulty understanding each other. There's no doubt, she does need the company of others."

"Was she angry that you came?"

"Not a bit."

"So, see you at the weekend?"

"Yes, and I'll cook you a really good dinner, so you'd better be there!"

Niels Peter scratched his head. He phoned the hospital and got through to the nurse on the ward.

"Yes. A few times we've found your mother crying when

we've gone into her room."

"Oh, no!"

"It's a very difficult time for her. She insists on washing herself when she goes to the bathroom. Sometimes she takes up to an hour doing it. She's quite exhausted afterwards. But she won't let us help her."

"She's very determined to keep us all at arm's length," he said. "She says she wants almost no visitors. What do you think about that?"

"Well, it's hard to say, really. But deep down, I think she'd like you to come."

"Would you mind going and asking her if it's all right for me to visit her this evening? Even though I'm under strict orders not to come until the day after tomorrow."

Permission was granted! He took the train to Lindebjerg, and then a taxi the short distance from the station to the hospital. Ran along the corridors — past aluminium tables, stretchers...

Lay across Bett's bed and buried his face in her quilt.

"Why, what's the matter?" said Bett calmly, stroking his hair. "Have you been talking to them? Have they told you something? Do you know something that I don't?"

"No, no, no!"

Apart from the fact that he knew she was dying.

And that they had such a short time left together.

He wiped his eyes on her quilt.

"If you only knew," he whispered, "how awful I felt over the row we had — the evening before you came here."

"But you help me think clearly, Niels Peter. You always have."

He sat upright as Bett went on.

"You make me see things from a different angle. I'm a very free and easy person, and I have this tendency not to face the facts. You're different, though, and that helps me."

Niels Peter took her hand.

"Will you listen to me?"

She nodded.

"It's far too much for me to cope with all on my own. I feel so unsure of myself. Couldn't you open up a little more? You've got so many really good friends. Why can't you let them in too? You mustn't isolate yourself so much, which is what you're doing now. There are a lot of practical and psychological aspects to your illness..."

Something changed in Bett's gaze.

"Yes there are," he went on. "And it'd be helpful if we could discuss them more freely. With each other. With friends. And with the hospital... So that we can draw on them for advice and help."

Bett gave him a hawkish look.

"I still can't see why! I've always been quite used to managing on my own."

Niels Peter let out a sigh.

"When you get back to Marstrand Street, I'd very much like you to have your friends and family coming to see you."

"Oh, but then you wouldn't be able to work, Niels Peter!"

I can't work anyway, he thought. But he said:

"Yes I would. They can come one at a time, in turns. That really would be a help to me."

"Well, all right... if you think so."

He pulled his chair up to her bed and opened his shoulder bag. Took out a screw-topped jar — and a small bouquet of anemones in a clear plastic wrapper.

"Thank you, dear. Who made the soup for me?"

"Lajla did. She's also cleaned your room and ironed your blouses."

"You know," said Bett, "the hospital food here is terrible. And monotonous. If I ask for some soup, they say they can dissolve a soup-cube for me."

Niels Peter cautiously put his hand on his mother's stomach. He had been looking at it and had noticed it had grown bigger. He felt it now with his hand. It was hard. Was it the tumour? Was it her liver? Or what? Suddenly Bett straightened up and looked him sharply in the eye, one hand clenched.

"I'll have you know I was furious about Gertrud visiting! Did you know she was going to come?"

Niels Peter couldn't lie and never had been able to, even if it meant getting himself into trouble.

"I knew she would probably visit you one day."

"So I can't trust you! Not even you, Niels Peter. I *don't* want any unannounced visits. I'll make up my own mind when I want to see people. I don't want anyone coming to see me — not now that I'm weaker than usual. I've written to Gertrud to say she *mustn't* come unannounced. Will you post the letter for me?"

"I'm very sorry."

"Please, don't let it happen again!"

Bellows and gurgling noises came from the next room.

"There's some poor mental patient in there," said Bett.

Then she held her hand out to Niels Peter.

"What worries me is — you're thinking about me far too much, Niels Peter."

He nodded. She was right.

"Sometimes your thoughts feel like a heavy quilt, weighing down on me," she said.

"I'm sorry," he sighed.

"The best thing for me would be if I knew that you were working every day, concentrating on your studies."

"But I do," he replied sullenly.

"That translation you've just handed in may turn out to be really important to you."

A nurse opened the door.

"Would you like a cup of coffee?"

"Not for me, thank you," said Bett. "I'd rather have another glass of iced water. But my son would like some."

The nurse handed him the coffee and closed the door.

"Would you ask Mette to bring me some more ice-bags? You know, the kind you fill with water and put in the freezer to make ice-cubes."

"Don't they have ice-cubes here in the hospital?"

"Believe it or not, they don't. And there is a fridge out in the kitchen."

Bett was becoming exhausted by the conversation and was breathing heavily, her eyes feverish.

"Also, would you mind not phoning and having conversations with the staff behind my back," she said. "It humiliates me, seeing my right to decide and be responsible for myself taken away from me."

He didn't reply.

"I enjoy being allowed to lie for hours entirely with my own thoughts. Without interruptions. I lie here going through my memories from childhood. Memories that I've not given time to before. I don't mind being alone. I'm surrounded on all sides by friendliness and care, which is a great luxury... "

"That's good," he broke in.

His mother was not going to be interrupted.

"But there's one thing that very much surprises me, Niels Peter. One thing that no one seems to understand. Not even you. That is that I want to be left in *peace*."

"Nothing wrong with that."

"But I'm not left in peace. I've even been visited by a priest. A very nice young priest. But I sent him away. I have nothing to say to a priest."

She calmed down.

"Now, tell me how are things with you and the boys?"

"We're going to see Gertrud at the weekend."

"Why? Why there all of a sudden?"

Here we go again!

Niels Peter was beginning to get quite angry. What the hell was it to do with his mother where he went at weekends!

But he controlled himself.

"Because Gertrud invited us," he said coolly. "And because I'd like to."

Bett changed her tune.

"Well, I should think it'll do you good."

He got up and looked at his watch: "I'd better not miss my train."

"Give my love to the little ones."

"Would you like to have a photograph of the children here? On your table?"

"No. Don't bother," said Bett, who used to keep hundreds of photographs of her grandchildren. Maybe she doesn't think of them as her grandchildren any longer, he thought.

As he left the hospital and walked down the narrow streets to the station, he knew that this was the very last time he would weep for his mother. Never again.

Everything would be handled more dispassionately from

now on.

The sun was a huge red sphere in the pale sky over the railway yards. The trees in the gardens were in blossom — tender, trembling.

The hissing of car tyres in Copenhagen. Bluish-white street lighting. Long shadows on the asphalt. Lights in windows and pleated white lamp shades. Bicycles at rest for the night, locked. Children's chalk marks on the asphalt, half worn away.

The tulip heads all closed up for the night.

Stars in the sky. Small and large.

He saw his window from the street. The front door shut. The wind was getting up.

He was fond of his street.

The children, in coats too big for them, running to meet him. Casting long shadows. They flung their arms around him.

Fumbling blindly. As if drunk.

It was wanton destruction. The person he had loved so much had now disappeared. Love distorted and gone.

His sleep was confused and heavy. His dreams seemed to carry him off somewhere. To an obscure country whose language he did not understand, whose manners and habits were alien to him.

The postman stood outside his door, dressed in red, carrying a black bag. He held several white envelopes in his hand.

"You're looking cheerful this morning.

"Actually, my mother's got cancer and she's in hospital."

"Oh, I know all about that. I had to look after my own mother myself. It was terrible. And we didn't get any support from anywhere."

"We're lucky. We do."

"We had to handle the whole thing ourselves. And it damned well nearly ruined us. Cancer! It's a terrible thing."

A dark-skinned man was standing on his doorstep, his hand held out. A beggar. Quite clearly a beggar.

"Got anything for the unemployed?"

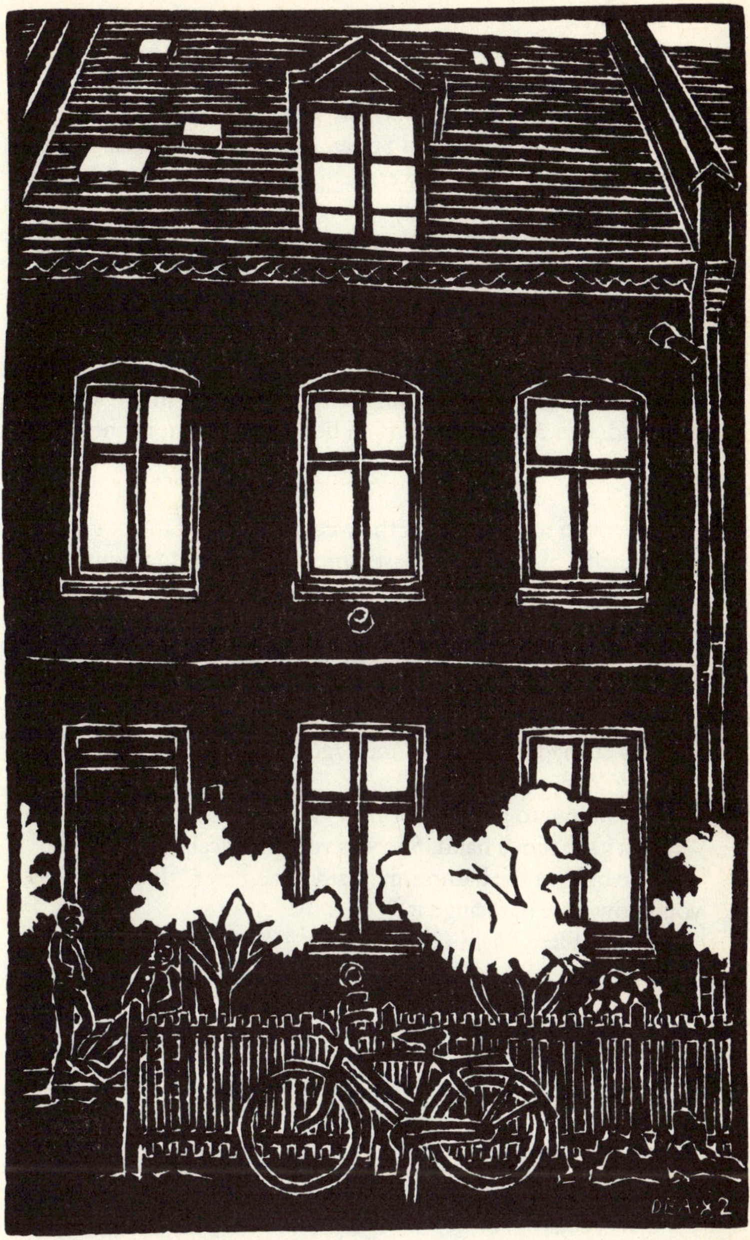
DEA·82

"Like what?"
"Some food? Or a little cash?"

The sun dipped below the horizon. A ball of fire.

It was quiet in Marstrand Street. Brilliant green trees. White narcissi. Cherry trees in flower.

The rustling leaves of May. The crisp nights.

This was about the time they had been due to go to Greece — himself, Bett and the children. It was a pity they'd told the children.

Instead Bett had ended up here, in hospital — fighting the hardest battle of her life. And the loneliest.

If she'd had a husband, it might have helped. With his love — if he had any. As she lay here, in her single room, in the most bitter situation imaginable.

They went to see Gertrud at the weekend, he and the boys. She spoilt them. She cooked roast lamb. They talked late into the night. Slept in beds with freshly ironed sheets. Got up late. Had breakfast in the garden.

Afterwards Niels Peter spent a couple of hours playing football with Jacob and Zigzag and Gertrud's grandchildren.

He was at the university. A message from Isia was waiting for him.

Went home to prepare for Bett's arrival.

Lajla gave him a hand. She was very practical.

"The bulb in the bathroom," said Niels Peter. "It's gone. Do you know how to change it?"

"No problem," said Lajla.

At last Bett returned to Marstrand Street. After twelve days in hospital.

She sat on the sofa with the boys and Niels Peter. Lajla brought them tea and white bread.

"They've drawn up my programme of treatment," she said, showing him the timetable.

"For a whole year, as you can see."

She looked proudly at Niels Peter, brushing loose hairs from her blouse.

"Let's see, let's see!" cried the boys.

"Shh," whispered Niels Peter. "Be quiet now."

"From now on, I have to go to the hospital every Thursday, as an out-patient, for a blood-test. And every fifth week, I go in for five days for chemo-therapy."

There was a knock at the door. Oh no! he groaned inwardly. He was just helping Bett to the table.

Isia appeared.

"I've just got back from Yugoslavia."

Niels Peter felt himself stiffen. He looked away, avoiding eye contact.

"I hope I'm not disturbing you," said Isia. " I just wanted to see how things are going. And I've got a message for you..."

They were standing in the hall.

"My mother's just come out of hospital. She's very tired."

"You look very worried. Is something wrong?"

"So much has happened, that's all."

"Tell me what's happened."

Isia's questions were a torment.

He was aware of his own hostility. A barrier seemed to be forming between them. Impenetrable. She said a few words. He wouldn't answer. Then he saw that she was obviously disappointed.

"Shall we go upstairs for a moment?" he suggested.

She followed him up the stairs and began to tell him about the conference in Dubrovnik. He didn't want to hear it. Not now, anyway. He was thinking about his mother's treatment being fixed — for a year — and about having to transport her there and back, there and back, between home and the hospital. But this was hardly something to bother Isia with, not at the moment, anyway.

"I'll be going soon," said Isia. "I just wanted to see how you were. Is there anything I can do to help?"

He shook his head.

"You look awfully miserable," she whispered.

"I am."

Tears came into Isia's eyes. He leant forward and stroked her hair, then her cheek and down to her neck. They looked at each other. The barrier began to dissolve.

"I don't know what I'd do if I didn't have you," whispered Isia.

Something was changing again, between them.

He looked at his watch.

She stretched out her arms towards him.

He glanced at the closed door. Got up and put the latch on.

They embraced each other. Started undressing. Flung their clothes across the floor. On to the bed in a close naked embrace, exchanging long kisses.

Suddenly there was the sound of footsteps outside the door.

"Dad, Dad, open up!"

Jacob was shaking the door.

"Someone wants to speak to you. Gran and Lajla said I had to fetch you."

"I don't want to be disturbed for the moment," called Niels Peter, seeing the latch about to give way. "Go away now."

They heard Jacob stamping off down the stairs, obviously in a temper.

Isia and Niels Peter lay for a moment without moving. Paralyzed.

"We'd better get up," he whispered.

They dressed and smoothed out the bed.

"I'll come down with you," she said.

"You needn't."

"But maybe I can help with something before I go."

"You don't have to. But couldn't you come back tonight at about eleven, when everyone's asleep?"

Bett was sitting on a chair by the window like a small shadow in the light. The dishwasher was rumbling. The boys running noisily through the house. Some friends had come round to play.

The problem that Niels Peter had been called down to deal with had already been solved. Just the chimney-sweep on a routine visit.

Isia and Niels Peter sat down at the table next to Bett.

"I've just come back from Yugoslavia," said Isia. "I thought I'd call in to see how you all were."

Bett was annoyed, and frowned as she watched them lighting their pipes.

"You smoke too much, Niels Peter. I've begun to notice that recently. And it's bad for you, with your weak lungs."

He nodded.

"I can't see the point in destroying yourself like that. Both of you smoke and drink far too much."

Bett looked at Isia.

"You don't give a thought to the the situation he's in."

Niels Peter placed his hand on his mother's thin arm.

"So much has happened the last few years," he said quietly. "Divorce and work and illness — you'll have to forgive me if I use stimulants now and again."

"There's a horrible smell of tobacco in here."

Niels Peter got up and made a sign to Isia.

"See you, then?"

"Yes," said Isia. "Hope all goes well."

Then she left.

He got the boys into bed. Now he was standing with Bett at the bottom of those fourteen stairs. They looked up them. They seemed to be endless.

She put her left hand on the banister rail and her right arm round her son's shoulder. He grasped her firmly around the waist with his left arm.

Slowly, they took the bottom step. Then she took a rest, and sighed. With his right hand, he grasped her trouser leg and lifted her foot on to the next step, then leant forward and pulled her up with him. Her legs were heavy. With no strength in them — as if the muscles had gone completely.

The last two stairs were the most difficult.

There was a strange acidic smell from her body.

He had a momentary vision of letting his mother go, watching her hurtling backwards down all those stairs...

Helping her into bed, undressing her, giving her his father's old nightshirt, which was roomy and light.

"Would you wind my watch, please?" she said.

Taking the various pill bottles out of her toilet bag. Going down for iced water. Giving her the pills one at a time: the white one, the pink one, the grey and the black one.

Slowly, she sank back on to the bed.

"Would you help me bend my legs. Yes, that's it."

"Listen," said Niels Peter, his face turned away. "I'll tell Isia we won't be seeing each other any more here in the house. You two just don't seem to get on well together. In future, I'll arrange to see her in town. Every now and then."

"Yes, that's probably best," said Bett, putting her hands under her cheek. "Sleep well. It's nice to be home again."

Isia came as agreed at about eleven. Niels Peter had put out two glasses and opened a bottle of red wine. He reminded himself to buy some more wine.

They were sitting in separate chairs. He put Nielsen's "Sinfonia Espansiva" on the record player.

"Things aren't going too well."

"I think I know why."

"Why's that, then?"

Isia looked thoughtful. She lowered her gaze.

He looked at her, irritated.

"I don't think we were very considerate this afternoon. My mother had just come out of hospital. And we disappeared up here."

Isia lit her pipe and puffed out a cloud of smoke.

"But wasn't that young girl here to see to things... ?"

"But, all the same... "

He nodded in the direction of Bett's bedroom.

"I can't cope with this mixture of death and sex. I'll have to concentrate completely... on seeing to... all this."

"Is your mother very jealous?"

"Probably. She probably finds it very hard to accept my taking an interest in you. She demands my full attention, and she's got a fair claim on it. She's dying, after all. But on the other hand, all this could drag on for a long time."

"Purely theoretically, you might even die before her."

He managed a smile.

"So might I, for that matter," Isia went on. "But you're right — concentrate on your mother. You should — I can see that. You can come over to my place if you get a chance."

A moment later he leant over again.

"Isia, I find it very difficult," he whispered, "to accept that she was so abrupt with you this afternoon."

Isia was cleaning out her pipe with a pipe-cleaner.

"I found it painful," he whispered.

"You shouldn't worry."

He made up the camp bed in his room. He'd decided to sleep alone. Isia sat on his bed, not knowing what to make of it.

"Why don't you come over here with me?"

"I can't."

"Just for a while."

"It won't work. I prefer to sleep by myself."

He lay down on the camp bed and pulled the quilt up over his head.

Isia lay on the other bed, smoking.

They were both wide awake. Then Isia got up and dressed.

"I'd better go."

Rain was falling heavily as he let her out into the darkness.

In the night he was woken by a loud noise coming through the wall from one of the other houses.

He could hear voices but couldn't make out the words. Maybe it was just the sound of the water pipes. On the other hand it did sound like two people quarrelling. Like two lovers having their very first fight.

For a few days he heard nothing from Isia.

Then they met at the Institute.

"How are you?" he said.

"I've had a dreaful migraine," she said. "It's been years since I last had one as bad as this."

It had been difficult then.

It's not quite so difficult now.

And maybe things might even get better.

Niels Peter is up in the attic. It is late evening.

Burning your bridges, selling your house, moving, forming new focuses in life — isn't that what most people have to face up to?

A short while before, all the lights and heating in Forest House had gone out with a bang. The fuses had blown. Bett used to fix things like that. Now Simon did.

There was a roaring sound like the sea out there.

On the floor beside Niels Peter is a large old trunk full of his letters. Letters he had brought over to Forest House so as not to clutter up the place in Copenhagen.

Letters from the whole of his life. Letters from friends — about school and studies. Love-letters from girlfriends, full of little drawings, photographs and pressed flowers. Copies of job applications. And all Bett's letters to him — written in her characteristically spidery hand.

Where on earth was he going to keep all this stuff?

Mette had even found all his letters to Bett one day when she was clearing up.

"These are yours," she had said. "You'd better deal with them."

Bett can't have read them more than once.

He takes a few of them from the pile and looks through them.

Should he take the stamps off the earliest ones and off the letters from abroad? No, that'd be too much like desecrating the envelopes.

He puts all the letters back into the trunk and carries them down the stairs, across the yard, now quite dark, and out into the grounds, out to the place where they used to burn the garden rubbish.

Shakes the letters into a large heap and puts a match to them.

He feels a desire to tidy up behind him and to live each day as if it were his last. This involves him imagining that he might die at any moment.

He's ready to.

But is he prepared to live?

As he stirs the bonfire with a branch to make sure that everything has burnt, a thought strikes him. Something about his mother that has been puzzling him now becomes clear.

That time when Bett was lying in hospital saying that she wanted peace!

The peace that he didn't understand. Then something in her appeared to change. She became more resolute. More precise in her relations to the world.

She was finding a way to free herself from him!

As the dying free themselves from the living.

TUESDAY 21 OCTOBER

The coffee-maker is bubbling away in the kitchen; the bread is in the toaster. They're sitting round the big table.

"Everyone's got a grandmother except me," says Milla.

"No," says Mette. "Not everybody has a grandmother. Lots of people don't."

"Everyone at the kindergarten has one. I'm the only one who hasn't."

Simon is sitting gloomily at the end of the table, wearing an Icelandic sweater.

"I can hardly bear thinking about clearing out the studio."

"Shall we help?" says Niels Peter.

"No. I'll do it myself."

"When are you going to start?" says Mette. "Today? Tomorrow?"

"When I've got my head together."

"What else do we have to do today?"

"I think we ought to look at the larger pieces of furniture," says Mette. "The big bench and the chest-of-drawers and the cupboards and... "

She is the most level-headed of the three of them. The brothers are constantly asking for her advice:

"What shall we do now?"

"What do you think?"

"What shall we do with the chest-of-drawers?"

"Do you want it?"

"No, it's too big."

"Then we can leave it here in the house."

"Or take it to the flea market," says Mette.

"I haven't a lot of room at my place," says Niels Peter.

"And I've got even less space," says Simon. "But if there are any kitchen things left over, we could certainly use them at the collective."

"We'll bear that in mind."

They re-organize Bett's little bedroom as a room for all the special things.

In it they put all the things to do with their family or Bett's old school, things they don't want to keep themselves — but which they don't want to throw away either: books, old letters from long-dead relatives, tied with silk ribbons, pictures, photographs, glasses and other fond mementos.

They have agreed with Bett's sister, Elin, that she will come on Friday and help decide what to do with all these personal things.

Outside the windows of Bett's bedroom, the fields in the filtered October light, blue hills merging one behind the other as in a painting by Brueghel.

They're in the barn opening a box of Christmas decorations.

"Here's a whole packet of sparklers."

"Can we have them?"

"Yes, but light them in here. You really can't see them outside in the light."

"Got any matches, Dad?"

"We'll have to shut the barn door or it won't be dark enough."

The faces of the three children are lit up by the cold light of the sparklers.

The air was full of midsummer sounds, a murmuring and whistling and the bubbling light of the chestnut trees. One blue evening in May when Niels Peter took Jacob, Zigzag and Milla to the Tivoli Gardens.

While Mette stayed in with Bett at Marstrand Street.

Just before Whitsun.

They were standing outside the Pantomime Theatre looking at the peacocks on the curtain.

"Let's go on something exciting," said Jacob.

"Not yet. First let's go round the gardens and look at all the free things."

The water in the fountains changed colour, fanned out, came together and then spread out again. There were performers riding one-wheeled bicycles and waving their arms about. Balloons in every colour imaginable, anchored to heavy concrete weights.

They walked through the alley behind the roller-coaster.

"Can we have some candy-floss?"

"It's bad for you."

"Oh, Dad!"

"No, I said. No!"

"Not even if we pay for it out of our own pocket money?"

"It's too messy."

"Well, we're going to buy some anyway... !"

"You know what... ? A girl at our school cut her finger."

"Did she?"

"It looked disgusting, it did. And all the insides poured out."

"Can you die of that, Dad?"

"No, or at least you'd be very unlucky if you did."

"I can't eat my candy-floss."

"Throw it away then."

They walked past the bumper-cars — electric sparks were showering from the netting above — past shooting-galleries and amusement arcades and past a place where people were dancing behind huge coloured windows.

"I wish Gran was here!"

"Me and Zigzag thought we'd give her one of those huge big striped lollipops for her birthday."

"For her seventieth birthday?"

"Yes."

"Look, you can have your photo taken like Superman and Batman!"

"Look at that tattooed man swinging the clubs."

"Hey... man... Dynamo... man!"

"Again, do it again! Cor, that must be really hard!"

"Hey, look, those boats are sailing on real live water."

"Brilliant! Can we have a go, Dad?"

"Watch for a while instead."

"Oh, Dad, *it's much more fun to have a go!*"

All round the lake hung festoons of little purple, red and green lights, their reflections in the pale blue water forming circles. Beds of narcissi. More beds of tulips, some with several heads on the same stalk.

The clock on the City Hall tower struck the quarter hour.

By now they had been once round everything that was free, and again found themselves in front of the Pantomime Theatre, its little stage bright in the dark. It was very crowded. The children couldn't see very well, so they walked on past the white Pierrot statues and the orchestra scraping away on the platform.

"Now, you can go on three things each."

"No, four!"

"No, three. That's the deal. I'm not made of money, you know."

"Me for the roundabout!"

"Me for the Blue Wagon."

"No, the Fishpond. You always win something there!"

"Can we have a balloon?"

"No."

"Please, Dad, oh please, please."

"They're ridiculously expensive and you'll only lose them."

"Then we'll go to Purgatory!"

"I hate that."

"But we're going in all the same, you old fogey. You can just watch."

"If we can't go to Purgatory, then we want to go on the real roller-coaster."

"It's too dangerous."

"We're *going* to Purgatory!"

Purgatory! It was indeed like being on the way to Hell! The noise was deafening. Hyperactive overgrown adolescents in denim jackets, baggy trousers and panama hats. Rushing all over the place, in and out. Making the suspension bridges sway. Shrieking. Pushing. Tyrannizing the younger children. Wheels turning. Moving staircases going up and down. No synchronization. Slides. Swinging ropes. Little girls crying and adults with headaches, looking desperate.

At last Jacob, Zigzag and Milla had had enough.

They stood there panting in the chilly evening.

"We've never been on the Big Wheel before."

"Let's try it, shall we?"

After waiting a quarter of an hour at the steps, in among an elegant and cosmopolitan crowd, they got up into one of the Ferris Wheel's balloon gondolas.

Jacob and Zigzag sat on one seat, Niels Peter and Milla on the other.

The children gurgled with laughter.

"I'm not holding on to anything — look!"

The huge wheels creaked into action.

Milla pressed against Niels Peter with little shrieks of delight.

"Fantastic!" cried Zigzag, his hair flying.

Slowly they were lifted up and through the lights in the chestnut trees. Hanging still. Swaying in the air. The twinkling garden lay beneath them. Far away out there — they saw the harbour.

"There's City Hall Square!"

"There's the Railway Station!"

"And there are the lakes right over there! Hooray!"

A brilliant, warm and sparkling city on all sides; below them the little roller-coaster roaring into its papier-mâché tunnel. They could hear the crash-bang of breaking china in The Crazy Kitchen.

Then with a sigh and a sinking movement, the wheel turned the top of its cycle and started coming down. They clung to each other and to the safety bars. Phew, as they felt the fall. The exhilaration of being scared.

"Oh, isn't it brilliant!"

"It tickles!"

Niels Peter saw three radiant pairs of eyes and happy smiling faces.

Now they were up again among the planes and stars.

They swung round and round in gigantic circles. The City Hall clock shone white — opposite the oval, scared-white face of the moon in a violet-coloured universe.

And the swans flying by.

That night he read Ross and Feigenberg on death. And Isia had given him Frankl's *Psychology and Existence*.

He read in the hope of understanding more about what he was going through.

Opened the window out on to a great emptiness. The lights on Marstrand Street were winking at him, every wink a summons. To what?

Found the two boys in with Bett in the morning. Zigzag was

asleep, snuggled up close to her small body; Jacob squatted Buddha-like at her feet.

"You're not bothering Gran, are you?"

"They're so sweet," said Bett, giving him a smile.

"I've given Gran her breakfast," said Jacob proudly. "I made tea and yoghurt, and carried it up on a tray."

Outside — dazzling sunlight. A dazzling forecourt to life itself.

During the day, he derived great satisfaction from being able to devote all his attention to his mother.

The translation had gone to the typesetter, and now he was waiting for the proofs. Meanwhile he was going through the projects for his students' oral examinations.

It was clear that Bett had now slipped into a calmer phase.

By now, the antagonism she had shown during her long stay in hospital was gone.

She very much wanted to talk to other people.

Share herself with others.

This took a great pressure off the family.

"Do you want a bath this morning, Bett?"

"No, I was given a bath the day before yesterday. That'll have to do."

He brushed a few white hairs off his mother's shoulders.

"Don't you want a bath every morning?"

"If only you knew what a lot of bother it is. Once a week will have to do. I just sit here, so I don't get dirty."

"Even if one doesn't get dirty, one does sweat."

"Well all right, twice a week then."

She looked like a dirty mirror, all blotchy, but didn't see it herself.

It suddenly struck him that perhaps it was actually for the staff's sake that they washed patients every morning.

"Do you want a clean blouse?"

"Do you think I need one?"

"Well, I don't know about need... It'd be nice if you had one, though."

The washing-machine was constantly on the go. He and Lajla

washed Bett's clothes in secret in the hope that she wouldn't realize how often she had to change. Naturally she found out when the clothes came out the wrong colour, because they had been careless with the wash.

He also washed his own clothes, extremely carefully. And the children's. And towels and teatowels and bedclothes. Everything that could be washed was washed.

"I do wish you wouldn't use that violet rinse," said Bett. "It looks deadly."

"Yes," he said, but went on using it.

Luckily, Lajla was now coming in every day to help with the house and with Bett. She was young and unemployed and a thoroughly lovely person.

It startled Niels Peter: In theory I could be her father.

Bett didn't regard Lajla as a home-help, but more as a friend of the family. They talked about everything under the sun.

And Lajla kept a record of her hours, which she gave to Niels Peter on the quiet.

They spent most of their time in the little garden behind the house.

Sometimes Ditlev sat with them, talking or reading a book. The house did actually belong to him, a fact they somehow forgot.

A wild vine tumbled over the wooden fencing. Jacob sat on the steps with a magnifying glass and a piece of wood.

"What a lovely month May is," said Bett. "I'm so glad I'm here."

Friends started coming.

Every morning, Bett and Niels Peter checked with the diary. This way, they could organize people's visits, so that there was at least one and at most three a day.

Her friends willingly fell in with the arrangement; they would bring Bett small presents, flowers and home-made soups.

There were bunches of forget-me-nots, lilies-of-the-valley and narcissi everywhere. In teapots and jamjars, for there were no vases in the house.

Bett had very definite ideas about whom she wanted to see. The older the friendship, the better. Members of the family, friends from her youth and childhood took pride of place. And she had increased her circle of friends for every year of her life.

But sometimes the ways in which she chose among some of her longer-lasting friendships were inexplicable to Niels Peter.

Bett wanted to take her afternoon nap on the camp bed in the back garden. The bunches of flowers were placed at the head of it. Lajla put a rug over her and a pillow under her feet.

Niels Peter sat at the garden table with a pile of exam papers and watched his mother sleeping silently.

Then his gaze wandered above the fence to two pale grey collared doves swaying on a wire. The male was trying to cover the hen. They flapped about, unable to find a foothold on the wire, stopped for a moment and then tried again. The hen stretched her neck and spread her wings. The male hunched up. They swayed, unable to keep their balance, gave up and disappeared in different directions.

At about two o'clock, Bett woke, smiling. Her eyes had become yellower. She looked tanned. Yes, noticeably so.

Slowly Lajla helped her out of bed and over to an armchair at the end of the garden table, then put a pillow behind her back and lifted her feet in their blue Chinese slippers on to an upturned beer crate.

Bett sat there like a queen on her throne, ready for the day's audience, a bright red silk scarf over her white hair and wearing the blouse that Lajla couldn't get white or well-ironed enough.

She had three thin gold bracelets. A present from her husband. One for each of her children.

"Isn't it lovely here?" she said. "Look how the roses are growing."

"Do you want the newspaper?"

"No, I'd rather just sit and look."

The first guest of the afternoon arrived — her sister Elin. Elin had brought her a posy of artemisia.

"I'd very much like to come and stay with you at Forest

House for a couple of weeks this summer," said Elin.

"Oh, if only you would," said Niels Peter, throwing his arms around his aunt's slight waist.

"Come and sit down here next to me," said Bett. "And tell me what you've been up to."

Before a visitor came, Niels Peter would ask his mother: "Would you rather I left you alone?"

"I'd rather you were somewhere near. Maybe over there at the table, reading or writing."

"But don't you want to talk about... more personal things, perhaps."

"They all want to talk about serious things. As if there's something important that I *have* to tell them. And I simply can't imagine what that might be!"

Sometimes he wondered if she was keeping something secret. Something she didn't want to reveal? Was this why she didn't want to be left alone with anyone? Or was it that her surroundings were closing in on her?

Dazzled by reading the paper in the sun, Niels Peter eventually left the back garden and went into the house. His eyes took a moment to get used to the dark.

As far as possible, he always tried to be there to greet her visitors at the front door, taking the flowers and whispering:

"You have to reckon with her wanting to chat about everything under the sun."

"Fine," they would say, and then the talk would start. About work and children. Homes and holiday plans. Journeys and things they'd bought recently.

Niels Peter had a feeling that he was putting his mother on display. The others, like me, need to see what it is, he thought. Maybe they can learn something that they'll be able to use later.

Then the wine merchant arrived with a crate of white wine from Viggo, Bett's brother.

In one way, it surprised Niels Peter that Bett's old friends found it so easy to talk to her. No one seemed to feel awkward or shy. All of them talked to her naturally and with affection.

This filled him with pride. He felt that his family was hugely privileged, a privilege which he had to ascribe to his mother.

He was sitting at the garden table with a dictionary and a stack of papers. He had just been sent the galley-proofs of his translation and was going through them. But one ear was listening to Bett and her visitors talking.

It struck him how much of the general conversation was about *food*! Magnificent dinners described by the visitors; loin of beef, sea food and French wines discussed with enthusiasm. It didn't seem to embarrass Bett. But perhaps her friends had simply not realized that she had long ago eaten her last meal and now survived on a monotonous diet of liquid foods she could hardly taste.

Many of them brought letters from abroad, from France, the United States, Sweden, England, Norway, Yugoslavia. Large colourful stamps on the envelopes.

The art of letter-writing was far from dead!

Many of the letters had to do with Bett's old school. The same letters were often read aloud, the photographs were passed round. Anything to do with her school — teachers and pupils — interested her greatly.

They agreed in the end that Niels Peter should answer the telephone — in Bett's presence. Then she could make signs if she wanted to speak to whoever it was. Or not, as the case may be. If she waved eagerly, he took the phone over to her on its long extension cable.

Now and again, she would say: "I'd like to be alone now. I need to rest. Gather my strength."

For what, he wondered.

The kitchen sink was full of dirty water. Scummy.

An hour later he looked at the sink. It was still full of water which had not run away.

"What shall we do?" he said.

"I could run across to the paint shop and get some of that stuff to put in it," exclaimed Jacob with enthusiasm. "I can do that, Dad!"

Jacob fetched "that stuff", the waste pipe cleared and the water soon ran away.

Now half a kilo of potatoes lay in the sink.

Reaching out for the Chinese coffee flask that stood against the background of flowers and the green wild vine. Closing his eyes and drawing in the aromatic scent of the flowers. Thinking about Isia. A flash of anxiety that she might leave him. That they would never meet again. He consoled himself — she has *said* that she loves me.

Opened his eyes and saw Bett sitting on the chair at the end of the garden table. A small basket-work case on her lap. She kept things of special importance in that case. Family silverware that was all wrapped up; on the outside she had written the names of her children and grandchildren. A number of small boxes containing a medallion with a photograph in it, a coral necklace, little red Indian beans with tiny elephants inside them, an amber heart, a thin gold chain, a brass ball, a splinter from the Holy Cross in Jerusalem, made in Hong Kong.

In the case she also had her father's letters to her mother, two leather-bound volumes of poetry with gold lettering on them, and a posy of everlasting flowers.

She raised her head and said to Niels Peter:

"That fine black leather case with the velvet cover — I'd like you to have that. You know, it's under my bed, in a plastic bag. But remember, don't let it go flying!"

"Yes," he replied. And he thought: either I'll take it with me next time I go flying... or else I'll give it away. From then on, he always thought of it as the flying case.

Bett was beginning to give things away. Things that had hitherto been too good to use. She hadn't had the heart to use them, but over the years she had kept them stored in bags and cases. A pink straw hat with a veil, that Elin had once given her, a twin-set, an elegant tailored suit from the fifties, smelling of lavender.

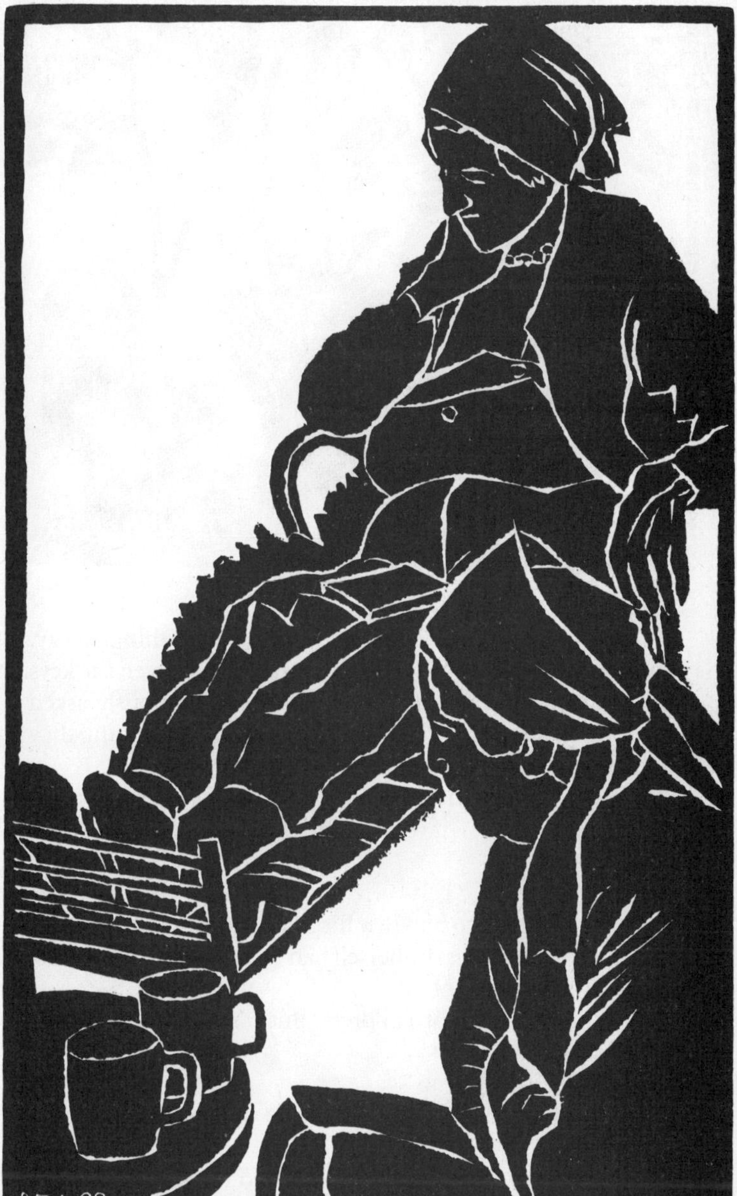
DEA 82

A little while later, she started giving larger things away. Furniture and pictures. The recipient was simply given the keys of the apartment in Havne Street. And they cautiously asked Mette, Simon and Niels Peter whether it wasn't something they would have liked for themselves.

But the three of them replied truthfully, as if with one voice:

"By all means take it, if you want it — Bett loves giving things away."

Sometimes it seemed to him that his mother was trying to tempt those around her, just as she herself had been tempted all her life. Tempted to own this or that.

One can always tempt children. But it's also quite easy to tempt adults.

For his own part, Niels Peter wished to own nothing but the bare minimum.

Only what was necessary for himself and the boys to live.

He didn't want to store up old things and keep them piled

away in bags and cupboards. Nor did he want to get involved in shifting things about.

Every year he spent a couple of days at Marstrand Street just going through his possessions and discarding everything that was unnecessary.

He fought a daily battle to keep "things" at bay. All those "things" that arrived via the letter-box. All the "things" that the children found in rubbish skips in the street. All that expensive packaging, the jars and plastic containers food was sold in in this competitive world.

Never before, though, had the battle to keep things out of his life been as great as today — now that they were sharing out the Forest House furniture among themselves.

October is a beautiful month. But June has something strangely flat and subdued about it. June lacks an independent character of its own.

He never longs for June; in fact he's generally glad when June and July have gone.

That feeling was especially strong this year.

The garden at Marstrand Street — which had been so dazzling and concentrated in April and May — had lost its attraction now.

Or was it that the leaves of the trees were losing their strength? Was it that the chestnut leaves were beginning to droop? Was it that the holidays were beginning? The unwelcome obligation of having to relax? Perhaps it was just those lazy, sunlit streets of Copenhagen, which seem to become wider in June.

The nicest things about June were the long afternoons and the changeable weather. The light was strong. But things lacked real colour. The colours did not come from within, but seemed pasted on the outside.

Only the long bluish evenings of June were beautiful.

Bett clutched her breast.

"Oh, June depresses me," she said. "I can't bear to think that it'll soon be Midsummer Day... and then the days will start drawing in."

Lajla put the new garden barbecue on the table.

"It's for you. Bett asked me to buy it. It's a present."

Cutting the boys' hair. Then their nails.

"That's too short!" they cried out.

"Look what you've done to my thumbs!"

They wriggled and fidgeted so that he cut their hair unevenly and so had to trim it even shorter.

"Into the bath, boys."

"Oh, not again, Dad!"

Jacob and Zigzag under the shower and Niels Peter washing them. Rinsing their hair. Drying them on blue towels. Drying their hair. Cleaning out their ears. Looking at them. Rubbing body oil into their skin.

The two boys were standing in front of him. Fresh and healthy. Silky-soft. The smell coming from their hair and mouths was like the smell of freshly-licked kittens.

They were purring.

He was intoxicated by their strong young hair and their dark eyes.

"I hate socks," said Zigzag.

"Why?"

"Because they get so stinky."

The window was open on to the blue stillness of dusk.

Niels Peter had begun to believe that his mother was going to live for much longer than they had first imagined.

Began to adjust to that.

Talked to his brother and sister about it.

It started all over again. Some of Bett's best friends came to visit again. Like pearls in a pearl necklace being drawn through someone's fingers.

She was taking a purposeful farewell of her friends. One by one. They took it as a pleasure and privilege. Without sentimentality. Without excess. Appreciating being given the opportunity.

The city rumbled on around them, all that was green growing greener. They sat in the garden eating ice-creams with the neighbour's three children.

This period of time was meaningful.

It had substance.

Was it the treatment they had to thank for this?

Then came another twist.

Ditlev came down and sat with them.

Suddenly Bett asked him a very direct question. As if he were a doctor or Our Lord, and not a mere teacher of Russian.

"Tell me," she said. "Can a single small liver test like that really show that it's cancer?"

Ditlev took off his glasses and looked at her short-sightedly.

"Didn't it go to microscopy at Finsen?"

"Yes, but I still can't understand that they're really in a position to make a diagnosis like that."

Ditlev put his heavy glasses back on again and looked thoughtfully at his old friend, this teacher of the art of living. He cleared his throat and said in a quiet voice:

"Are you saying that you're not sure you have cancer, Bett?"

"Yes. How can I be? I don't feel ill at all."

"I doubt that they would start you on a course of chemotherapy if they weren't absolutely sure."

"Just one little test," Bett said angrily. *"How can that prove anything?"*

Niels looked from Ditlev to his mother and back again.

Ditlev drew on his pipe.

"There's one thing you have to remember, Bett. Cancer develops very much more slowly in older people than it does in younger people."

"Does it really?" she exclaimed joyfully. "Did you hear that, Niels Peter?"

Zigzag came in from the street, pale and tearful.

"I fell off my bike and hit my head."

Niels Peter took him up on his lap. Bett watched from her chair.

"And there were all these amazing colours. Everything turned red and green."

He put the boy down on the empty bed and Ditlev covered him with a rug. They kept him under observation, in case he was sick.

There was a new look, something distant and detached, in Bett's eyes — she, who had always been so attentive and painstaking with the children.

Bett leant on Ditlev. Painfully, slowly, they mounted the three garden steps and went into the porch.

Her face was dark. Yellowish. Sunken, as she said with a little smile:

"You know I'm trying to get an apartment here in the street? Preferably in the house opposite. I'd very much like to have my own place. You understand that, don't you?"

"I'll tell you if I hear of anything," said Ditlev.

At seven o'clock, the sky grew darker. Then came the thunder. Then the rain. Now the rain was rattling down on to the asphalt.

Niels Peter went upstairs to see Ditlev, who offered him a beer.

"Some of the things that Bett says embarrass me," he said. "Her mind's going."

"You're wrong," said Ditlev sharply. "Her mind isn't going. However, she has got jaundice..."

Constitution Day. A day off school for the children. Cloudy. The boys were going to Fælled Park, to their old kindergarten, where they flew kites every year on this day.

Niels Peter packed their backpacks with fizzy drinks and sandwiches and sent them off.

"Gertrud's coming soon," said Bett. "You go upstairs and get on with your work. I'll be all right on my own, for heaven's sake."

When he came down a few hours later, Bett was alone and looking very much alive. It was clear that Gertrud's visit had had a very special effect.

"Oh," she exclaimed enthusiastically. "*We had a wonderful cry together.*"

Niels Peter managed a smile.

"You've no idea how good it felt," said Bett.

She had cried until the tears ran dry.

Maybe this was what was wrong — that he and his mother hadn't cried together? They didn't do that. They couldn't. They had found no reason to — not since that day at the hospital, when he'd decided that he had cried for his mother for the very last time — and that now everything was to be more matter-of-fact.

Bett's eyes were shining.

"And do you know what Gertrud said? She said they only offer you such expensive treatment if they can really see some point in it."

Jacob had lit the grill. There was a smell of methylated spirits and charcoal.

Ditlev came and gave each of the boys a present — a white plastic crash-helmet for when they were on their bikes.

A blackbird was perched high on the television aerial, whistling cheerfully, with one eye on the sun. Then the flags were lowered and that was the end of Constitution Day.

Fatigue, fatigue, fatigue. The day had been a long one.

"I've been thinking," he said to his mother. "I'd really rather *you* told the boys about you having cancer."

"I'd be happy to do that, if that's what you want."

She took off her scarf and shook it out. Leaving a scattering of white hairs on the table.

"I'm moulting like a little cat."

She was moulting — it was that wretched treatment.

The boys helped her up the steps.

"Why do you get so tired, Gran?" said Jacob.

"Because I've got a disease called cancer."

"What's that?"

"It's when some of the cells in your body start to grow wild. And that makes you very tired."

"Is it dangerous?"

"Yes."

"Can you die of it?"

"Yes, you can."

"Will you die of it?"

"Yes, sooner or later. But it can go on for a long time."

Jacob hid his face in his hands and started crying.

When she was lying down, she raised her hand and beckoned to Niels Peter to sit on the edge of her bed.

"It'll soon be time for my next five days' chemo-therapy at the hospital."

"Yes?"

"I'd thought of asking if you'd take me with you to the country. Then I could live at Forest House and just go back and forth in an ambulance and not have to be admitted."

He remembered how bitter everything had become last time she had been admitted.

"Yes, of course," he said. "That'll be fine. I'd like that."

"Do you think it can be done — practically speaking, I mean?"

"Yes, as long as I can get Karin to take the boys. Their

summer holiday starts next Friday."

He took off his glasses and polished them on her quilt cover.

"It's very unpleasant, the chemo-therapy, isn't it," he said.

"Yes. They pour a fluid the colour of red jelly-babies into my veins. I wondered whether you'd like to come with me to the treatment, so you can see what happens."

He put his glasses back on and saw a shrivelled little yellow concentration-camp prisoner.

She had once been his mother. She'd had large soft breasts and thick dark hair.

"Can I think it over?"

"Of course."

"Are you afraid of the treatment?"

"Not really."

"Would it help," he went on, disingenuously, "if I was there?"

A proud person always says no to a question put like that. And that's exactly what she answered:

"No, no. I just thought you might find it interesting."

"You know, it's an experience I think I can do without."

"That's all right. Don't worry about it."

Traitor, traitor, that's what he was.

He had denied her request. He'd not thought of the nausea the chemo-therapy caused her, but only of his own queasiness.

Jacob crept into the study.

"Dad, you mustn't be cross about what I'm going to say."

"Go ahead. But whisper!"

"Is it infectious?"

"Cancer?"

"Yes. Somebody at school said that cancer's infectious."

Niels Peter raised his eyebrows.

"No, that's not true. If it was, then it'd be criminal to let people's families look after them when they've got cancer. No, you really mustn't believe that."

"Can you inherit it?"

Maybe the children were afraid.

As he was.

As everyone was. Afraid of this terrible disease, the modern equivalent of the plague.

He dreaded the thought of being alone at Forest House with his mother for the period of her treatment. He had to have someone to talk to. Someone who could help. But who? In his mind he went through his friends and members of the family. The lot fell to Simon.

"You'll have to come with me to Forest House."

"No. You know I'm in the middle of preparing for my exhibition."

"You must. I won't take no for an answer."

How many times music had helped! In the small hours of the morning, Chopin's piano concerto, which Simon had given him.

Now the record player wasn't working. How was he going to get it mended? Should he take it to a repairer? But it was too big to carry. Could he get someone to come and mend it? Yes, but that would probably cost a fortune.

It sounded as if someone were trying to get in through the front door, which was locked for the night.

He lifted his head from the pillow; pricked up his ears.

Sat up in bed. Wide awake. Was that the noise of the electrical appliances in the house? Or was it someone trying to get in?

It was raining. The wind was rattling the doors. It had come to fetch someone. It had come to fetch them to Forest House.

Since that day when everything had become horribly clear, he had occasionally noticed a kind of curtain coming down on his life. Everything turning black. And a deadly anguish creeping up on him. He was not fit to live.

He was not fit to nurse a dying person. The thousand daily details left him confused and unsure of himself.

Karin came to fetch Jacob and Zigzag, and Bett and her two sons set off for Forest House. She in an ambulance, they by train.

She was on a stretcher in the ambulance, although she had

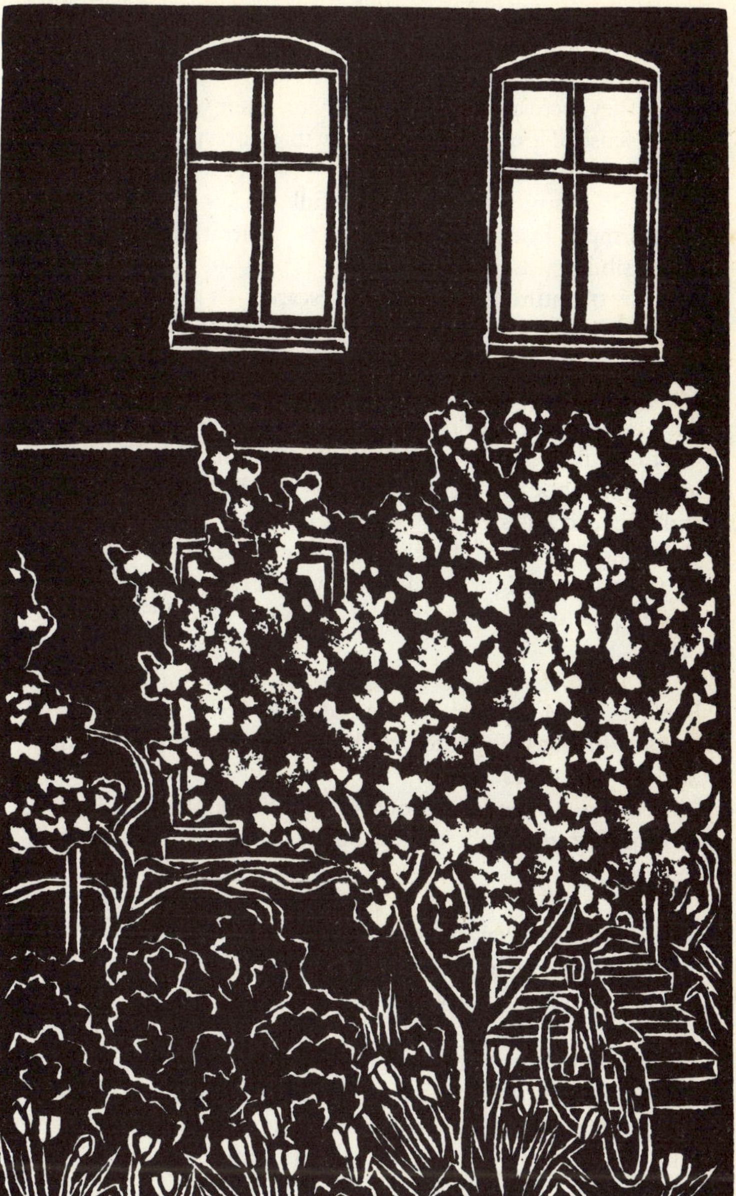
DEA·82

insisted on sitting. This was a constant source of conflict between mother and son.

There they were at Forest House. Niels Peter walked the fields with a sense of great sorrow. Sorrow that Forest House had lost its enchantment. It would never, never be the same again!

His life was slowly turning full circle. He was being transformed from second to first generation. Now the responsibility was his.

A law of nature that no one can escape.

You look for a chance to run, but you have no choice.

The good thing about Forest House was being the second or third generation, with Bett always seeing to everything.

She could get the neighbours to work miracles. There was something about all those offers of help which both impressed and offended Niels Peter.

But now he and his brother and sister were to be responsible for the house, and their generation wasn't capable of asking the neighbours to help in the same way. Things were different these days.

Bett was at the hospital. Simon and Niels Peter sat on the steps that led down to the garden, backs against the doorposts, as they had so many times before.

Listening to the sounds of the house and looking around.

Enjoying the sight of the birches that they had planted themselves.

They sat there taking in the countryside as if it were an unconscious *you* that they could talk to.

Nature was a whole, and they were part of it.

"It worries me, what's going to happen to Forest House," Niels Peter told his brother.

"What do you mean?" said Simon, chewing on a straw.

"Well, when the time comes, I suppose that Mette could be here on her own with Hans and Milla. But I couldn't really cope with there being two families in the house at once. We'd probably end up arguing. I tried it once before."

"Then we'll just have to go on sharing the house at different times," said Simon. "I'd like to be happy here — whether it's with Mette or with you."

"But if it's the two of us, I think we'd feel very isolated. Unless we had friends to stay. And we'd have to look after them, wouldn't we? And we've no car. What about food and stuff? I'm just beginning to see how hard it's all going to be, and how time-consuming..."

"Come off it now," exclaimed Simon. "The shopkeeper's always brought everything we need."

"It's always been Bett who's organized it, though."

"Then so can I, damn it!"

"What about the oil for the heating? And getting the grass cut, and mending the roof — and all the damned expense?"

"You can always bring Isia with you."

"Yes, but a family collective like that wouldn't necessarily be right for her."

Bett came back from the hospital every day after her treatment. Clearly exhausted.

"Will it be all right if I go out this evening?" said Niels Peter. "I've arranged to meet Isia in Lindebjerg. We're going to go out for a meal. And Simon wants to read to you from Colette's *Sido*."

"Wouldn't you rather bring Isia back to Forest House tonight?"

"Yes, but don't you remember our agreement?"

"Can't you bring her back after I've gone to bed?"

Bett was rubbing her hand up and down her arm. He looked at her.

"Does it itch?" he said.

"Yes," she said. Tears in her eyes. She stopped rubbing.

He brought Isia back when Bett was asleep. The brothers showed her the house and then they all went for a walk together over the fields.

"It's a lovely place," she said. "So unusual."

They were sitting in the pergola in the blue of the evening. Simon had lit a fire and they listened to a tape that Isia had brought with her, a recording of a radio broadcast about Alexandra Kollontai, the Bolshevik writer and diplomat.

They undressed in silence in the attic room; Isia now naked.

But in the tension of the moment, he saw his own body as shrivelled and greyish-yellow, a diseased body about to embrace her healthy one.

It began to grow grey behind the window pane. Isia kissed him. On the mouth. On the eyes. Slowly, his anxiety faded.

In the morning she drove off — without waiting to see Bett.

The fifth and last day's treatment. Simon went with Bett to the hospital and sat in the waiting-room while she had the red liquid poured into her veins.

After the treatment, an ambulance drove them to Copenhagen.

Niels Peter stayed behind at Forest House for a few hours, on his own, to clear things away and lock up.

Then he went back home to Marstrand Street, by taxi, train, and, finally, by bus, and was met by Bett and the boys.

Bett usually felt very poorly for several days after her chemotherapy. She took a dive. Down and down!

Then — slowly, interminably — she came back up again. She was stabilized. Had a brief reprieve. And then, just as she was improving, the next five-day treatment would start.

It rained. The roses grew.

Bett was so tired that now and then she cried from sheer exhaustion. Then they would talk together, and it passed.

On the one hand, it was a terrible burden.

On the other hand, in a way, astonishingly easy...

Niels Peter phoned Simon to see if he could help look after Bett and the boys one evening.

"I'd like to," said Simon. "But I've got to go to a meeting of the Society of Artists. It's my union work, and I can't afford to miss it.

So Niels got Lajla in to look after the house while he went on a run round the lake.

The little track around the lake was in a bad state. Cracks in the asphalt and the banks of the lake falling into the water. Huge fish, seemingly without colour, sluggishly moving their tails;

gulls bobbing on the water and breaking up the reflection of the berberis bushes. Clover and burdock in flower. And elm seed slowly floating down from the sky. Murmuring. He remembered the seeds in the school yard when he was a child.

All appointments cancelled. No meetings. No parties. Nothing. Apart from this one thing: this last time in the city with her.

Just before Midsummer Day, Mette and Hans arrived in their car. Milla in the back with a scrap-book on her lap.
 Bett's things were all packed and ready in the porch.
 Bett set off for her summer holiday. No problem; everything went smoothly.
 The last thing she said was:
 "You will phone, won't you, Niels Peter? Once a day, just to let me know how things are."

Now he had three weeks to himself. After that, he and Simon would be going to Forest House to relieve Mette and Hans.

He had been curious about how he would react once Bett had gone. Would he feel that he was being denied an essential part of their time together?

On the contrary. From the moment the car disappeared, he felt an enormous sense of relief.

I'm free!

Isia was in Århus and wasn't due back for a couple of days.

Ditlev, Niels Peter and the boys had a little midsummer party in Marstrand Street.

The neighbours had made a bonfire with some old bits of wood. Lajla sang and the others joined in. Her father passed round a bottle of sloe-gin.

Bett's roses were still in a jamjar on the window-sill, withered and dying. He left them there. Without a sound, the petals fell and lay on the sill in bright, slightly yellowed heaps which then fell to the floor. For some reason or other, he felt no desire to clear them up.

Sometimes he saw an acquaintance or one of his students in the street. He hadn't the energy to talk to them. Glanced away. Crossed over. Passed at a distance.

Occasionally, though, he couldn't escape.

"Hi, how's things?"

"All right."

"Your mother's a very strong woman," one of them had told him. "And long may she go on being so... "

"I don't think it's quite that easy, really... "

"Yes, but you can't expect things to be easy... "

June was warm. He felt a pent-up excitement. He began seeing things.

Young women, cycling past in the streets, in shorts and white rubber-soled shoes.

Women looking at him from all directions.

Suddenly he'd feel frightened of being alone with women. Frightened he might start kissing and embracing them. Pressing himself up against them.

Ready to leap, just like a frog.

Then, at last, Isia was back.

It was light on the other side of the curtain; the morning star in the sky, the evening star transformed into the morning star. In the old days they were thought to be two different stars, until it was discovered that the planet Venus was actually a wandering star.

A bird was singing in the tree outside.

He saw Isia's face in the shadows below him and heard her say: "I'll always love you."

"Don't say that!"

"Why not?"

No reply. But he was thinking: because then you'll probably leave me, like the others.

For the first time in many months, he took his guitar down from the wall and started playing.

His students had finished their oral exams, and he had good reason to be satisfied with their results.

The boys were sitting at the garden table, drawing robots and space ships and skull-and-crossbone flags.

The roses were blooming, white, yellow, red... incredibly insistent.

Naturally he phoned Forest House. Every day. To see if there was any news.

Mette or Hans would answer the phone. The conversations were painful, but necessary. He had promised.

But he didn't understand the purpose of these phone calls. So that he could be kept in touch. But why? After all, for a short while it was no longer his burden.

He was told that Mette and Hans, with the help of Bett's doctor in Lindebjerg, had got a system of home visits under way. A nurse came in every morning, a home-help twice a week.

They had also got hold of a wheel-chair for Bett. She now spent her days in the wheel-chair, out among the fruit trees of Forest House.

Mette had found a big box of family photographs. They were looking through them all and writing names and dates on the backs.

Bett was growing quieter and quieter. She would often just sit and stare.

"Are you finding it hard?" said Niels Peter.

"No," said Hans. "We're grateful for these weeks together with Bett. You know how much she means to us, and that includes me."

Lapis lazuli; that is how the sky above Copenhagen was one day in early July.

Niels Peter and the boys walked through King's Park, down Gother Street, across King's Square, and then down through Nyhavn to Havne Street.

It was a still Saturday morning with people poking around under the bonnets of their cars, or sitting with a beer on the quayside.

"It smells of Gran here," said Jacob as they went into the apartment. "I love that smell."

They stood in Bett's apartment and looked around for the things she had asked them to fetch. Two quilts. And a gold watch in a creaking drawer.

Everything was clean and tidy, all in order; just one unwashed cup in the kitchen. The water was running in the lavatory cistern.

Shadows slid past him.

Voices and sounds from childhood.

"This is the last time we'll be here," he said to the boys. "In a few weeks' time the flat'll be empty and everything moved to Forest House. So that Bett can have everything in one place. You've got to say goodbye to the flat... today."

Jacob's mouth trembled. Zigzag looked at his father enquiringly.

"But why can't we keep it? Even if Gran can't get up the stairs?"

"Because you can't have more than one flat. And the people who own the house have their own use for it."

He hugged the boys and stroked their hair. They helped him

to say goodbye; with them he could look forward to the future.

"Can we take our toys back home?"

"You can fill one carrier bag each."

This cheered them up a little. Jacob went along the window-sill dismantling a Polish toy train. Zigzag found a football in a basket and two picture books in the bookcase.

Bett had told him: "Niels Peter, if you find anything you'd like to have, just take it."

He took a few cups and some coloured glass. A chair with a rush seat. Found the two quilts and the gold watch. Also a bottle of Campari on the top shelf in what had once been his room — and poured himself out a glass.

Got down on his knees and pulled a big flat wooden box out from under one of the beds. The box was full of drawings. Simon's drawings, all the way back to his childhood. And also from the time when he was apprenticed to a decorator. There was a whole file of the things he had sent in with his application to the Academy of Arts, sketches of animals in the zoo, model drawings, still-lifes. Bett had carefully kept them all. There they all were, together with notices of exhibitions he had been part of.

He pushed the box back under the bed and looked out of the window at the gulls rising and falling above the ships at the quayside, soaring away and re-forming, gliding on bluish-white wings. They never collided, their instinct somehow keeping them apart.

Went round tidying up a little, although it wasn't really necessary.

"Home now, boys," he said. "Pack everything up."

They stood in front of him, each with a plastic carrier-bag crammed full.

He phoned for a minicab.

The pheasant season had begun. They could hear shots in the forest.

Simon had been playing with the children for most of the day, while Mette and Niels Peter had unpacked the bags from Havne Street.

Simon showed the children the game he and Mette used to

play when they were young. They threw a loosely folded rug on to the floor, and pretended that it was a mountainous country. They had a little box of clay animals which they used to put in the caves and on the plains of the rug.

Mette and Simon would sit for hours, just moving the animals about and talking.

Bett loved watching them play.

"Don't disturb them," she would tell Niels Peter. "They're having such a lovely game."

Niels Peter used to think that his brother's and sister's game was childish.

Time should be used more sensibly. He used to read while the others played. He made plans. He drove himself on, worrying that he'd not complete everything he had set his mind on.

WEDNESDAY 22 OCTOBER

The reflection off the water is thrown on to the ceiling. With a huge sense of relief, Niels Peter sees his mother sitting in an armchair in Havne Street.

He opens his mouth and says:

"There's something I really have to talk to you about... "

She lifts her head and looks at him with interest.

" ...I have to tell you that I'm feeling terrible about everything that happened this summer."

She holds out her hand to him.

"It torments me terribly," he says.

Now everything will be cleared up. Niels Peter will be forgiven. He will receive the forgiveness that will give him peace.

Then he is shattered, as if struck by a blow from a club.

"But you can't speak," he cries. "You're dead."

The vision immediately dissolves. His mother disappears, as does the shimmering light from the harbour.

He wakes in bed at Forest House, covered in sweat.

Bett's store-room in the barn is the worst. Box after box of things that she's inherited, been given by friends, or bought at the flea market.

Simon and Niels Peter bring the boxes out on to the floor of the barn. Mette stands by the table, unpacking them.

There is a box of bed linen, white, with crocheted borders and the year and people's initials embroidered in the corner. There are polka-dot curtains, and some lavender-scented seersucker.

Another box contains their own toys, toys from the forties

and fifties. Dresses that Bett had made for Mette. With buttons and hems.

There are sailor's jackets, knitted jerseys and anoraks.

And a box of ski boots, tennis shoes, beach shoes and wooden-soled shoes.

They go through everything, sorting it all and putting things into heaps. Thermos flasks. Bicycle bags. Mirrors. Portable easels. Empty picture frames. Oval frames. Gilded frames. All kinds of tools. School books. Poetry books. Old illustrated magazines. Pottery and kitchen things. Baskets

There's a whole box of games — playing cards, chess, dominoes and halma. These would have to be hidden until the grandchildren are older. Or kept for a rainy day.

Bett's children had grown up after the war. They'd never known great shortages of anything. They often used to make fun of the way she would tuck things away — half a tomato until the morning, a plastic bag carefully folded and put away in a drawer.

A pheasant shrieks somewhere nearby. Through the barn door they can see the children trying to get their black kite up into the air.

Who would have dreamt that Bett had so much stuff stored away?

"I wonder why she hasn't cleared things out more," says Simon.

"But that's just what she *has* done," says Mette. "Bett's spent ages clearing all this out."

"Yes — moving things from one place to another."

"Oh, do shut up, Simon."

They divide all the things into seven heaps, one for each of the three of them, one for friends and family, one for the flea market, one for the auction and the second-hand bookshop — and one pile containing things to be burnt. The last pile seems to be the biggest. Perhaps because it's such a mess.

Niels Peter keeps sifting through his own pile. So that it doesn't get too large.

Like Bett, Mette was a collector, too. Her house is full of pictures.

All kinds of things on the shelves.
And they have a considerable collection of books.

"When exactly was it that we came here this summer," asks Simon, "to take over from Mette and Hans?"

"I finished at the university on the tenth of July," says Niels Peter. "So it must have been sometime around then."

Simon and Niels Peter had seen immediately that their mother's condition had deteriorated. She lifted her hand and made a faint attempt to smile. Jacob and Zigzag kissed her and disappeared out to the fields with Milla. Bett's face was dark and emaciated, her eyes clear, with a strange glow in them.

She was lying in the big bed in the living-room, clearly no longer able to change position by herself.

Hans and Mette showed the two brothers how to help Bett to walk.

First Hans raised her from the semi-lying position so that she was sitting up. She sat on a rubber ring and a lambskin blanket. These were gently removed. Then he went down on his knees and put both arms firmly round her waist, while she put her hands round his neck.

"Now let's try," said Hans, leaning back, then rising and lifting her into a standing position.

The amazing thing was that she, who was so small, seemed so incredibly heavy.

Upright with his mother-in-law in his arms, Hans moved backwards step by step. In this way, they went from bedroom to bathroom to living-room and back again.

Simon and Niels Peter shuddered.

"Tell me how it's going," said Niels Peter.

They were sitting in the pergola. Bett was having her midday sleep. Hans leant back and rubbed the small of his back.

"Does your back hurt?"

"Yes."

"It's all been going very well," said Mette.

"Sometimes she's almost manic and gets on at us," said Hans.

"To find things, mend things, tidy things up..."

He was finding it difficult to hide his weariness and irritation.

"Twice it's happened," said Mette. "We've found Bett on the floor outside the bathroom. She's got up in the middle of the night to go to the bathroom. Then she's fallen and been unable to call down to us. Once she managed to open a cupboard door and get a towel to put under her head. It was terrible. I thought that I'd heard a noise. But I didn't go down to see — I find it hard to forgive myself for that."

"I suppose we can't avoid that sort of thing happening," mumbled Hans. "And we should also expect that worse things are going to happen in the future."

"At least the nurse comes every morning now," said Mette, looking a bit brighter. "She gives Bett a bed-bath. That's a great step forward. There are two of them — one younger, the other older — and they do shifts. They're both very nice. Bett appreciates their help a lot."

"And we've got a home-help three times a week. She drives here and does some shopping for us."

"What about a night-nurse?"

"We've not been given one yet."

"Apart from that, we've had a lot of visitors coming."

"Someone's made a very good job of the lawn."

"It was me," said Hans, looking at his watch. "Are our bags packed? And where's Milla?"

He turned and whispered to Niels Peter:

"I have to tell you that I think Bett is really depressed."

"Can you write me out a prescription?" Niels Peter whispered back. "I'm finding it very hard to sleep."

Just before they drove off, something happened which really surprised Niels Peter.

Mette and Hans were sitting on Bett's bed, and all three of them were crying. Niels Peter had never seen his brother-in-law cry before.

"Thank you, my dears," said Bett. "Thank you for being so marvellous."

Then she carefully took the three gold bracelets off her arm and put them on to Mette's wrist.

Sometimes if they went unexpectedly into the living-room, they'd find Bett lying right back, quite silent, her eyes closed and her mouth half open.

They'd steal across the room, lean over her and take her cold hand. Was it all over... ?

Until a tiny sound from her throat told them that she was asleep.

There was something wrong with the drains. The toilets wouldn't flush properly. The others must have noticed. Although they had left without saying anything. Perhaps they'd had more than enough to do. And what could they have done about it, anyway?

The phone rang. It was Bett's sister, Elin.

"What would you say, if I was to come over tomorrow?" she said.

"We'd be delighted."

"And I'll stay as long as... "

"Isn't it lovely to see Elin," said Bett.

It was pouring with rain. They were in the living-room, sitting at the little round table beside her bed, the boys bunched round Bett.

"Move over, Jacob," said Zigzag.

"I was here first."

"Shut up or I'll kick you in the balls."

"Where on earth did you learn such language?" said Bett, shocked.

Zigzag leaned forward and thumped his older brother on the back.

"Now he's hitting me," exclaimed Jacob.

"There was a fly on your jersey."

"But you don't kill flies with the side of your hand."

"Boys," said Niels Peter. "Would you go out. *Right now!*"

"What are we having for dinner?" said Jacob. "Tell us that first."

Simon's hands were shaking slightly as he lit one cigarette from another.

The situation was getting out of control.

"Do you mind if we take a little medicine?"

"Not at all, my dear, as long as I don't have to."

Simon went out and fetched a cold bottle of aquavit from the refrigerator.

Jacob put two fingers up in the air.

"Can Zigzag and I get the dressing-up clothes out?"

"Whenever you like."

Simon poured out two glasses.

"Cheers," said Niels Peter.

"Cheers," said Bett, as she lay there drinking soup through a Donald Duck straw.

Half an hour later: the boys had used a felt-tip to draw moustaches, eyebrows and scars on their faces. Wearing coats, belts, pistols and patches over one eye, they stood duelling with wooden swords in the middle of the living-room.

Cigarette smoke hung in the room.

The wooden swords clashed and clattered.

"Have you heard the one about... " said Simon, trying to drink aquavit through a straw. " ...the one about... "

He had tied a check-patterned headscarf round his head, under Bett's straw hat.

He gave up trying to tell his story and got up, swaying, in front of his mother.

"Can I lie down beside you for a while?"

He collapsed on to the bed beside his mother. In amongst the powder, the rubber ring and the lambskin blanket. He began to laugh, a low chuckle.

Jacob pointed his pistol at him.

"What's so funny?"

"Oh, just *everything*!"

Simon and the boys were watching television, still in their pirate clothes.

Niels Peter was walking backwards, manœuvring his mother towards the bathroom.

Avoiding eye contact.

From the bathroom on into the little bedroom.

A tortoiseshell butterfly was quivering on the window.

The morning nurse gave Bett an enema and a bed-bath, rubbing carbamide cream into her patient, then massaging her feet and giving her her medicine. Then she helped her to dress.

"Thank you, my dear," said Bett. "It's so nice of you to come."

"It's a pleasure to be here, really it is."

They taught the boys to shoot at a target, using an airgun and a tin can.

"Bang."

Jacob and Zigzag were impressed.

Neither Niels Peter nor Simon had done military service, although for a while they acted as though they had.

"What's the matter?" said Niels Peter, when he saw the expression on Simon's face.

"The day-after feeling. Why do we do it?!"

"You had too much to drink yesterday."
"Look, don't mother me..."

The water would not flush down the lavatory. They lifted the cover off the septic tank and saw the scum. The system had finally collapsed.

A taxi stopped outside in the yard. A tiny little white-haired figure in a linen dress and sandals got out, carrying a case and some parcels. The boys flung their arms round her neck. It was Elin.

"You've hardly eaten a thing, Simon."
"I'm not hungry."
"No one in this family's hungry," said Elin. "I'll have to think up some exciting meals for you."
Simon's mind was roving elsewhere.
"What are you thinking about?" said Niels Peter.
"It's strange," said Simon. "I've been obsessed with the thought that you shouldn't help anyone, if you can't help everyone. I thought that was socialism. But I seem to be wrong."

The pergola was green, the clover in the grass thriving.
The boys were half-naked, going round with their fishing nets and catching water snails in the little lake of bobbing water-lilies.
The home-help came. She emptied the waste-paper basket, hung out the washing and put the clean clothes away when they were dry. Everything smelt so good when it had hung out of doors.
Elin was cleaning up in the scullery.
"Shouldn't we eat up what's in the freezer?" she said. "Wouldn't it be better if we gradually emptied it?"

Elin moved silently over the floor with trays and glasses of water, lovingly tending to Bett's needs. They looked at photographs. Talked about the old days and their childhood. A great intimacy between the two sisters.

The one created a calm space around the other.

The children became calmer, too. They would lie down carefully beside Bett. Zigzag took her hand and placed it on his head. Jacob read aloud to her from the newspaper.

Simon and Niels Peter didn't know how they would have managed without Elin. For a distance had developed between the mother and her sons that was threatening to turn into... hostility.

"I wonder whether the water from the washing machine runs into the septic tank," said Elin. "Something tells me it does."

She sat down and phoned all and sundry. Got hold of the builder who had built the bathroom. Dug out the plans of the house.

The result of all this was that a plumber would be coming to empty the septic tank.

"You're a tremendous help, you know," Niels Peter told Elin.

"I'm not helping — I'm learning," she replied.

"But don't you ever get cross with us?"

"Not in the least. You must remember I love you. My problem is that I often feel... sort of grey. But here at Forest House I find that I can be useful. It's a challenge."

"You're very patient with Bett."

"I should think so! I've always admired her good humour. Bett's the sort of person who thinks everything will work out. When you think like that, it does. Faith and trust is what counts in this world."

Niels Peter smiled.

"Do you think that, then?" he said.

"Yes. Doubt and distrust just make everything difficult."

"What kind of faith are you talking about?"

"Faith that there's something good in life," said Elin. "Faith that there's something good in people. Feeling a fellowship and finding... how can I put it? ...the eternal in life on earth."

Later that day, Bett said: "The only thing I want for my birthday is a great big feast. I want it carried down the hill. And all the children should be allowed to eat as much as they want."

"Yes," said Niels Peter. "But don't you remember we talked about not inviting all that many people?"

"That doesn't matter. I want a good feast — a party."

Early in the morning, something terrible on my mind. My mother's face changed beyond recognition.

The clock ticked mechanically. Isia's letters lay in a heap on the table.

What is Bett thinking at this moment as she lies awake in her bedroom?

Alone. Unable to change position.

Wonder if she's thirsty? Maybe she can't reach her glass of water.

Maybe she knows everything but drives her spirits to the limit in order to live up to her guiding principle — always make the most of everything. In the most hopeless of situations, look round for something positive. Make the greatest effort to be friendly to others and to show interest in them.

That's what she expected of herself.
That's probably also what she expected of others.

They were always pleased to see the nurses when they arrived.
They were incredibly gentle.
And easy to talk to.
They gave a straight answer to every question.
Yes, in a way the two nurses were the reason that each day started so well.

One day the older nurse arrived earlier than usual in order to get her patient ready. Ready to be fetched by ambulance and taken to the hospital for another five days of chemo-therapy.

She bustled and fussed over Bett as though she were a newborn baby.

Then she came out into the kitchen where the others were, closed the door behind her and sat down on the bench.

Elin poured her some coffee.

"You know," whispered the nurse, "I can hardly bear the thought of what she's got to go through for the next five days..."

"Simon and I will go to the hospital with her," said Niels Peter. "I've phoned the consultant and asked him to see my mother himself today. It must be at least two months since he last saw her."

"Say goodbye to Gran," he called to the boys. "We're off to the hospital."

Jacob and Zigzag came running up, their mouths red from eating cherries, and each gave Bett a cherry-flavoured kiss before the ambulance door closed.

They stood with Elin in the yard, smiling and happy. They had no way of knowing if this was the last time they would see their grandmother.

They waved.

Then ran back to their cherries.

"I have examined your mother," said the consultant inside his small office. "And have come to the conclusion that she is in no condition to stand further treatment. She has arrived at what we call the terminal phase."

"The terminal phase?" said Simon.

"Yes — the body has a deadline. That means that any further treatment becomes meaningless. Up until now the chemotherapy has stabilized the patient. It can no longer do that."

"Have you told her?" asked Niels Peter.

"No," he said quickly. "I don't think one should ever say that to a patient, however serious the situation is. One mustn't take away a person's last hope."

"What have you said to her?"

"I have told her I think we should have a pause in the treatment. And then see again later — in August sometime — what we should do."

Niels Peter looked steadily at the doctor.

"How long do you think she'll live?"

"We-ell, I can't really say with any accuracy."

"But you must have some previous experience of how long the terminal phase can last."

"From three to six weeks, depending. By the way, she's asked to stay here for a few days."

Dressed in a white hospital gown and lying in the big hospital bed, she looked tiny. She resembled a bright-eyed baby bird.

"Well?" said Niels Peter, sitting down on the edge of the bed and taking her hand.

"The doctor examined me and suggested that I take a kind of summer holiday from the treatment. We're going to skip the next session."

"And what do you feel about that?"

"I'm glad. But I also told him I'd rather stay on here until Monday so that you and I can both have a bit of a rest."

"Do you mind being here?"

"Not in the least. Anyway, I know everyone here. They're so kind and they all come and say they're glad to see me again."

"Don't you want us to come and visit you?"

"No, no, no. Just for these few days. Make the most of your freedom."

The ward nurse said to them:

"No wonder you've got bad backs. We can send your mother home in the bed she's in. In the ambulance on Monday."

"Thank you."

"If there's anything else you need, just say so."

Had a feeling of rising through dark earth and breaking through a cold layer of cloud into a blue sky. At last.

At last the end is in sight.

Yes, they enjoyed their freedom. Simon oiled his printing press in the studio. Elin lay by the little lake and read a novel.

Everything was green and lush.

There was the scent of wormwood.

Niels Peter set about typing up his scribbled notes. He was behind with his work. He was restless and couldn't concentrate. He checked through his bank account and what he saw worried him. Elin had offered to lend him some money. But how and when would he be able to pay it back?

The boys were building a platform, a lookout post in the copper beech. They disappeared into the reddish-brown foliage of the tree.

Yes, the two boys had disappeared from him. They seemed remarkably unclear to him during this time, blurred, in a way, as if they didn't really exist.

Isia phoned. She was busy moving her mother from her own apartment to a nursing home. Driving back and forth with her mother's possessions and helping her to settle in.

"What do you feel about your mother going into a nursing home?" said Niels Peter.

"Great relief. She couldn't manage any longer."

"You've no qualms of conscience?"

"Not at all. My mother's pleased about it."

Ditlev came from Copenhagen to visit Bett in hospital.

In the afternoon, he went on to Forest House.

He had a small volume of Shelley's poetry with him.

"When Bett comes back, will you read this to her?"

They went for a long walk across the fields.

Ditlev told them he had trouble with his eyes. He was going blind in one eye. Sclerosis.

Karin's friend Bjarne the carpenter phoned to ask if he should get started on the cupboard Bett had sent him drawings of several months earlier. The cupboard was to be a surprise for Jacob.

"No," said Niels Peter. "I don't think we'll be needing it after all. But can I speak to Karin?"

Karin came to the phone.

"Bett hasn't long to go. They've stopped the treatment."

"How are you feeling?"

"I'm very tired. I hardly ever get a proper night's sleep."

"Shouldn't we come and fetch the kids? They really shouldn't be around while all this is going on."

"Can I think it over?"

"Sure. But I'd like to send the boys over to my parents in Fyn. And let them stay there until school starts."

Would it be sad for Bett to find that her grandchildren were not there when she came home? Or would it be a relief?

"What about the boys?" asked Simon. "Wouldn't it be better for them to be with Karin's parents?"

It was raining when Karin and Bjarne came.

Pouring with rain. They looked around the house for a while, and Niels Peter again felt what he had felt several times before during the past six months — that Bett's things, her clothes and so on, became a little, yes, a little ridiculous when other people looked at them.

Her poor things.

He was confused and had not packed the boys' gear properly. They almost left without any clothes, without their wellingtons or any socks.

"We'll find some," said Bjarne, "just relax."

Jacob and Zigzag could be seen in a blur, waving through the rear window of the car. When would he next see them?

Late that evening, Elin, Simon and Niels Peter went and sat in the studio.

Simon was talking about women. After a while, their conversation turned to sexuality. The brothers started asking Elin questions, and she answered them more freely and openly than they could have imagined.

There was one thing about their present situation — Bett dying — which Niels Peter generally left out of account: it did tend to crystallize certain observations, certain thoughts and ideas.

Niels Peter looked at Elin in the way that one looks at one of those puzzle pictures where you have to find the hidden objects.

A good thing about the situation was that it helped him to see the life in others.

The grass was long. The raindrops fell into the white elder flowers, reinforcing their prickly spicy scent.

Elin and Niels Peter went round getting everything ready for Bett's arrival. Simon was asleep in the studio. He had drunk too much the night before.

The ambulance wheels crunched on the wet gravel in the yard. Two ambulancemen jumped out.

"We've brought the hospital bed with us."

"Where do you want it put?"

They opened the garden door and the ambulance rolled across the grass. The ramp was lowered.

"Have you any plastic? So that her quilt doesn't get wet."

Elin fetched a big yellow plastic sheet.

The ambulancemen spread the sheet over the bed — then lifted it out of the ambulance and down the ramp. Lifted it up over the step and into the living-room, heaving with all their might, their faces turning bright red.

"It's heavy," said one of them.

"The water-bed alone probably weighs about sixty kilos," groaned the other.

At last the big metal bed was in the living-room. Niels Peter removed the plastic sheet and lifted the quilt. He couldn't see Bett. Where was she?

"Try the other end," said the men.

At what he'd thought was the foot of the bed, he found his mother's white face.

"You poor things," she whispered. "What a lot you have to do just for my sake."

The bed was wheeled into place. The men showed how to get the bed-head up; with a screeching metallic sound the cot bars slid up and down.

"We've brought a commode too," they said. "That's it, then. We'll be off now."

And off they went, leaving nothing but the sound of falling rain.

"How are you?" whispered Elin, bending over Bett.

"Everyone was really sweet in the ward. But I slept so badly..."

The rain eased off; the raindrops slowly fell away.

Elin had put on Bett's raincoat and wellingtons and gone for a walk in the woods.

Simon was leaning against the bookcase.

Niels Peter was sitting on Bett's high bed.

"How did it go?"

Bett looked round, searching for something. Simon handed her a glass of iced water.

"Would you move my left leg? Just a little."

"Like that?"

"Sorry. Now the right."

There was a strange trembling tenseness in the room.

Two clear eyes were looking at Niels Peter from the sockets of a skull.

"I just don't understand. They can't really mean that I..."

"That you?"

"They can't mean that I'm to lie like this for seven years."

Niels Peter took her hand in his.

"Has someone told you that you're to lie like this for seven years?"

"No," she replied in a thin voice — as if he had caught her out telling a lie. "But I couldn't bear to live like this without knowing what's going on in the world. And be looked after and nursed like a baby... if I don't get my health back."

"Have they promised you your health back?"

Bett made no reply.

"Have they?" repeated Niels Peter.

"No."

"I don't think so, either. They only promised us that the treatment would help you — so that the sickness doesn't become too unbearable."

"What am I going to do?" she whispered. "I simply can't bear the thought of carrying on like this."

"I know, I know," said Niels Peter, noticing his brother's eyes on him.

It was deathly quiet. Niels Peter stroked his mother's arm and thought: Now's the time to say it. Simon must stop me if I'm on the wrong tack. He looked calmly at Bett.

"I don't think," he said, "you've got long to go."

She looked at him questioningly.

"I think you've only a short time left. Maybe a couple of months. Maybe just one. Maybe even less."

Then she opened her thin lips and said in a weak voice:

"That's good."

Simon shifted position over by the bookcase.

Her newly won strength left her. Her eyes turned blank and her mouth opened for a question. Niels Peter remembered a line of a hymn: "And see so many mouths... "

"Are you thinking about how you'll die?"

Scarcely audible — like a slight expelling of air.

"Yes."

"I think I know something about that. Shall I tell you?"

"If you want to."

"I think that what will happen is that you'll get more and more exhausted. You'll sleep more and more. And be less awake. You'll glide into what they call somnolence. And then you'll die — quite still and calm. And we'll be with you."

"How do you know all that?"

"Because I had to. I asked the doctors. And I've also read books about the psychology of death."

The expression in her eyes changed. As if she was drawing her tears back.

For a moment he thought: Now she's angry again. Angry because I've gone behind her back to find things out.

He looked at Simon.

"And all that doesn't worry me," he said. "I just think we shall do everything we possibly can — to make it good between us."

"Yes, of course we will," she whispered. "I think I'll have a little rest now."

They were standing in the kitchen, the door closed. Simon thrust his hands into his trouser pockets and nodded to Niels Peter. There was mutual agreement between them.

Half an hour later the little china bell rang.

"Yes?" said Niels Peter, leaning round the door of the living-room.

"I'd like you both to come in again now."

They took up their places.

"You know what I've been lying here thinking? I'm going to tell the doctor I don't want to have any more treatment. I think it's pointless. Would you phone him, Niels Peter?"

Quiet evening meal, no sound except the clink of knives and

forks on white plates.

"Maybe I should sleep in with Bett tonight," said Elin.

"Yes," said Niels Peter. "But you know what, Elin? We need to be careful of you, too. I think you ought to go home soon — in the next few days... "

They tried to lift her down on to the commode. But it didn't work. They couldn't get her out of bed properly. And even if they managed to get her down, how would they ever get her up again? They had to forget about it and use the bedpan instead.

"Shall I do it?" said Elin.

"Or me?" said Simon.

"It's all right, I'll do it," said Niels Peter. "You go on, the two of you."

The moment he had feared. What does one do now?

He thought about Karin in childbirth — how the bedpan was pushed in beneath her.

He turned back quilt and nightgown. Using all his strength to turn his mother on to her side, he placed a waterproof underlay on the sheet, pushed the bedpan in and gently drew her over on to her back again.

Her eyes closed. Her face contracted. From the pain of the hard metal? Or because what they had never dared talk about was now happening?

Her body was not yet frightening. It was intact. No sores. Face, neck, torso and arms. Just so terribly brittle, as if made of glass. But the lower part of her body was swollen with fluid and her skin colourless. Cold. As if numb.

She was still full of feelings, though — he could see that from her mouth.

When her mouth tightened, it seemed to him that he must

have done something to make her angry.

That hurt Niels Peter as if a hundred razor blades had cut him all at once.

Her poor sex.

He had never seen it before. Only — as if from afar — when he was a child and she was undressing — a comforting triangle of black hair.

Now it was defenceless, naked. Like a child's.

She was looking to one side. He to the other. Their gazes crossed like searchlights in the night.

He had once lain in that womb. His way out into life had been between those legs. He had drunk from those breasts. Those hands had caressed him a thousand times.

And now, here he was, perpetrating violence on her.

The cancer had been transferred to him as a punishment. Planted in him.

"Does it hurt?" he said, rolling her over on to her side again and pulling out the bedpan of urine. Drying her. Rolling her back. Putting her nightgown and quilt back into place.

"It's so hard to lie on," she whispered.

"Maybe we can cover it with something."

Began putting out one medicine glass after another.

She was watching him with steady eyes. "Can't I skip those big calcium tablets? I can hardly swallow them. They almost choke me."

Desperately:

"But the doctors said it's important that you take them. What shall I do?"

"Can't I skip them?"

She had tears in her eyes.

So did he — from pent-up rage.

"I could break them into smaller pieces?"

She nodded her consent.

Placed the small white bits like pieces of blackboard chalk on her stiff tongue one by one. Put the glass of water to her lips.

Then the other pills, the white, the pink, the grey and the black.

Absurd. Here he was, forcing pills on to somebody terminally ill.

He opened the door and said to Elin:

"You can come in now."

Elin stood at the end of the bed massaging Bett's feet.

"Could you try turning me over on to my side?"

They put their hands flat against her back and turned her over. Placed a rolled-up pillow at the small of her back, and little pieces of lambskin beneath her heels, where the skin was red and thin as silk.

"Thank you, my dears, that's much better."

And a little later — as the medicine began to work.

"I feel good now. I hope you do too."

Just before they switched off the light and closed the door:

"I'm very glad they're not going to continue the treatment."

He wrote to Isia:

> It's terrible. She's got so small. She's disappearing. All my joie de vivre has gone. My love of work, too. I have a feeling it'll never come back...

The young nurse came the following morning.

"Could you show us the proper way to do it?" said Niels Peter.

She showed them how to deal with the bedpan. The rest — the enema — she did herself. She taught them how to change the bedclothes, how to turn the patient from side to side by pulling the drawsheet.

They wheeled the bed up to the garden door so that Bett could look out on to the fruit trees as she lay.

They gave her vegetable juice.

"Thank you," said Bett. "Please could you phone for Hans now?"

Simon and Niels Peter were sitting on either side of the nurse.

"She's amazing, your mother is. Do you realize that? You never hear her complain. She's never sorry for herself, and she's grateful for everything you do for her. The first thing she always asks me is how my family are. I see a lot of things in my job, sometimes not all that pleasant. But I must tell you, it's a great joy for me to come to this house."

Gertrud came as arranged. She parked her car under the hazel trees. She got out. Tall and lean, wearing lovely pale leather shoes, her glasses on a chain round her neck.

Niels Peter and Elin met her and explained the situation briefly. A dragonfly hovered in the air. They could see Gertrud trying to adjust to the situation — thinking what she would say to her old friend.

"Gertrud, dearest," said Bett. "Well I never. So you've driven all this way just to visit me."

They were all sitting by the open garden door, looking out on to the brilliant summery space.

Gertrud handed round roll-ups and talked about her childhood. Bett broke in with questions and comments.

Now and then she would consult her sons and her sister in order to add some detail to Gertrud's stories.

Simon was sitting on a high office chair, one leg over the other, rocking the chair slowly to and fro.

"I'd like to buy one of your pictures," said Gertrud.

"No question of buying," he replied, pleased. "You can have one."

"Certainly not."

"Do as he says," Bett said. "He knows what he's doing."

Just before Gertrud left, she said to Bett:

"You know that when you die, you can be with all your loved ones at once? And watch over them. So you can watch over Milla. The dead watch over the living. They're our good spirits."

Bett smiled — as if she found the idea amusing but not particularly convincing. She looked as if she were thinking: far be it from me to take your childish faith away from you, Gertrud.

Gertrud set off for Copenhagen. Niels Peter repeated his question to Elin:

"Don't you think you should give yourself a break? Wouldn't you like to go back home soon?"

Hans came a few hours later — at Bett's express wish.

They stood round her bed. The sheet and the lambskin blanket were crumpled.

"Let me try to lift you, Bett," said Hans. "Put your arms round my neck."

But she couldn't. Simon and Niels Peter stepped in. The three men couldn't even lift her enough to get the sheet out. She seemed to be glued to the bed.

Her face contracted.

Hans picked up the jar of pink Doloxene from her bedside table.

"Would you like one of these?"

A quarter of an hour later they could see her features begin to clear.

"I'd very much like to speak to you alone for a while, Hans," she said.

Elin, Simon and Niels Peter were sitting in the pergola waiting for Hans. When he came, Simon asked him at once:

"What did you talk about?"

"I don't think I want to tell you."

"Then don't."

"Don't worry, I won't."

They were helping themselves from a saucer of raspberries on the table.

"Hans, can I come into town with you?" said Elin. "If that's all right with you, I'll nip in and pack my things. I'll be back for Bett's birthday."

A short while later, Hans fixed his dark blue eyes on Niels Peter.

"Bett spoke of suicide," he said. "She asked if I could help her..."

"She doesn't mean it, though," Simon said.

"She's talked about that for ages," said Niels Peter. "It's too late now."

"Agreed. And it's pretty impossible for me to help — but it shows she's understood the reality of the situation."

"I think it's her way of appealing to us to be more understanding."

"That's probably true. But why? Surely, you understand her

well enough, don't you?"

"Not me."

"Why not?"

"I can't face identifying with her. I keep trying to avoid it all the time. And that makes me hard."

"You don't help another person with pity. You don't have to suffer, too. You have to be what you are."

"I can't distance myself," said Niels Peter. "I can't find that professional distance — not when it comes to my mother."

"I don't really know whether children should ever nurse their parents when they're dying," said Hans, hesitantly.

"But sometimes they have no choice," said Simon.

"Hans, do you know what the biggest problem is?" said Niels Peter. "It's about what we really should be doing here at Forest House. I feel that her old friends can't keep coming any more. They've come over and over again, and I think the pressure's beginning to tell."

"She should go to Copenhagen," said Hans, "to Marstrand Street."

"But wouldn't it be a pity to move her from Forest House?"

"Yes, but on the other hand, who's going to be able to join you out here? You're beginning to crack up."

"I don't know how long I can cope, either," Simon said quietly, his face strangely pale. He tapped his front teeth with his thumbnail. "If you ask me, I think it'd be best if she went into hospital."

"Out of the question," said Niels Peter. "Definitely not."

"Anyway, you're much too isolated here. If you come to town, at least we can take it in turns looking after her. We'll manage. Otherwise you're not going to be able to cope. You must decide soon."

"It's simply that I can't decide anything at the moment," groaned Niels Peter.

"Listen then," said Hans, "Can't we get her into hospital a few days after her birthday? In the meantime we can have a hospital bed put in at Marstrand Street. Then she can be taken there... "

"Yes, and she can stay with me until... "

Niels Peter drew his hand flat across his Adam's apple.

"Yes."

"What do we do if she's in pain?" said Simon. "She never asks for painkillers herself."

"In the old days, patients weren't allowed to become addicted to morphine. You always had to hide some for the last moments. But it's not like that today. Today no cancer patient is allowed to suffer pain. That'd be intolerable. Here's a jar of pain-killers. Give them to her as you think necessary. But don't forget — don't wait until she's already in pain. It needs to be nipped in the bud, so she must have it in good time."

"Incidentally," he added, "I think you're looking rather poorly yourself, Simon."

Simon raised a hand resignedly and scratched his head.

Niels Peter nudged Hans: "Why is she so heavy?"

"There's twenty to thirty litres of fluid in the lower part of her body. That's why we can't lift her. In hospital, the porters do it..."

"And why is there a smell of cat's pee?" asked Simon.

"Because she's got cancer of the liver. When the liver ceases to function, waste products seep through the skin. It happens with kidney diseases, too."

"What do they do in hospital?"

"There's a ventilator going all the time."

Elin came back in. She had packed her belongings and said goodbye to Bett. But the two brothers still had questions to ask.

"What shall we do if Bett starts with her stupid thoughts again?"

"Just appeal to her good sense over and over again," said Hans, gazing out over the fields. "Has she talked about her own death before?"

"Yes, often," said Niels Peter. "All through my childhood, she was forever telling me that she didn't want to live past seventy."

"Do you take it from that that she was afraid of dying?"

"Of course."

"I'm inclined to disagree with you. I don't think she's necessarily afraid. I think she accepts her death at an intellectual level. But definitely not emotionally. Don't you think we would all react in exactly the same way?"

"Yes."

Niels Peter gave his brother-in-law a searching look.

"As a matter of fact, I find it very moving, the way you are with Bett," he said.

"I'm very fond of her," said Hans. He fell silent, crossed his legs and cleared his throat.

"No one's ever been... "

His eyelids fluttered.

"No one's ever been... as good to me as Bett has."

Turned his head so that they couldn't see the expression on his face.

"When you think how Bett accepted me as part of the family... "

Then he slapped his thigh and said in a loud voice:

"Well, now. Shall we be off into town, Elin?"

Hans went home to Mette. Mette phoned every day to see how things were going.

She had accepted the ending of her mother's treatment more easily than Niels Peter had imagined she would. She seemed almost calm about it.

"You needn't feel duty-bound to phone so often," he said.

"I can't *not* phone," she said.

One morning, the nurse used a catheter for the first time.

"I'm sorry," she said. "It'd take too long otherwise. But give me a ring if any problems arise."

"It's the weekend and you've got your own family to look after."

"Don't worry — just phone."

Everything was dripping wet and glass-green. They loved this summer rain which every year made Sjælland so lush and fertile, and the flowers and the earth so fragrant.

The curtains were drawn when Bett asked for the bedpan at midday.

For the first time in ages she was unhappy.

She lay on the bedpan for a long time. With no result. Niels Peter went out and turned on the tap in the kitchen, letting it run so that she could hear it.

Nothing happened. He got her off the bedpan.
Tried again a quarter of an hour later. Still no result.
She became more anxious.
"It's simply hysteria," she explained, " ...that's why I can't."
She stared up at the ceiling.
He took her hand.
"You've never been hysterical. And neither are you now. I'll phone the nurse."
"Oh dear, is she to be troubled again?"

"I'll put in a catheter now," said the nurse.
"Permanently?"
"I think so."
She instructed Niels Peter how to use the bags and tubes. It was a hundred times easier than the bedpan. And far cleaner.
Bett moaned.
"Don't worry about it," whispered the nurse, wiping the tears from her cheeks. "You'll hardly notice it. It's much more pleasant for you than the bedpan."
She packed her things.
"I'm off now. I'll be back early tomorrow morning to see to you."

They were alone in the room — Bett and Niels Peter.
At the sight of how miserable his mother looked, his heart started thumping in his chest. She had more invested in avoiding a situation like this than he had imagined.
He held out his hand, but then checked himself. His hand poised in mid-air.
The rain had stopped.

He went out into the garden. The lawn was full of wet daisies, dandelions and clover. White, yellow and green. Walked round the house to where no one could hear. Sat down under the copper beech and blurted out: "It hurts so much, it hurts so much. It hurts me so much for you, my dearest Bett."
Sat there staring vacantly.
Went back.
Bett was lying there, gazing at the ceiling, and didn't notice

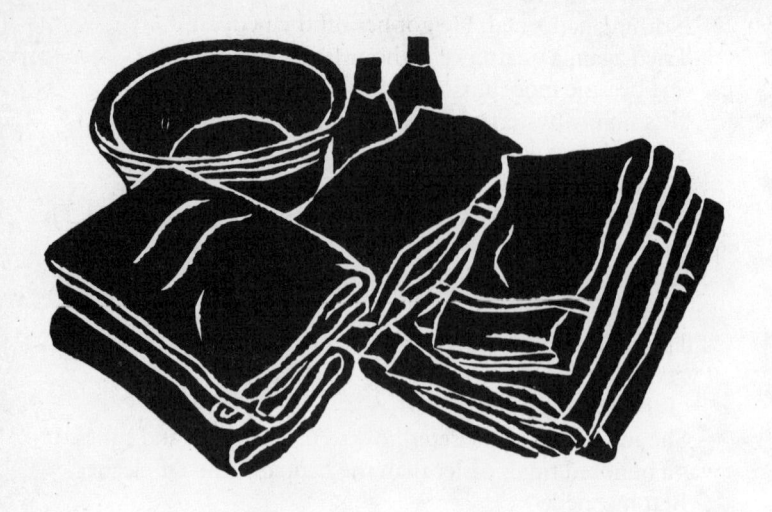

him.

There was a bottle of aquavit on the table. After he'd emptied his third glass, he went over to his mother and kissed her on both hands.

"It's hard for you," he whispered. "You mustn't think I don't know. I do, only too well. If only I could take some of this pain from you."

She touched his arm.

Her eyes were turned away up towards the ceiling.

Rather sombrely, they emptied the bags of dark yellow urine. Straightened her quilt and pillow. Went round the room with the fly-swatter.

They went for walks at night and heard the grasshoppers chirping, the mosquitoes buzzing, the distant roar from the motorway. They saw layer upon layer of trees. Light shading into dark. Dissolving like stage-scenery in the moonlight.

At this moment the moon was staring in wickedly at the brothers in the kitchen. Pale through the glass, puffy, like a patient on cortisone.

A mosquito was flying round under the light.

Simon kicked the kitchen cupboard: "Shit! Piss and shit!"

From his earliest childhood, Niels Peter had had a recurring dream.

He was to move into an old, decaying apartment. With lots of rooms. Large and small. Long Kafkaesque corridors. Niches and stairs. The walls were rough, more or less raw plaster. Dust and mortar everywhere.

A sensation that other people were going to live there, too. But he didn't know them and never met them.

He was always given a small, out-of-the-way room.

There was never any possibility of his protesting against the move.

That night the apartment was more decayed than ever.

The room he was given also had no windows.

A letter from Isia: *Your love of work will come back. You can be sure of that.*

Mette phoned. She and Hans had spent all day packing things at Havne Street.

Niels Peter asked why they didn't get the removal men to do the packing.

But Mette thought that would be too expensive. Anyway, she wanted to go through every single item and make sure things were properly packed.

"How are we going to pay the removal firm," she said.

"We'll have to share it. Then later on, see if the estate... "

A little later, his hand clenched round the receiver, he said:

"I think this is all too much. Too hard. Cancer, moving, transport, the birthday and all. Shit!"

"What are you on about?" said Mette. "This is the way you wanted it. And now you don't seem to want to."

"Anyhow, I want to die in hospital. I've decided that."

"Why on earth are you saying this?"

"Dying at home in comfort. It's just a huge illusion. It's defeat after defeat... "

"You and Bett have always had this special thing... "

"Yes," he replied. "But sometimes I wish Forest House

would be struck by lightning and the whole shitty lot would burn down."

"You're tired."

"Tired? I'm exhausted."

Finally, more subdued:

"Didn't you want to go to the Women's Conference?"

"Yes, but there's no question of that now, not with things as they are."

Simon put some Bach on the record player.

"Isn't that wonderful music," said Bett. "Do we have any more?"

Simon went out into the studio.

"Come and sit over here with me," said Bett to Niels Peter.

He sat at the foot of her high hospital bed.

"Your glasses are crooked," she said.

"I know," he replied.

"I'd like 'Denmark — now closes the bright night' sung on my birthday."

"What kind of birthday would you like?"

"I want you all to enjoy yourselves and be happy."

"And tell jokes and do things like that?"

"Yes, that's right."

"Then I don't think we should sing that, because it's far too emotional."

She was lying by the garden door, a pillow under her knees and her hands across her breast. Looking, almost without blinking, out on to the gentleness of the garden.

"I'm so happy things are so good for us."

There was something lovely about her. Especially her eyes. They were as clear as glass, and deep at the same time.

But it pained her to speak. Her teeth seemed to have become too large for her mouth.

"You must never get rid of this place."

"No," whispered Niels Peter.

"You'll never find anything so good."

And a little later:

"Do you think you'll find a way of sharing the house?"

"Yes, I think so. We'll share the holidays between us, then either Mette or Simon or..."

"Oh, Simon. I'm so worried about him..."

Niels Peter frowned.

"Stop worrying about us. We'll manage all right."

Niels Peter phoned his children — for the first time since they had gone away. Their grandfather had bought them a machine for making ice-cream. There was a cave, too. And new playmates. Everything was great.

"I thought we'd have chicken on my birthday," said Bett. "That'd be simple."

"How shall we do them?" said Simon.

"You can roast them first and put them in the freezer."

"Do you think they'll be all right eaten cold?"

"I expect so," she said. "And the French bread can be heated up in the oven."

Simon put on a record of Bartók, but it was too violent. He took it off again.

"Ditlev has given us a little book of poems by Shelley," said Niels Peter. "Shall I read something aloud from it?"

Simon sat down at the table with paper and ink and started drawing.

Niels Peter read.

Bett lay with her eyes fixed on his mouth, following the words closely.

"You do read well," she said.

Suddenly he discovered that there was a small screw in the frame of his glasses, a screw which could be tightened with the point of a penknife.

"Would you read that again?" whispered Bett.

So Niels Peter picked up Shelley again. Simon put down his pen, leaned back and listened.

> Whether the Sensitive Plant, or that
> Which within its boughs like a Spirit sat,
> Ere its outward form had known decay,
> Now felt this change, I cannot say.
>
> Whether that Lady's gentle mind,
> No longer with the form combined
> Which scattered love, as stars do light,
> Found sadness, where it left delight,
>
> I dare not guess; but in this life
> Of error, ignorance, and strife,
> Where nothing is, but all things seem,
> And we the shadows of the dream,
>
> It is a modest creed, and yet
> Pleasant if one considers it,
> To own that death itself must be,
> Like all the rest, a mockery.
>
> That garden sweet, that lady fair,
> And all sweet shapes and odours there,
> In truth have never passed away:
> 'Tis we, 'tis ours, are changed; not they.
>
> For love, and beauty, and delight,
> There is no death nor change: their might
> Exceeds our organs, which endure
> No light, being themselves obscure.

It was one of the last mornings in July; the birds had all fallen silent.

He lay in bed, hoping to be there when she died. Wishing so desperately... as long as I can be with her. As long as I can see it.

To help her over the threshold.

A huge truck drove in slow motion through the avenue of half-grown birches.

Was manœuvred across the yard, with its rear to the barn door.

Two men in white shirts and leather aprons started carrying crates and furniture out of the truck and stacking them in the barn.

All the things from Havne Street were at Forest House, so all Bett's worldly goods were now gathered in one place.

Simon and the removal men sat down at the kitchen table and poured themselves a beer. They were talking about boxing. About Stevenson the Cuban. Everyone — with the exception of Bett — was following the Olympics in Moscow.

"What does it look like in the barn?" said Bett.

"Very neatly stacked. They don't take up nearly as much space as you'd expect. And Mette's written a label for what's inside every single box."

That same evening at dusk, Isia arrived and parked her Mini under the hazel trees. She brought with her a bunch of poppies she had picked on the way. And two bottles of wine.

"Bett's ready for sleep," said Niels Peter. "Wouldn't you like to go in and say goodnight. Just look at her a little. And tell me what you think."

Isia, Simon and Niels Peter were sitting by the lake, calm as a mirror, with its floating water-lilies and the grass caught between the stones.

"Your mother's incredibly clear in her mind," said Isia. "I think she may live for many more weeks. But it's hard to tell, really."

"I think I'll go inside and sleep with Bett," whispered Simon.

"Stay here for a while," said Isia. "Wouldn't you like just half a glass of wine?"

"All right, just for another couple of minutes, then."

"We ought to talk about what's happening in Poland."

"We can do that another time."

"But the workers in Warsaw and Gdansk have been on strike for a week."

"And the government has agreed to a ten per cent wage rise."

"Going on strike in a socialist country!"

"Why shouldn't they?" asked Simon, getting up and disappearing across the yard.

"Why did you let go of my hand when Simon was here?" Isia asked.

"Did I?"

"Yes. You do that occasionally... when there are other people around."

"If we touch each other," said Niels Peter hesitantly, "that's an open declaration of our relationship."

"Is there anything wrong with that? Don't you want to admit to it?"

The evening was light. He put his arm around her and she leant her head on his shoulder.

A smoke-ring floated away.

If he opened his eyes, he could see her face, defenceless.

His own body was so dry. Unlike Isia's mouth. He drank in its moisture, as if he were a cactus which would retain it for months.

She put a cushion under his head and bent over him, on all fours. He looked up into her dark eyes.

She kissed his forehead, his throat, his shoulder.

He hardly dared breathe.

She tensed and clung tightly to him. Her eyes clouded over. He lifted his hands and stroked her back, immersed as if in a warm bath.

As they embraced, he slid into her.

Lay still. Vibrant.

A vision appeared to him. An almost perpendicular clover field in bloom, the clover bright green, the flowers endless. They began to tremble and were transformed and enlarged into convoluted cotton heads as thin as spiders' webs, white, with faintly pink...

"Oh, it's there now," he whispered. "And it's going on and on and..."

At nine in the morning, they said goodbye under the hazel trees.
"Goodbye, my darling," he whispered.
"Goodbye, my darling," she echoed.
"See you again soon."

The plan had now been decided. On Friday it would be Bett's seventieth birthday.

On the following Monday she was to go into hospital, while Niels Peter arranged a sick-room in Marstrand Street — which Bett would go to on the Thursday.

He embarked on a whole string of telephone calls to organize borrowing the things they'd need from the hospital in Copenhagen. Water-bed, lambskin blanket, bedside table, bedside lamp. Everything to be arranged in accordance with proper nursing standards.

All the preparations were channelled through the social

welfare officer at Lindebjerg Hospital.

Late that night, Niels Peter wrote Isia a letter: *Darling, if I wrote to say I've never been happier about you than just now, it would not be the truth. But that's how I feel.*

The quilt and pillow you lay on are with me tonight. The towel you dried yourself on hangs over my chair. I can still feel your kiss.

He wrote her unfamiliar summer address on the envelope and put the letter first into one envelope, then into another.

No one but Isia was to be allowed to read these letters. No one but Isia must know that he loved her.

The larks were singing loud and clear that sunny early morning over Forest House.

"Good morning, Bett, and happy birthday to you."

"And see how lucky we are with the weather!"

The nurse brought French anemones. The home-help brought everlasting flowers. Several taxis arrived with telegrams. A heap of greetings piled up in a basket on the table.

"You really mean that all these letters have come today?" exclaimed the home-help.

Bett nodded proudly.

"What a lot of friends you've got."

"Yes, I have."

Neighbours came by with flowers and chocolates and brought birthday greetings to the invalid.

Before they left, one said:

"Oh dear... you know, my brother went just like that."

And another said:

"My mother, she had it, too... "

The shopkeeper's young wife and her father brought the food. Drink too. And also an orchid for Bett.

Bett heard their voices.

"Come on in," she said. "And tell me how things are going with you."

At two o'clock, they woke Bett from her midday sleep and got her ready. Dressed her in a freshly-ironed white blouse with silver cufflinks shaped like small hearts.

There was a bouquet of bright red roses in every window in the house. A man had brought them from Lindebjerg, a gift to Bett from Elin and Gertrud.

Cars arrived in the yard. People got out, laden with parcels and flowers, and embraced, delighted to see one another.

First came Mette and Hans. They had brought Ditlev and Elin with them. Then Gertrud. And Bett and Elin's brother, Viggo. A handsome, white-haired, quietly spoken man. He had driven all the way from Halland in Sweden.

The home-help had laid the table for coffee out on the lawn in front of the garden door, so that Bett could see it from her bed in the living-room.

"Wouldn't you prefer your visitors to come in one at a time?" said Niels Peter. He straightened her pillow, pulled up the bedhead and discreetly hid the tube and bag under the drawsheet.

The guests drew lots for the order in which they would go in to wish her happy birthday.

Viggo leant over her and said: "Happy birthday, my dear."

Gertrud gave her Vivaldi's "Four Seasons".

Ditlev had brought a little bouquet with a red ribbon around it.

"How are your eyes these days?" asked Bett.

The first bottles of white wine were opened. Glasses in hand, the guests walked round admiring the house and the view, the gifts, the many bunches of roses and the telegrams. A great many of the letters were read out.

"Isn't it a wonderful place?"

"And have you seen the view of the forest from the hill?"

"Isn't it amazing how fast the vine in the pergola has grown... ?"

"I wonder if I should try Viggo's medicine, to see if it works," said Bett with gusto.

Elin fetched a schnapps glass and poured some out. They drank to Bett, and Viggo told them about life in the forests of Sweden, about elk-hunting and sailing. And about mutual old friends in Sweden.

Niels Peter drew Hans out into the kitchen.

"This morning she's got some dark red spots of blood on her chest," he whispered. "Little dots or splotches. What do you think they are?"

"I'll have a look," said Hans.

They crowded round the table alongside Bett's bed. All very close together, but hardly shoulder to shoulder, as the chairs were of different heights.

Mette and Elin brought dishes of cold chicken with hot French bread. Earthenware bowls of green salad, olives, tomatoes and fennel were passed round.

They discussed children and schools. They talked about boxing in Cuba. Or rather, Ditlev and Simon talked about their idol — the Cuban Teofilo Stevenson — who was to go into the ring the next day against one of the Soviet champions.

"Do you remember the Games when the Cuban boxers took most of the medals?" said Ditlev.

"Yes, and ran round and round the ring waving little Cuban

flags."

The hour turned blue.
The trees turned blue.
Melancholy descended on Forest House.
Then Elin gave the cue and Viggo started telling his stories.

Mette lit the candles and put them on the table and on the window-sills next to the roses. The window-panes reflected the light, doubling their number.

Bett was happy. Radiant, as she lay in her bed, occasionally lifting a transparent hand when she wanted to say something.

"Viggo, tell me again about that time when..."

Niels Peter made doubly sure that she took her Doloxene.

At about ten, Bett said:

"I think I'll go to sleep now."

One after another, her guests said goodnight. Mette led them over to the studio, where Simon — who was wearing Bett's straw hat — had lit candles and opened a few bottles.

Then she was given her pills; the white one, the pink one, the grey and the black.

"What a lovely day," she said. "Thank you, my dear."

"It's us who should be thanking you."

"And isn't Viggo a good story-teller."

She smiled.

"And wasn't it a good thing that we didn't sing."

"Yes," said Niels Peter. "I'm not sure they could have coped with it. Ditlev in particular."

"Now you must just go and enjoy yourselves and not think about me."

Niels Peter went on a mosquito hunt with the fly-swatter. Placed a piece of net over her to protect her face. Put out the light and left.

He stood out in the yard with his guitar in his hand, looking at the lighted studio and thinking: What a lot of good parties we've had in this house. With the lights on like this. With the night lying thick and dark-blue around us.

He was aware of a warm feeling of friendship, a feeling of

lifelong friendship and loyalty.

His first thought when he woke in his attic room on Saturday morning was God knows whether Bett hadn't died a short while ago. Now that she had achieved it all. Now that she can feel content. Now, with her best friends all here in the house.

Mette had slept with her that night. He imagined Mette on her way up the attic stairs to tell him. They could cancel the admission to hospital, the journey there and the business of setting up a sick-room at Marstrand Street. How easy that would make it...

But instead it was Hans who came.

"I've had a look at Bett," he said. "Those spots she's got on her chest are burst arteries. That's a sign of metastases."

"What do we do about it?"

"There's nothing we can do."

"Shall I stay?" said Elin. "It's fine by me."

"There's no need to," said Niels Peter. "We'll manage."

They took their morning cups of coffee and had breakfast round Bett's bed. Mette took photographs. Simon did a disappearing act with Gertrud's cigarettes. Bett was in fine spirits.

At about three on Saturday afternoon, the farewell ceremony began.

Viggo gave Bett a quick kiss on the cheek.

"Goodbye, my dear," he said.

"All the best to you, dear Viggo."

They smiled and waved to each other. He was going back to Halland. It was the last time brother and sister were to see each other. They knew it. As he got into his car, Viggo said:

"Oh well. Sad that this is the way that things have to go."

He had tears in his eyes as he got behind the wheel and wound down the window.

"You coped really well, both of you," said Niels Peter.

"So did you, my boy."

Then Viggo disappeared up the avenue of birches. Hans and Ditlev drove off a short while later. Gertrud took Elin with her in the car.

Bett was left with her three children.

They set about clearing up. Mette and Niels Peter collecting up bottles and cutlery. Emptying ashtrays. Wiping tables. Carrying chairs back to their places and washing up.

Meanwhile Simon lay totally exhausted in the big bed, a half-empty bottle of white wine in his hand, watching Stevenson — with some effort — defeating his Soviet opponent.

"Are you enjoying it?" said Bett.

"It's fantastic," said Simon. "Shall I pull your bed over so that you can watch too?"

"No, thanks all the same."

They went to bed early that Saturday night. There was a crescent moon in the sky.

"What are your plans?" asked Bett on Sunday morning.

"I must go back to Hans and Milla in an hour or two's time," said Mette.

"I'm coming with you," added Simon with a grimace.

Niels Peter was disconcerted.

"Do you have time to talk now?" said Bett.

They sat down round her bed.

"Would you raise the bedhead a little, Niels Peter? And get the papers from the Cremation Society. They're in my bag."

Mette and Simon lowered their heads. Niels Peter got up.

"Do you mean the ones marked *My Last Wish*?" he said soberly.

"Yes, would you read it out?"

He opened her bag and in among her address book, diary, purse, keys and tissues, he found the envelope.

"It's a kind of questionnaire," he said. "You can put down how you wish the burial to be carried out."

"Would you fill it in?" said Bett in a faint voice. "Put that I want to be cremated and that my ashes are to be put in the common grave at Bispebjerg."

"That's a fine thing. You've always wanted that."

Mette gave Bett a glass of tomato juice.

"May I make a suggestion for the death announcement?" said Niels Peter.

"Yes, do," said Bett.

"Well, first your full name and then the two dates... signed family and friends. Then underneath, that the burial has taken place."

"No," said Bett in an astonishingly loud voice. "Just the date and time of day."

"The date and time of day?" exclaimed Niels Peter. "You don't mean a religious service?"

"No, no," said Bett, frowning. "Naturally, there's to be no priest, nor a coffin. Just flowers."

Mette sobbed and Simon shuddered violently. Niels Peter's eyes blurred over — but that was with anger. What was going on?

"Yes," said Bett. "And I want all the children in the family to be there. And my old pupils and all my friends."

Niels Peter tapped the paper with his pen.

"Then you have to say what hymns you want. There's room for three."

Without hesitating, Bett said:

" 'Hark! Hark my soul'. Then I'd very much like a hymn by H.C. Andersen or Grundtvig... "

"What about 'Tender Shepherd, Thou hast still'd'?" suggested Mette.

"Yes. And last of all I'd like you to sing 'Now the labourer's task is o'er'."

"Do you really mean that?" said Niels Peter.

"Yes, I do," said Bett. "Also one of you has to make a speech."

"I couldn't," sobbed Mette.

"Neither could I," wept Simon.

"Well, I'll do it then," said Niels Peter. "If you think that's all right."

"Thank you."

They sat in silence for a while. Then tears welled up again in Bett's eyes.

"And afterwards I'd like you all to go back to Hans and Mette's house."

"Everyone?" said Mette with a note of alarm.

"Yes, everyone who wants to."

"I've written all that down now," said Niels Peter. "Would you sign here, Bett?"

They propped her up and with a great effort Bett signed her name at the bottom of the form. Would that be the last time she'd hold a pen in her hand?

"Just tell me if there's anything else you'd like," said Niels Peter persistently. "Just say so."

"Yes, there is one thing," said Bett. "You must promise me that you'll never get rid of Forest House."

All three of them lowered their heads and nodded.

"Now I'd like a little rest," said Bett. "If you'd just help by lowering the bedhead."

It had rained in the night, flattening the corn.

They were sitting in the pergola.

Simon wiped his eyes on his sleeve.

"What about a drink?" he said.

"Thanks, a double," said Niels Peter. "I need one. So she wants her funeral announced! There's to be some kind of ceremony at the crematorium!"

"It's strange," said Mette. "I thought Bett didn't want a funeral. This goes against everything she's always said before."

"That's right... she never wanted it before," said Niels Peter, his voice rising. "I'll have nothing to do with it. It's something she's just thought up."

"Sssh," said Simon, putting his finger to his lips.

"What on earth do you mean?" said Mette.

"I'll talk to her just once more," whispered Niels Peter. "And try to bring her to her senses."

Mette opened her eyes wide.

"You mustn't. Not when she's so weak."

"Yes, I will."

"No, you won't," said Mette. "I'd do anything for Bett. Even crawl to the moon."

"Don't get so worked up," said Niels Peter, beginning to get worked up himself. "You wouldn't. That's just hot air. We've just celebrated her birthday. She's had guests and telegrams and gifts. Do you really want us to inconvenience all those people — and many, many more — so soon again? And stand there having to shake hands, and mumbling. I simply couldn't do it."

"You're really unkind," said Mette, trembling.

Simon said nothing, but busied himself filling up the glasses.

Niels Peter placed his hands flat on the table and leant over towards his brother and sister.

"She thinks everything — *everything* — is to do with her."

"*But so it is*," exclaimed Mette. "And I wouldn't promise a dying person anything I couldn't stick to."

"Yes, you would," said Niels Peter coldly, "if you saw it was blackmail."

Mette stared dumbly at him, her hair lifting in the wind.

"Maybe *you* feel you're being blackmailed, Niels Peter," said Simon, intervening in the conversation for the first time. "But we don't. Neither Mette nor I. You must realize that."

"Yes, this is your problem," said Mette.

"Then I want to say one more thing to you," said Niels Peter furiously. "If this ceremony is to go through, then *you're* going to have to arrange it. I won't. I'll go with her all the way as long as she's alive. But I won't be part of a theatrical performance after she's dead. That'd be the end. But you can go ahead if you want."

He stopped, astonished at the loudness of his voice.

"We can't do that," said Mette, looking at Simon.

"You may have to," said Niels Peter. "If you want to fulfil your mother's last wish."

Then he added a second or two later:

"Because I don't."

Simon lay face down on the bench. He looked and sounded as if he were drunk and incapable. Not for the first time.

"Take him away," said Niels Peter to Mette. "Didn't you say something about having to get home?"

"Can you manage with Bett until tomorrow morning?"

"What if I said no, I couldn't?"

"What do you mean?" said Mette, looking at him in bewilderment. "You've always... "

He knew that he would manage, and said in a cool voice:

"Off you go now. It'll work out. Simon can help me lock up the studio and the barn. That'll be one thing less to think about tomorrow morning."

With his pipe in his mouth and his hands in his trouser pockets, he stood watching the Citroën drive away.

It disappeared from sight. He started thinking about how he was to deal with this, his last evening with Bett at Forest House.

Tomorrow she was to be admitted to hospital and from there she would be moving back to Marstrand Street.

First and foremost, surely, they must avoid sentimentality. Perhaps they should be quite quiet, and underplay the situation?

He went in and sat with Bett, her cold hand in his. She smiled at him, her eyes brilliantly grey and clear.

"Tell me," he said. "Do you really think 'Now the labourer's task is o'er' is a good hymn?"

Bett looked at her son with interest.

"Don't you think so?"

"No, to be honest, I don't. And neither do those words 'Leave we now Thy servant sleeping' suit you."

"Have you a better suggestion?" she said.

"There's lots of better ones. What about all the old ones? I'd be happy to go through the old hymn book, if you like — you know, the one with all the good old hymns in it.

He had put on Vivaldi's "Four Seasons".

"I've always wanted that," whispered Bett.

The house was back in order again. He could find nothing else to do.

Then it occurred to him that he might take some of the smaller objects back to Marstrand Street with him. A milky-white glass off the shelf. The children's small gifts from her bedside table. A pair of framed photographs of Bett's parents. And one of herself at five years of age.

He wrapped the things up in kitchen paper and put them into a plastic carrier bag.

The garden door was open. They could hear the grass and the leaves breathing.

The water in the lake. The animals moving in the forest.

The sun was low on the horizon, throwing a long golden light over the yellow cornfield, in over the hedgerows, through the windows of the living-room and out on to the yard and the little avenue of birches.

He wished that he and his mother could simply glide away on those rays as they shone into the house. Just glide away on a tangent of the earth and disappear...

The light released its hold and drew darkness behind it like a cloak.

The white campions opened their heavy white flowers and spread their fragrance.

Night fell, enveloping the house and grounds in the immensity of its gentle darkness.

On Monday morning he straightened everything in the house, over and over again, so that everything lay perfectly parallel and symmetrical.

The older nurse came for the last time.

While she was saying goodbye to her patient, Niels Peter put a gift on the back seat of her car. It was a book, from Bett.

They were alone again. They were expecting the ambulance at eleven, but it was late coming.

Niels Peter lay down on the big bed so that he and Bett could see each other. What did they talk about? They talked about love. They talked about his father. About the mystery play called love.

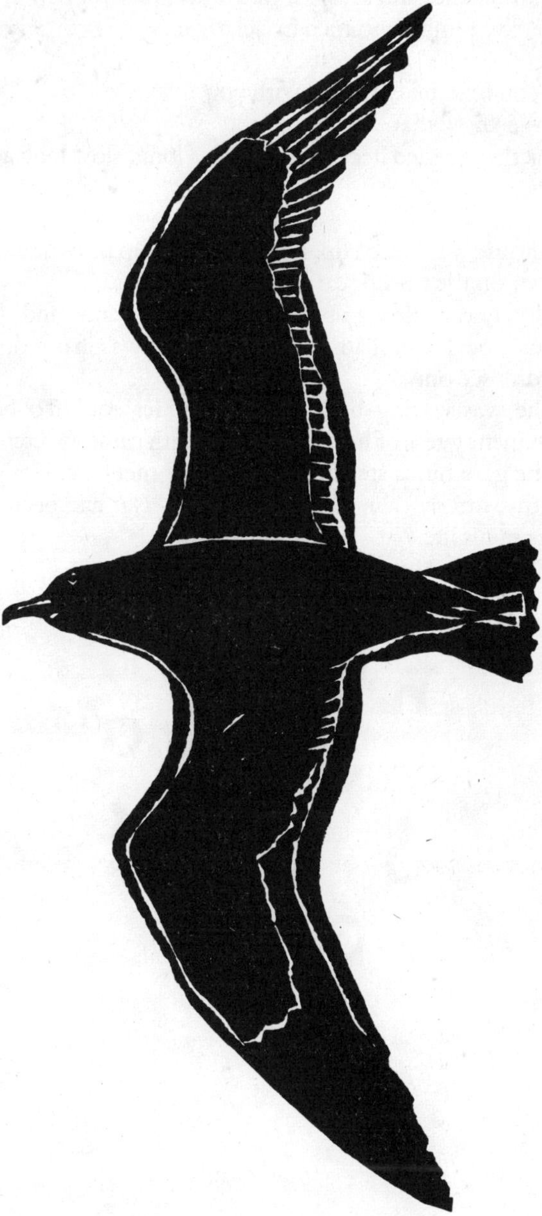

The ambulance slid into the yard and reversed up to the garden door. Two ambulancemen in clean starched shirts came into the room. Friendly, courteous.

"You're to take the bed with you."

"We know that."

As they carried her out, she took a long, slow look across the fields.

The house was locked up. Niels Peter got up into the ambulance and sat on the tip-up seat next to his mother.

Slowly they drove up the short birch avenue and the green slope. The lower half of the window was frosted, so Bett couldn't see out.

She was leaving her house now. Her soul. To become a permanent guest of her son's, until death came to fetch her.

She gave him a steady look. His eyes met hers. Her gaze was lengthy, utterly calm and approving — as it had been so many times in his life.

That look. He would never forget it.

THURSDAY 23 OCTOBER

The sound of coffee being poured into a thermos. A sound that gets louder and louder.

The postman has just brought a letter from her. Together with a couple of bills.

Niels Peter is sitting at the kitchen table reading Isia's letter.

They write to each other almost every day. They could be together from morning to night — if reality didn't keep them apart.

Zigzag is lying face down on an ironing board. On the floor beside him, Milla is thumping her cousin's back and saying:

"Cough now."

"What are you playing at?" Simon asks.

"That Zigzag has cystic fibrosis."

"Do you know what that is?"

"Yes, one of the boys at the kindergarten's got it," says the little five-year-old.

"Can I join in?" Simon asks.

"Would you like to be thumped?"

"Yes," says Simon, lying face down alongside Zigzag.

"Isn't today the day you're supposed to be starting on the studio, Simon?"

"Do I have to?"

"Yes, you most certainly do," says Mette. "It's Thursday. And we've agreed to clear everything out by Sunday. You really must get a move on."

Simon has no choice but to get up from the floor.

"Oh, and we were having such a good game," says Milla.

Simon tries to pull himself together. He has to go through all the cupboards in his studio, through all his drawings, sketches, oil paintings, equipment and suchlike. Clear things out. Make decisions.

"I think I'll chuck all this shit out."

"Not without looking at everything, surely!"

He pulls on his boots and a working jacket.

"The only thing I want to keep is the printing press."

"Wait a bit, first!"

Simon disappears over to the barn.

Returns a moment later with a large pack of clean drawing paper.

Gives it to the children.

"Use it," he says. "Draw on it."

He feels like a stone. Good for nothing. Lifeless. Totally grey. The terrible sound of the alarm ripped into his sleep and everything inside him was about to stop — that morning in Marstrand Street.

Simon had been there the day before. They had screwed hooks in all the windows. Small hooks and storm-hooks. They had hung the ship's clock from Havne Street up in the kitchen, so that they could keep track of the time.

He had painted the window frames white. Painted her little commode white. And laid out the children's little presents and the oval-framed photographs.

They had talked to each other as if what they were going to be involved in now was a mere nothing — a click of the fingers. Simon had said, for instance: "You know Fidel's sent a telegram to Stevenson?"

"To Moscow?"

"Yes, and offered him the job of Minister of Sport."

"Isn't Stevenson a member of the Cuban parliament?"

"Yes, and becoming Olympic champion three times in a row — how many members of parliament can do that?"

In the evening, Niels Peter had been up in Ditlev's flat and had talked with him about his mother's crazy plans for her funeral.

"I want to do what's right while she's alive. But when she's dead, then that's in the past. If there's to be a public funeral and all the hoohah that goes with it, it'll have to be without me. Count me out. Mette and Hans and Simon will have to cope with it."

The rain was drumming on the zinc coping outside the window.

"I know you mean what you say."

"I feel she wants me to stand there like some kind of husband and round off her life. I refuse to do that. Because it's playing to the gallery. And anyhow, I haven't the energy. It seems like she wants to punish me."

"May I say one thing?" said Ditlev quietly. "She does *not* want to punish you. It's only that her sense of being excluded is tormenting her. I think she's suffering from lack of oxygen, which is affecting her brain."

"Well, she's not the person she was."

"Do you mind if I talk to Mette and Simon about it?" said Ditlev.

"Might do some good."

Niels Peter had gone back down to his flat and had taken some sleeping pills to knock himself out.

Now the alarm clock was ripping through his sleep.

It was Thursday morning. In a short while the bed and all the other equipment would be coming from the hospital. The intensive care department at Marstrand Street would be ready for Bett's arrival a few hours later.

A fair-haired hospital porter assembled the bed in the living-room. Placed an empty water-mattress on it. Filled it — with the help of a hosepipe he'd brought with him — with lukewarm water from the kitchen tap. Niels Peter shuddered when he realized that he would have filled it with cold water.

"Then she'd have frozen," said the porter, smiling.

An ambulance stopped out in the street.

There was a knock at the door.

The ambulancemen carried the tiny figure wrapped in a white sheet into the house.

Niels Peter was at once at her side.

"Welcome home."

Two bright eyes looked up at him. Dark skin taut across her face. Her ears had grown bigger, more transparent. Her hands white. Nails white.

"How grand you've made it all," she whispered.

An hour later, a district nurse appeared, a woman of authority who addressed her patient as *we*.

"Are we tired? Do we need to rest a little after our long journey?"

She read the report from the hospital and went through everything to make sure nothing was missing.

Before she left, she told them that the night-nurse would arrive at about eight.

He read the report from the hospital:

> Dosages at discharge:
> Kaleorid tablet 750mg (morning) — 750mg (evening)
> Aldactone tablet 25mg (morning) — 25mg (midday)
> Lasix tablet 20mg (morning) — 20mg (midday)
> Magnesia tablet ½g (morning) — ½g (midday)
> Ketogen tablet at night
> Doloxene at night
> Patient increasingly listless, oedematous, tired, no appetite. Patient given daily bedbath, turned according to need. Patient eats and drinks little. Patient denies it but looks in pain. After some persuasion, patient willing to accept pain-killers. Patient is welcome to return to the department at any time.

Long phone conversations, here, there and everywhere. Hectic activity in the house. Or was it just that Niels Peter was feeling confused?

Elin came.

"Look what I found down by the lake," she said, holding out her hand to Bett. "A mushroom."

"You can find mushrooms all over the place," whispered

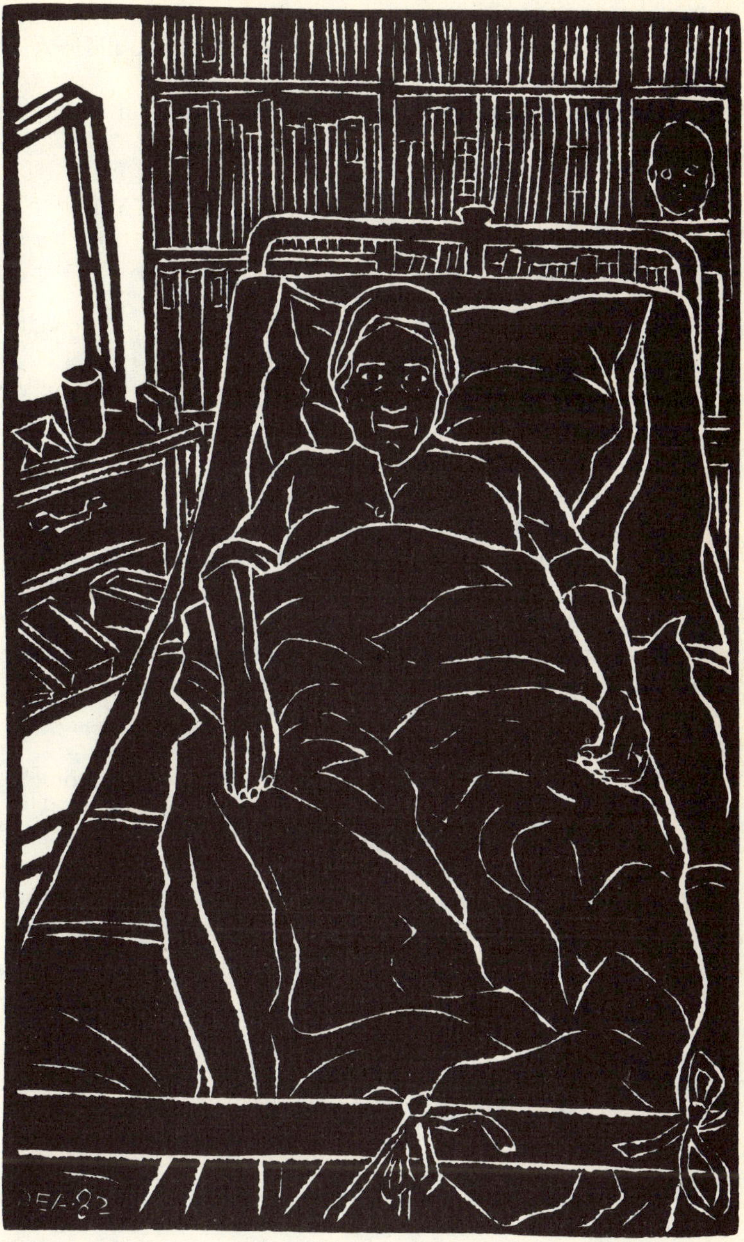

Bett.

"But it rained last night," said Elin, "and I always go and look when it's rained."

Elin stayed with Bett while Niels Peter cycled off to buy straws, ice-cube bags, fruit juice and a kitchen roll.

When he got back, Mette and Simon were there with Milla.

Milla clambered up on the sofa so that she could stroke her grandmother's hair.

"Can I come up and sit with you, Gran?"

"No, treasure, I'm afraid I'm too tired."

"Then I'll go out and play for a while."

Simon gave Bett a little picture he had painted.

Mette read letters out aloud. Niels Peter went out of the room to switch on the dishwasher.

"We must get it framed," whispered Bett.

A little while later Milla came back in.

"Can the other children in the street come in and see you, Gran?"

"Yes, of course they can."

Three little girls appeared and stood gaping in the doorway, quiet as mice. Then they walked round the hospital bed, looking at it from all sides, and said:

"Gosh, isn't that something!"

Milla was about to start showing off to them by doing some P.E. exercises against the headboard.

Bett raised her hand a few inches above the covers.

"Now, now, little ones, that's enough now."

The children left the sick-room in single file.

The dishwasher stopped for a moment, and then went on with its mechanical labours.

Bett's hand touched Simon's.

"How're things with you?"

"All right," mumbled Simon, tears trickling down his cheeks.

"We're going now. We'll be back tomorrow."

"Yes, we'll come every day," whispered Mette.

The night-nurse turned out to be young and pretty. She seemed experienced.

After making Bett ready for the night, she whispered to Niels Peter:

"Yes, you're right. Your mother seems confused, and she's in some pain, Give her Ketogen as and when you think she needs it."

Alone together again. He pointed at the camp-bed.

"I'll sleep here tonight," he said. "Just beside you here. I'll go up to my study for a while, but I'll be back down shortly. You can go to sleep now."

He had just an hour to himself. Played some Bach on the record player. Needed to feel the music sweep through him. His mother would only be able to hear it faintly.

Sat down on his chair and thought: If only we had someone to guide us. Someone who could tell us what's going on. Someone who could assess the ethics of this situation... and who would take the responsibility...

The hands of the clock moved towards midnight. The months of light nights were now at an end. Now — *now* — the two hands were perpendicular, held together with a tiny screw — pointing at the figure twelve.

Niels Peter ran downstairs and stood by her bed; the nightlight was still on.

He couldn't bear to look at her.

"Can I go to sleep now," she whispered.

"Of course. I thought you were already asleep. It's midnight."

Perhaps she meant something else by her question.

Suddenly he understood. He was to stay by her side all the time — not leave the house any more.

He undressed. Gulped down a sleeping-pill and drank two glasses of wine. Lay down on the camp-bed a few feet away from the hospital bed, wishing and wishing that he would fall asleep immediately.

He wished there were something he could put between them. If only one had a kind of carbon paper, so that the impression of one's thoughts would be fainter. He thought about the word carbon. Where did it come from? The great forests that grew on earth two hundred million years ago — they were called carbon.

In his mind's eye he managed to put himself out in some dark and rumbling space, as if he were on a cold ocean covered with carbon dioxide snow — and he saw the lighted windows of a low house. Behind those windows lay his mother, deserted and in enormous pain, lying in a white bed.

This evening Simon has begun to drag his old paintings and drawings outside one by one.

"Surely you're not going to burn all those?"

Simon has drunk himself into a state of determination.

"Yes. This stuff's all been here for years. And no one's ever really taken any interest in it."

"Can't you sell any of them?"

"I don't want to sell anything when I don't know if it's good."

"Well, give me a couple then," says Niels Peter.

"I've put some aside in the studio."

"You could let Mette and me store the rest."

"I won't have you storing things that I can't be bothered to keep myself," says Simon irritably. "What do you take me for?"

"Won't you regret burning all those pictures?"

"Depends what you mean by regret. Maybe I will. But what doesn't one regret? To hell with it all!"

Simon flings a picture on to the bonfire.

It's a self-portrait with red eyes, and a guitar with no strings. Two small figures in the background embracing each other.

"That's the one I'll miss the most," he says, taking a swig at the bottle. "But that's just self-pity, and I can't stand self-pity."

"I'd have liked that one."

Simon hands him the bottle.

"You should have said so before, then."

He's feeding the bonfire with pictures. Small square collages from his first visit to Poland, built up with oils and bits of newspaper, a hundred-zloty note or a page of a handwritten letter, all varnished.

"I was trying to make them look like old icons," says Simon.

Then a picture of Simon's great idol joins the others on the bonfire — the great Soviet poet Mayakovsky — against a background of scraps depicting ships and flowers.

Simon throws another idol on to the flames. A Jesus face with a black beret on. Che Guevara. Down in one corner. Simon has copied one of Picasso's harlequin figures.

The flames eat through the canvas, curling it up. The back frame breaks with a crack.

"I'm burning that," Simon cries, "because it represents the illusions of '68."

"You're burning them to punish yourself," mumbles Niels Peter, now almost as drunk as his brother.

"In future, I'm only going to do pictures on paper," says Simon. "Paper burns better."

Niels Peter thumps him on the shoulder.

"Mind you don't burn the whole house down."

"Shall we... ?" says Simon, drawing back his lips so that his silver front tooth catches the firelight. "Shall we get a can of petrol?"

He throws his arm back and flings the empty bottle into the night.

She was clinging on to life on the earth's surface. He knew it. She couldn't let go...

He disentangled himself from his bedclothes and stood at his mother's bedhead. It was seven in the morning on the last day.

"Did you manage to sleep?"

"Yes," she whispered, with tears in her eyes and trembling lips.

Perhaps she simply hadn't slept at all.

"Would you like a little water?"

She blinked.

That meant yes.

"How are we?" said the morning nurse as she gently and calmly prepared her patient for the day of her death. "A home-help is coming tomorrow or the day after."

The nurse and Niels Peter tried to get Bett into a shirt, one that Isia had bought for him in Italy. Bett had wanted it herself, because it was so soft. A few weeks earlier, she had asked Niels Peter if he would cut the collar and sleeves off, because they were uncomfortable.

It looked so disfigured.

He tried to get her arm through the armhole.

Her face contorted.

"Niels Peter," she whispered. "You're breaking my arm."

He almost wept. He kissed her hand — and the stubble on his chin scraped it as he said:

"Forgive me. Forgive me for being so clumsy."

Bett's eyes were blank. When she spoke, she had difficulty forming the words:

"I feel... feel... so strange. So listless... "

"Yes?"

"Are you giving me... some medicine... I don't know about?"

He showed her the jars of pills.

"It's only the Doloxene and the Ketogen — you know **about** them."

The morning nurse nodded in confirmation and packed her bag.

Bett looked dubiously at her son.

He felt as if his hair was turning white. As white as hers.

"Goodbye," said the nurse, and emerged on to the hot, suffocating streets of Copenhagen.

"Take my hand," she said all of a sudden.

Her hand was astonishingly cold, the nails ribbed and as white as paper. They both stared up at the ceiling, Thus they were united for a minute or two.

Then he did something that he knew immediately he would think about a great many times later in life. And regret.

"I'm just going to... "

He let go of her hand and went into the kitchen, where he added:

" ...turn off the coffee."

He turned off the coffee-maker, poured himself a cup, added some milk and lit a cigarette.

She said "take my hand", he thought. Now she's gliding into

the very last stage. I can feel it in the very molecules of her body. What wouldn't I have given earlier in my life, to be able to hold her hand in a situation like this? Why do I turn away now? I took her hand. Then I let it go. Instead of holding on as long as was necessary...

He went back in and took his mother's hand again.

But now it no longer mattered.

There, the search was over.

Folded the camp-bed up and placed it against the wall. Emptied the dishwasher. Ran up and down the stairs with various things in his hands.

Niels Peter's intention had been to create perfect calm. But instead he rushed about frantically, his thoughts flitting about... clothes, washing, pills, time, letters, finances, the family.

There was a knock at the door. Outside was Lajla. Radiant, her arms bare and sun-tanned.

"How are things?" she said breathlessly.

He jerked his head.

"Bett's having her midday sleep. It'll soon be over."

"It was so important to me that she didn't die," whispered Lajla, "before I came back from my holiday. Can I help with anything?"

"Yes, with everything."

They stole in and looked through the door. Bett lay groaning in the high bed, her hands in a strange position on her stomach.

He tried to write a shopping list for Lajla. He needed some small plates. Simon's picture was to be framed. Two litres of apple juice. Some more stamps.

The letters looked all wrong.

He found it difficult to spell.

No cash.

Wrote a cheque.

Sent Lajla off.

"Is there someone at the door?" whispered Bett. "Go and see..."

Ditlev was in the kitchen, the smallest bouquet in the world in his hand, wrapped in green leaves.

"How are things?"

He came in quietly and sat down on the bed with Bett. Stroked her hot forehead. Held her hands.

"How beautiful you are," he whispered.

She smiled happily.

"Thank you, Ditlev."

"Think what a lot we've done together," he said.

She blinked.

"Not enough," she said with some difficulty.

Niels Peter could see them through the open door. He put the coffee cups on the table, and got a bottle of schnapps out of the cupboard.

Ditlev closed the door behind him.

"She wants to rest a little."

"Come and sit down."

Niels Peter poured two drinks. Ditlev pulled up his chair and wiped his glasses.

"We could have talked to her about the funeral arrangements," he whispered. "But she's far, far too tired."

"But what are we going to do, then?" whispered Niels Peter desperately. "It's driving me mad."

Ditlev put a finger over Niels Peter's mouth.

"I spoke to Mette and Simon yesterday evening. They're changing their minds. They realize that it simply doesn't match up with Bett's life. They're realizing what a strain it would be to have a big funeral. They also realize that you really mean it when you say that you wouldn't be a part of it. Tell me, how many people know about that form you filled in for Bett last Sunday?"

"Only us."

Niels Peter took it out of his bag and pushed it across the table to Ditlev, who read it and shook his head.

"You mean — disregard it?"

Ditlev handed the paper back to Niels Peter.

"Yes."

"Niels Peter," a voice came faintly from the living-room.

He leapt up.

"I'd like... like to... see you again."

"Yes."

"Would you... straighten... my pillow?"

"Does it hurt?"

She squeezed her eyes tight shut. Tried to nod.

"Can I give you one of these?" he said.

Showed her the jar of Ketogen.

Her eyes were staring strangely.

Was it anguish?

"Shall I phone for Hans?" whispered Ditlev.

Perhaps the time had come.

Hans stepped quietly up to Bett's bed with his bag in his hand.

Leant over and kissed her. Stood up again with tears in his eyes.

"Shall we get hold of Mette and Simon?" said Niels Peter.

"Yes, definitely."

Mette and Simon arrived in separate taxis. Mette was devastated: "Who'll fetch Milla from the kindergarten?"

"I will," said Ditlev. "And I'll look after her tonight, at your house, if you'll give me the keys, Mette."

He left. Lajla came in like a breeze, loaded with bags of shopping.

"Will you watch Bett," Hans said to her, "while I go upstairs and talk to the others?"

The young girl went over to the dying woman's bed. Took her hand. Leant over her.

Bett stared at Lajla without blinking.

"How... pretty... you... are... " she whispered.

"Did you get my letter, Bett?"

"Yes... tell... me... about... your... summer... holiday... "

They were in Niels Peter's workroom.

"I think she'll die tonight," said Hans.

"Will you stay?" said Mette.

"No, I think it should be just the three of you."

He opened his bag.

"I'll give her some Pethidine."

"It's not anything that could give us trouble, is it?" said Niels Peter.

"Not really. It's only a pain-killer. It's what they use in childbirth. I'll put the ampoule on the bedside table, so that the nurse can see what it is. And here you have two more which you can give her if she gets upset or anxious. What you do is... "

He pretended to jab the needle into his thigh.

"Like that. Anywhere into the muscle. Then press the syringe right down — like that."

Lajla was standing in the same place — leaning over the bed — as when they had left her.

Bett was breathing slowly. Making a hollow sound.

"I'm going to give you something soothing," said Hans.

Bett glanced questioningly at Niels Peter.

He was supposed to be helping his mother to live. Not die.

The needle penetrated deeply into her thigh. She scarcely reacted.

"Come on," said Hans to Lajla. "We should go now."

Mette and her two brothers were calm — in a good mood, in a

way.

Simon went over to the Chinese take-away to get some pancake rolls.

The blue hour had come.

The night nurse came and took Bett's pulse. Fussed round her a little.

"I think I'll come back in an hour," she said. "I've two other patients to see to first."

She left. Simon came back. With the food.

The day was like that, the front door forever opening and closing.

They were sitting round the table, the door into Bett's room open.

Niels Peter took the *My Last Wish* envelope out of his shoulder-bag.

Simon nodded, lifted his glass and said: "Cheers."

Mette held out her hand. Without a word, she took the envelope and the paper.

Tore it into small pieces over the bin and put a match to it.

Niels Peter pulled out the telephone plug.

They finished their food in peace.

The room was lit with candles. Flowers on the window ledges in front of the drawn blinds.

Thus separated from the pale blue August evening, Simon, Mette and Niels Peter arranged themselves around the bed.

Bett's eyes were like glass, and there were large glass-like beads on her forehead. Her mouth was open — her teeth were like glass too. She was moaning rhythmically.

"Ah... oh, ah... oh, ah... oh... "

They stroked her arm.

"Bett," said Niels Peter. "Try to look at Mette. Mette's there. It's her hand."

Bett's eyes swivelled from side to side. Stopped when directed towards Mette's. But the pupils did not change. She wasn't focusing. Maybe she could no longer see?

Simon kissed her hand.

"And this is me, here, Simon... " he said.

Her eyes slid round towards him... and stopped... as if caught by his forehead.

"And Bett, it's me, Niels Peter here. All three of us are here. And we'll stay here. We won't go. Tonight we'll sleep here in the room by your bed."

He was pressing out the words. As if pressing them out of his limbs.

Her feet were icy cold. So were her hands. The cold was creeping in from the outside and getting closer and closer to her heart.

"Oh-oh, oh-oh, oh-oh," came from her throat.

Tick-tock, tick-tock, tick-tock, went the ship's clock on the kitchen wall.

A sound at the front door. Niels Peter went out to meet the night-nurse.

"My mother's dying now," he whispered. "No more phone calls out. No one is to come. We'll cope with this ourselves."

"Of course," whispered the nurse, following silently behind.

Mette was on her knees with her head against the edge of the bed. She was crying. Simon was standing beside her, his lower lip protruding, like a child trying to control himself.

The nurse moistened a piece of gauze with water. Wrapped it round some tweezers and pushed it carefully into the mouth that had been open for so long.

"Try to suck on this. Try to take a little of the water."

And the miracle happened. Yes, such things are seen as miracles. Bett gathered her lips together and tried to suck. Her hollow cheeks grew even more hollow.

So she could still hear. And understand?

The nurse went and stood calmly and expectantly at the foot of the bed — where in the old days no one was supposed to stand. For that was Death's place.

"Rrrrr," came from Bett's throat.

Resistance rose in her. The candles fluttered. Her face expressed one mute cry after another. She was like gold-leaf that curls up and becomes dust.

"No, no," cried Mette. "You mustn't die."

Mette and Simon were holding her hands. Niels Peter stroked her cheek.

213

"Try to be calm," he said. "You mustn't be afraid of anything."

She seemed... to relax.

"My dearest," he whispered. "Let yourself go now."

Her face was filled with peace. It became smooth. Her breathing became slower and slower. Finer and finer. Light little puffs.

Fading, fading.

Then disappeared.

There was total silence in the room. Tabula rasa. The candle flames quite still.

Beyond the blinds, out on the street, the light vanished with the sun. Their part of the earth now lay in shadow.

"Sometimes it is so beautiful," said the nurse, nodding, as if in appreciation of the dead woman.

She stroked Bett's forehead and closed her eyes, just as they had seen it done in films.

Mette was sitting on the floor, leaning against the wall, her face in her hands.

Simon was standing with his hands in his pockets, tears coursing down his cheeks, his eyes fixed on the body.

Death released a totally different reaction in Niels Peter. He leapt into the air, swinging his arms.

"It worked!" he cried. "Oh, God! That's it! It's over!"

A dry shell lay on that bed. A cocoon. The butterfly had spread its wings and flown.

"You must excuse me," cried Niels Peter to the nurse as he bounded past her. "Please excuse me."

"That's all right," she said quietly. "Everyone's different."

"Mette, Mette."

Shaking his sister by the shoulder.

"It couldn't have been better," he went on. "Here's a glass. You too, Simon."

"I'll phone Hans and tell him," murmured Mette.

The nurse was winding gauze round Bett's head to keep her mouth closed. In the old days, they would have used a hymn-book.

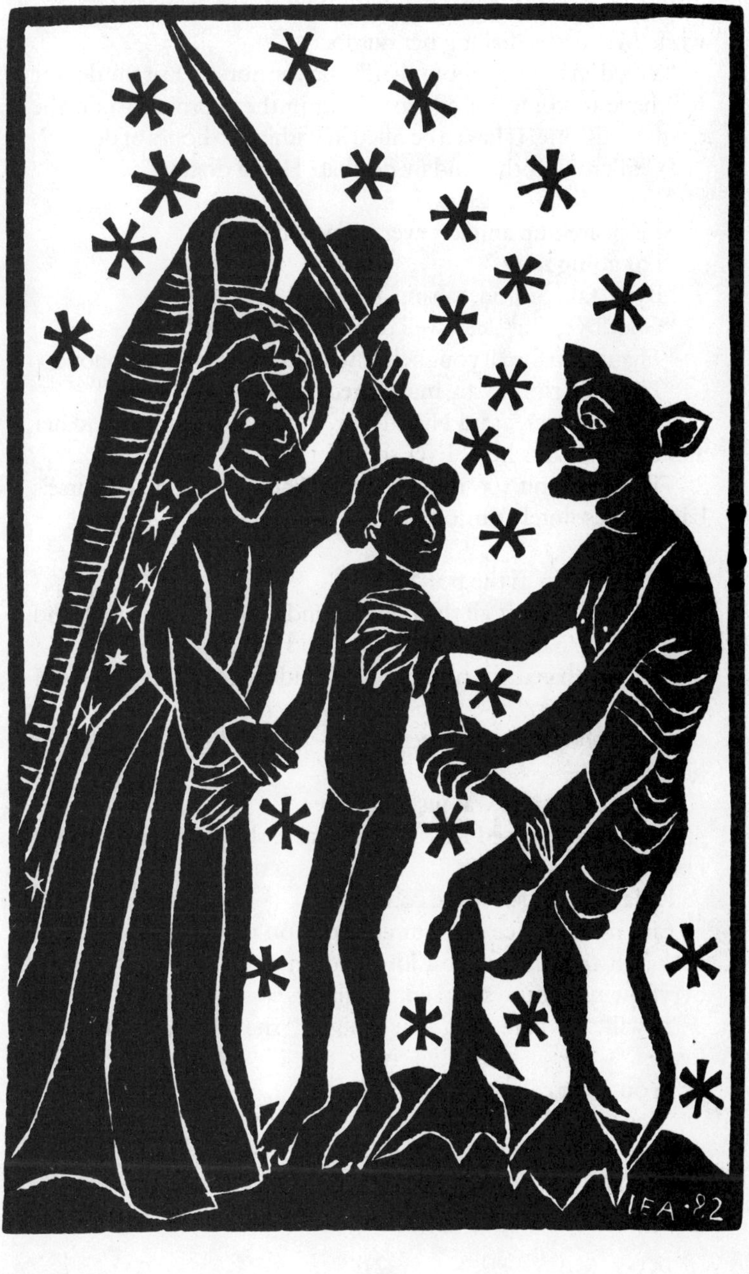
IEA·82

"Will you inform the registrar, and all that?" said Niels Peter, while Mette was dialling her number.

"Yes, don't worry about that," said the nurse. "But the doctor will have to come round first thing in the morning to do the death certificate. It has to be filled in within ten hours of death."

"Can't my brother-in-law do that? He's a doctor."

"Yes, by all means."

She cleared up and left everything shipshape.

"I'm going now."

"Bye," said Simon, raising a hand.

"Goodbye, and sleep well tonight, you three."

"Thank you for all your help," said Mette, still on the phone.

"That's all right," she murmured.

"You're sweet," said Niels Peter, flinging his arms round her and trying to kiss her. "Ever so sweet."

That was a bit too much for her. She picked up her nurse's bag and resolutely turned to leave.

She passed Elin in the porch.

Elin walked past all the lighted candles, over to the bed, and put a brown hand on Bett's white hand as it lay there.

"So Bett has died, has she?" she said quite calmly. "While I was at a concert."

"You should have been here. It was fine, the way it happened."

"No, it's good it was just you three."

Hans came, raised Mette from where she was sitting on the floor and embraced her.

Lajla came to see if she could help.

Elin made coffee and put cups out on the table by the sofa, although there was not a lot of room among all the candles, overflowing ashtrays and empty glasses.

"I will stay here with you tonight," she whispered to Niels Peter.

"You most certainly will not."

"Yes I will."

Hans looked at Simon.

"And how are things with you?"

"I feel... completely... empty."

They kept watch over their dead. They drank lots of coffee, as is customary, and spoke to the dead person as if she were alive.

"Have a good journey."

"And many thanks for all the time we've spent together."

Cool and peaceful she lay on the water-mattress in the big white bed, which now seemed even larger. Even wider. The ship's clock and all the watches in the room were ticking, the flowers in their vases listening.

Maybe she can still hear, he thought.

"Do you want to put something in her hands," said Elin. "In some places in Greece they put an orange in each hand. And hang a sheet over the mirror."

"Of course," said Niels Peter. "The mirror should be covered."

"And then you sing laments," said Elin. "Hymns for the dead."

"What about the funeral?" said Lajla.

"She's to be cremated," said Niels Peter — sounding like a teacher addressing a pupil. "But we're thinking of having a party. With all Bett's friends."

"Will it be next Sunday?" said Hans.

"Yes, here at Marstrand Street. We'll get in lots of wine."

"Can you cope with that, Niels Peter?" said Mette. "Do you think you can manage?"

"Yes, I can."

"I can come and help," said Elin.

"And me," said Lajla.

"And the rest of us, too," added Hans.

Elin and Niels Peter were alone. He covered the body with the sheet; then they set about clearing up.

They stood still and embraced. Elin's body was warm.

"Where will you sleep?" he said.

"In the children's room."

He put Bach's "B minor Mass" on the record player and switched off the light. Lay in the darkness and listened as Bett was borne away on the notes of the violins. This had been the most concentrated day of his life. And for his mother, too.

The choir sang *Kyrie, eleison*...

A stone thrown in the water. The water closes over it. The stone has gone. It is invisible, the grey film of the water covering the point where it struck.

The wind blows and birds fly. No amount of chemo-therapy, no achievement of human civilization, can change the direction of the wind — can make the water open and throw the stone back into your hand.

Tonight, an incredible full moon shining above Forest House. Sparkling. You can see that the moon is the earth's radiant satellite, surrounded by individual twinkling stars.

There it is — icy white — its head tilted, with its clearly marked mountains and valleys. With its characteristic expression, sleepy yet alert.

The light from the bonfire strikes Simon, Mette and Niels Peter, and casts their shadows far behind them on to the damp grass.

"What a wonderful *auto-da-fé*," Simon exclaims. "Truly terrible."

He has burnt his pictures, instead of flagellating himself as they do in certain countries. And they have dragged the heap of things marked 'to be burnt' out of the barn, and they are tossing them one after another on to the bonfire.

They watch the flames and the sparks flying, exploding in the darkness. Floating. Rising and vanishing. Spreading out and being absorbed by the darkness.

And so it is with love.

It has gone.

Nothing can be done about it.

"Do you know what the Middle Earth is?" says Niels Peter.

"No."

"It's a place where your soul goes between life and death. In hot volcanic countries, on its way to death, the soul meets an obstacle in the form of a burning fire. In colder countries the crossing to the kingdom of the dead is made by boat."

"And here, with us?"

"Here in the Nordic countries, the soul stops on a heath, in mist and sleet. On a spot rather like this, I suppose."

He wipes the sweat from his forehead.

"These obstacles have a double meaning. They mean that the soul must strain every nerve to enter the kingdom of the dead. And at the same time they stop the soul from returning to those who are left behind..."

A little while later, he sighs:

"The memory of the dead burns away, is watered down, washed away..."

"Well now we've blocked off the returning part, anyway," says Simon, quietly.

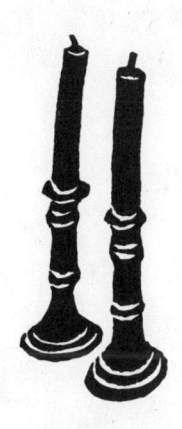

FRIDAY 24 OCTOBER

It is morning. A grey, dull day.

"Quite a fire you had last night," says Mette. "It's still smoking."

"Well, I feel much more relieved now," said Simon.

"That's good."

"Yes."

"I'm going to the station to fetch Elin now," says Mette.

"Can we come too?" says Milla.

"OK. Hop in, all three of you. In the back."

"Could you do some shopping for me at the same time?" says Niels Peter. "Keep a note of what you spend and we'll sort it out later."

"Get me three bottles of red wine, will you?" says Simon. "The ones at twenty-kroner."

Simon is stirring the bonfire with a hay-fork, cold drops of rain falling on to his forehead and hands, and hissing into the embers.

"What the hell!" exclaims Niels Peter. "Surely you're not burning that, too?"

He points at a portrait of Bett slowly being consumed by the flames.

"What's wrong with it?"

Simon scratches his head.

"What is wrong is that it was rather false. I was trying to flatter Bett when I painted it. I can't bear to look at it any more."

He leans his forehead against his hands on the hay-fork.

"Are you upset about something?"

Simon lifts his head and stares straight ahead.

"My brain's in chaos. Thoughts grinding round and round. How long do you think that's going to go on?"

"It'll probably take some time."

"What worries me... is that I'm so self-centred," says Simon. He takes a deep breath and goes on.

"I seem to need to be at the centre of things."

"I know exactly what you mean," says Niels Peter.

"I feel as if I've been playing the role of the child in the family. Now I've got to abandon that role."

"And what role have I been playing?"

"You've been playing the role of father. I think you should abandon that, too."

The car came back. Elin, Mette and the children are bustling around in the yard.

Mette shows Elin Bett's bedroom, where everything relating to the family and to her school has been put. Things that the three of them don't want to keep.

Elin sets about it with vigour. She phones round family and friends, and also phones Bett's old school to find out if they're interested in having some of the things.

Then she fetches boxes and baskets down and starts packing them, writing labels describing what's inside, tying them up with string and writing names on the outside.

Things have got much better at Forest House since Elin's arrival.

After breakfast, the sun comes out.

A van turns up in the yard — people collecting jumble for the sports club jumble sale.

Simon and Niels Peter help carry the things out and stack them in the van. They make up a whole vanful. Among them are a lot of things that Bett has bought over the years from the same jumble sales. Now they're being given back.

"Thanks," say the men, as they jump back into the van.

An endless procession of cars coming and going.

On the Saturday morning he was telephoning around for yet more motorized transport — a hearse.

Elin, Mette, Hans and Simon were sitting round the table, watching him and listening to what he was saying to the undertaker.

"My mother died Thursday night. The doctor is here now. Would you be able to come and fetch her soon. She wants... she wanted to be cremated and her ashes put in a common grave."

"Is there to be a funeral ceremony?" said the undertaker.

Niels Peter looked at the others, then answered in a loud voice:

"No, there's to be no ceremony."

No one said a word in protest. Mette was sitting quite calmly, holding Hans's hand in hers.

"We might be able to get a hearse to you by about midday," said the voice. "Do you want any special cerements?"

"No," said Niels Peter. "We don't want anything fancy. She is wearing her nightgown. Wouldn't just a shroud be sufficient?"

"Yes. What kind of coffin do you want?"

"Do we need a coffin?"

"Yes, that's compulsory."

"Then we'll have the simplest possible. The cheapest — with no extras."

Hans went up to the hospital bed. Turned back the sheet and looked at the bound head and closed eyes. Listened to the heart and lungs with his stethoscope. Found a hand and touched it. Covered her up again.

He filled in the death certificate.

Mette was incredibly attentive to Hans. He had only to glance at her and she caught his gaze. She needed to be at his side all the time.

Simon was trying to send a telegram to Viggo in Halland.

Niels Peter phoned the announcement of his mother's death through to four different papers.

He gave them her name, her date of birth and the date of her death.

Signed — Family and Friends.

Underneath, a note to the effect that the funeral had already taken place.

At midday, two heavy, elderly, solemn men came into the living-room. Dressed all in black.

"Would you like a cup of coffee?" said Elin.

"Wouldn't say no... "

They were given the necessary papers: birth certificate, death certificate, national insurance number, health insurance number.

"There may be problems getting the coffin out of the house," said one of the men. "We've had this problem before — the front doors in this street are too narrow."

"Couldn't you take the body out on its own?"

"Yes."

The undertaker's men lifted the plain white wooden coffin out of the hearse and placed it in the front garden. At the bottom of the coffin was a soft layer of fresh sawdust.

They wound the body in a sheet that they had brought with them and carried it like a white parcel through the door — like the Descent from the Cross, thought Niels Peter — and placed it on the sawdust.

They all followed. Elin had the idea of taking one of the bunches of flowers off the window-sill and putting it into the coffin. The others liked the idea and they emptied all the jamjars and teapots of their pale pink sweet peas and their roses.

The smallest bouquet in the world lay on Bett's breast — the one that Ditlev had brought.

Two children from the street had crept in and they stood with the family in a circle round the coffin.

"Maybe we should keep one bunch of flowers out," said the undertaker, "and put it on top of the coffin."

The lid was screwed down.

"Do you want to come with us?" said the men from the undertaker's.

"No," said Niels Peter, looking at the others in turn. "We won't be coming with you. We'd rather stay here."

The men from the undertaker's nodded and lifted the coffin into the hearse. A boy stood leaning on his bicycle, watching. It was Lajla's younger brother.

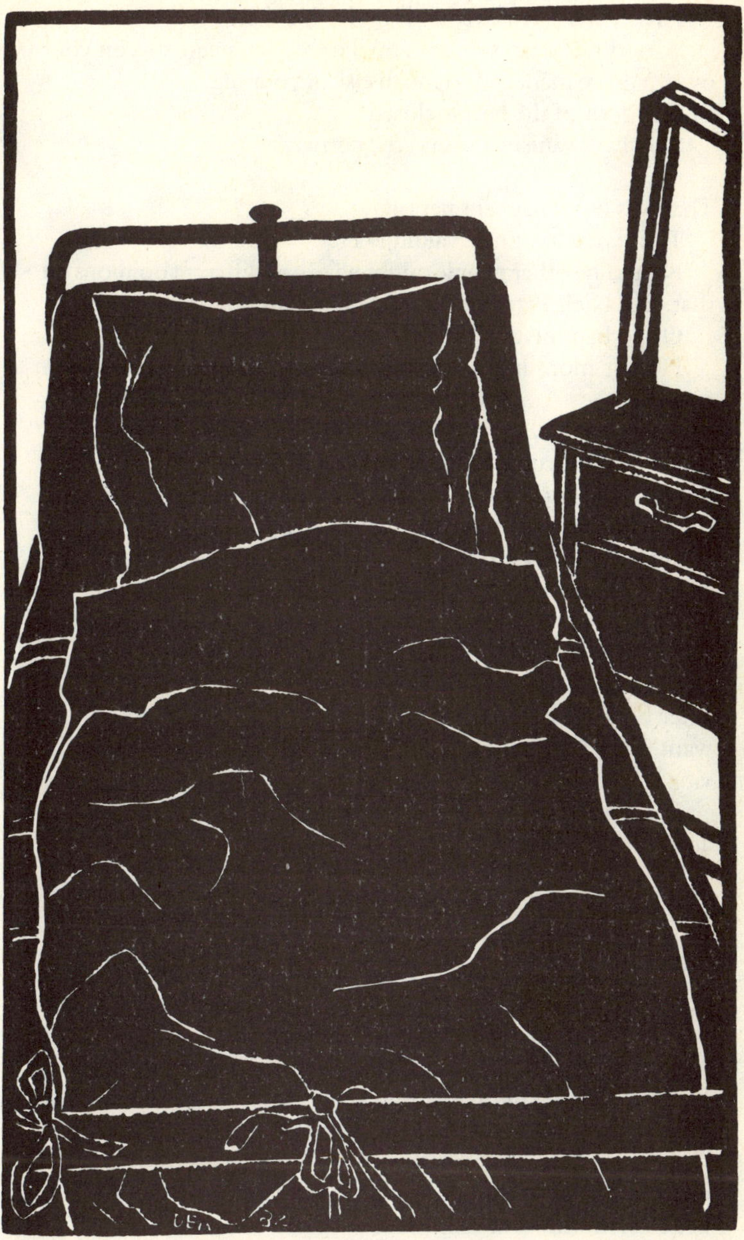

Niels Peter went over and laid his hand on the coffin.

"Goodbye, dearest Bett. You'll have to manage this on your own. You've managed so much else in your life."

The door of the hearse closed.

Slowly, it vanished round the corner.

That was how they sent her off.

They were not undervaluing her.

Naturally, other people might have had different opinions on that. But Niels Peter was certain. This was how it should be.

Or perhaps he was not that certain after all?

He felt more like a vacuum-sealed pack that has just been opened.

The water was running in the kitchen — for no apparent reason. No one had turned on the tap. Niels Peter heard the gurgling sound and had a sudden moment of anxiety.

Anxious that everything would disappear — like the water going down the plughole in the kitchen sink.

Then just as suddenly as it had started the water stopped, as if an invisible hand had turned off the tap.

They had breakfast in the back garden. Lajla came in. She didn't want to eat, and sat with her back to the others, looking at the vine.

She started to cry. Mette got up and went over and put her arm round her.

Late that night, Niels Peter was alone in his study. That strange amber-like atmosphere. A sense of the over-real.

Her body was now lying in the mortuary. Cold. Stiff. Feet pointing skywards.

A shooting star fell from the Perseides.

He put on the choral overture from the Bach "St Matthew Passion", lit a cigarette and listened with eyes closed. *Kommt, ihr Töchter, helft mir klagen*.

There seemed to be a scratch on the record which clicked every time the stylus reached it. A scratch that broke the link between mother and son.

As he observed the universe expanding, he thought: "I can't carry on being so neurotic about losing her love."

Sunday came. At midday Niels Peter heard his two sons come rushing in through the door, followed by Karin.

It was three weeks since he'd last seen them.

The boys looked at the empty bed and stopped in their tracks.

"Where's Gran?" they cried.

"I'm afraid she's dead."

"Dead?"

"Yes, she's died and gone away."

All four of them sat down on the sofa. Jacob sobbed loudly. Karin put her arm round his shoulders and let him cry.

"Poor Gran," said Zigzag, his head bent and his lower lip thrust forward. "Poor Gran."

"Sweet kind Gran," wept Jacob. "Where is she now?"

"She's been cremated," said Niels Peter. "And her ashes have been scattered on a big lawn."

"I can't believe it, that Gran's dead," wept Jacob.

"Neither can I," whispered Niels Peter.

"I'll stop soon," sobbed the boy. "I'll stop soon..."

"You don't have to..." said Karin. "...you just cry."

Zigzag leaned against his father.

"I'm just as sad as Jacob, even if I'm not crying."

"I know, I know," said Niels Peter. "I'm just as sad, too, even if I'm not crying, either."

He hadn't really wept at all.

Somehow it wasn't possible.

The two children were left with a feeling of great loneliness. Their grandmother had looked after them ever since they were little.

Human beings are very defenceless creatures when they're young. Some cope at fourteen. If they have to. Not a good thing. Others cope at twenty. Some never quite learn to manage without their parents — even if that's what growing up is supposed to be about.

Niels Peter was now — for the very first time — to take on his full role as father.

"Shall I help with the breakfast," said Karin.

"School starts tomorrow," said Jacob, his eyes red from crying.

"Yes, first day of term tomorrow," sighed little Zigzag.

"Do you think you two could find your school bags?"

"Are the boys coming back to live with me now?" said Niels Peter.

"Yes, if you like."

"I would, very much so."

"I think I'll be off home after breakfast," said Karin.

"OK, fine..."

The boys went round the house, a little uncertain of themselves, and moved back into their room.

The little presents they had given their grandmother had been laid out on their table.

"Are those for us?"

"Yes."

"Dear, sweet Gran," said Zigzag, tears pouring down his chubby cheeks. "It would have been so much better if I'd been here when Gran died."

"So that you could have helped her die?"

"Yes," said Zigzag, his eyes brimming with tears. "I wish I'd been here."

Niels Peter pulled the boy to him.

"You see... grown-ups can help each other to die... but you're only seven, and that's too young."

"No it's not."

"I was worried that it would make you too unhappy."

"Well. I'm much more unhappy now."

"Fancy you starting in class four tomorrow," said Niels Peter, running his hand through Jacob's hair.

"And me in class two," added Zigzag.

"Yes, you really are growing. And everything's OK?"

"Mm... no... yes..."

As a child, Niels Peter had always loved the first days back at school. Everything new and fresh after the summer holiday. The floor varnished. New books. Always a new boy in the class. The kids not yet defeated, and the teachers not yet exhausted.

Bett had also always had a special liking for August.

A warm night.
   The boys lay naked on their quilts.
   The windows were open on to the starry August night sky.
   On to the sleeping city.

Monday morning. After the boys had been sent to school, Lajla came round. Niels Peter asked her to clear everything out of the sick-room. Everything was to be thrown out — the bedpan, the plastic gloves, the drinking straws — everything to do with illness.
   All the doors and windows were opened.
   On the notice-board in the kitchen, Niels wrote bleach, detergent, washing-up liquid.
   Lajla stood in front of him with a broom in one hand and a dustpan in the other, tears in her eyes.
   "When you're dead, you're dead. I know that... and I shouldn't really grieve. But I'm very glad that I got to know

her..."

"What were you really thinking on Friday?"

"I just rushed around being unhappy. You were giving me the silliest things to do. One of them was to get a picture framed. I almost burst into tears. You were quite beside yourself, Niels Peter."

"I think I must have been drunk, too."

Lajla put the broom and dustpan down.

"But I kept thinking — what the hell am I doing... Bett's dying... If I was ever worried about something, I'd often tell her, and we'd talk about it. And she always thought that what I'd done was right. She was ever so supportive."

"I was glad you came back after she'd died — on Friday evening."

Lajla nodded.

"So was I. As long as I didn't have to go and touch her. I couldn't have done that."

"Were you able to sleep afterwards?"

"Can you bear to hear what I did? I didn't want to go back to my parents. I met my friends, and we went out dancing all night."

"And?"

"It was a wild night."

A truck stopped in Marstrand Street. It had come from the hospital to fetch the bed, the water-mattress and everything they'd borrowed.

"I'm sorry to have put you to all this trouble," said Niels Peter. "When it turned out to be for such a short time."

"The important thing was that your mother was happy to have the use of the bed."

"Yes, she certainly was."

"Do you have any of her medicines left?"

"Yes, lots."

"You mustn't put them in the dustbin or down the lavatory. Think of the sewage workers!"

"What should I do with them all?"

"Give them to us. There's an incinerator at the hospital."

He gave all Bett's fruit juices — in cans, cartons and bottles — to the children down the street.

"My mother sends her regards and says thank you," said Lajla's brother.

He took all of the plastic bags of ice-cubes out of the freezer and put them in the garden to melt.

Lajla came back with the shopping.

"It's strange," she said. "I've just seen Bett in the street."

Isia phoned. Wrote letters. Sent little messages.

If only he could turn to her with the same strength.

He looked long and hard at his reflection in the mirror. Nothing showed there. Nothing but the thin, dulled face of a man, a stranger of thirty-eight, soon to be forty.

Made coffee.

Opened letters.

Letters continued to come for Bett, as if she were still alive.

On Thursday, someone rang from the publisher's to say that the jacket that Niels Peter had suggested would be fine. Simon had designed it.

"But your brother's not too good at calligraphy," they said. "We'll have the title typeset."

Simon was pleased. He was preparing for an exhibition in Cracow:

"Could you help me with the text for the catalogue?"

"Yes, I'd like to. By the way, have you seen the announcements in today's papers?"

"Yes, and a nice obituary."

"I've cut that out too."

Turning on the tap. The flow of water grew thinner and thinner, more and more muddy, or perhaps rusty.

Then stopped altogether.

An hour or so later a high note could be heard ringing throughout the house.

"What do you think it is?" said Jacob.

"I think it's the water coming back on," said Niels Peter.

At that moment, Isia came into the kitchen.

"Oh... ! Wonderful to see you!" exclaimed Niels Peter, putting his arm round her.

"I've missed you," she said.

Jacob gave them a long, hard look.

"Things have been happening in this house," said Niels Peter.

"It hurts me," said Isia.

"You mustn't say that."

"I know."

"I want a shower," said Niels Peter.

"Why?"

"I don't feel clean."

"But you are."

"Not clean enough."

"I'll come with you."

At midnight, they were in bed in his study, listening to Nielsen.

Isia above Niels Peter.

Beneath her: fresh blood where her loins had touched his.

And there was blood on his hands and streaks on the sheet.

Sleep was coming.

I am being threaded through a dark corridor.

On and on through an endless, cramped, icy tube. Swirling away at a frightening speed.

At the same time, I can hear a long whining hum.

I am on my way, leaving the earth, out through the tube to sparkling galaxies beyond.

To a shivering loneliness.

Darkness and nothing beyond it.

Until consciousness explodes and becomes matter.

He woke in a cold sweat.

Now he knew what it was like.

Noticed a warm hand on his arm. Weeping, he half sat up in bed.

Isia put her hand on the back of his neck.

"Tell me about your dream."

"I've been in mortal combat all night. Now I know what it's

like. What it was like for her. How it hurt. It was so hard, so hard, so hard. And I didn't understand."

"I've been watching you," whispered Isia. "The dream only lasted a few seconds."

"It was more real than reality."

"Well, now you must wake up."

He covered his eyes with his hands.

"Maybe it hurts terribly to be dead? We say the dead don't feel anything. But we don't know. We only believe it because we see the body lying still. But what about the soul?"

Isia leant over and kissed him.

"Wake up now."

He pulled the quilt over his head. She turned back a corner.

"I'll go and make some coffee," she said. "And get some fresh bread."

He turned his head to the wall.

Half an hour later, she was standing by the bed with a thermos of coffee, two cups and a newspaper.

"Just listen to what's on the front page of the paper," she said.

> The Polish uprising is spreading. Workers are striking and demanding free unions. Sixteen thousand workers in the Lenin shipyard at the Polish port of Gdansk went on strike yesterday demanding higher wages and the reinstatement of their sacked colleagues, the right to form free trade unions and to publish their demands in the Polish press.

A Sunday in the middle of August. Two o'clock, and guests were beginning to arrive at Marstrand Street. In groups, in pairs, or alone. Ex-colleagues and pupils of Bett's. Her brothers and sisters, her nephews and nieces and their wives, husbands and children. Friends who had come to Forest House over the previous ten years.

A barbecue had been set up for the children in the front garden, with stacks of paper napkins, plastic cutlery and paper plates on the ground. Simon was supervising it.

He was wearing a white shirt, a black waistcoat and a fiery red scarf. His fair hair was ruffled as usual, a purple cigarette with a gold filter hanging out of the corner of his mouth.

Ditlev had arrived with a whole carton of scented Sobranie cigarettes — Black Russian — and Simon had taken a handful and put them in his waistcoat pockets.

Mette and Niels Peter were standing on the doorstep welcoming their guests, surrounded by an aroma of spirits and burning charcoal.

Mette was wearing a boiler-suit and leather sandals, her mother's three gold bracelets on her wrist. Niels Peter was in faded canvas trousers and shirt, crumpled and all the same colour as his hair.

"Hi," said Karin, giving Mette a quick kiss on the cheek.

"Hi," said Bjarne, giving Niels Peter a friendly pat on the back.

"Have you been to the people's festival yet?"

"Yes, we've just come from the park. It was great."

More guests came walking down Marstrand Street.

"Lovely to see you," said Mette. "We've decided to enjoy ourselves today."

"That's just what Bett would have wanted too," they said.

"There's white wine in the kitchen. And food. Just help yourselves."

The house filled up. Elin and Gertrud. Viggo. Hans talking to Ditlev. Isia and Lajla. The guests stood in groups, admiring one another's children.

"How you've grown."

Embarrassed children wriggled.

"Is it really you? The last time I saw you, you were no bigger than... "

"What school do you go to?" "Do you like it?" "What subjects do you like best?"

Before the child had time to answer, someone else came up to say hello. The questions remained unanswered.

Mette went from room to room.

"We'd like to say a few words, if you'd all come out into the garden."

He looked over all the people gathered in their little back garden and thought: How many people can stand on Bornholm Island? The entire population of the world? Or just of Denmark? Anyway, it's some amazing number.

Simon was standing on an up-turned beer-crate. He rolled his sleeves up, then back down again. He told them about the last six months with Bett, about how friendly and helpful people had been to the family. About the kindness that would be one of their strongest memories of a period that had otherwise been so sad.

Simon got down from his platform and handed over to Mette. Mette sought Hans's eyes, found them and felt calmer. Little Milla was perched on his arm.

Mette spoke of Bett's death.

People's faces were serious, everyone listening.

"Bett's ashes have now been scattered," said Mette. "And the long journey is over."

Niels Peter stubbed out his cigarette, hitched up his trousers which were hanging uncomfortably loose, coughed and got up on the crate. He wanted to say something about Bett's patience.

A jet roared across the sky.

Niels Peter ended by saying: "I've thought a lot about the meaning of death. Because there surely must be one. I think the meaning is that we are to give up and make way for others. The dead give way. And what we have shared with the dead person — whether it's confidences, love, affection, anger or property — must now be shared with others. We have to learn to shift our emotions and find new ways of relating to each other. The baton is handed on. That is what I feel very strongly at this moment. Thoughts and feelings that we shared with Bett, we now share with other people and with different people. With you. It was really marvellous. That's all I wanted to say. Thanks very much, all of you."

"I second that," said Viggo, raising his glass to Niels Peter.

Niels Peter felt a slender arm round his waist. Isia's. Cautious. Smiling at him. He wanted to give her a quick kiss but didn't. People were looking.

"Please stay and enjoy yourselves with us a little," said Mette. "There's plenty of wine. And do stay as long as you like."

Ditlev also made a speech from the beer crate, talking about Bett as a friend. About the hospitality he had always received, and how Bett had always made him welcome.

"She was so forgiving of people, too," he said.

He stood on the beer-crate and started to cry, unable to control himself. But he did nothing to hide it. It seemed to release something in the others, too.

While Ditlev was speaking, the children set about stealing the cigarettes he'd brought with him.

Then they started selling them to the visitors in the house, and then to passers-by in the street, chanting all the while.

They sold them for fifty øre and thus earned themselves a small fortune.

Milla and Zigzag were the main instigators. They stood in the corner of the yard counting their earnings.

"Can I have one of those?" said Viggo. "Two kroner?"

Milla thought for a moment before answering.

"No," she said. "Three."

Viggo put the three kroner into the child's outstretched hand

and gave her an affectionate look.

Voices rose and fell. The first guests started to leave, but most seemed to want to stay.

Some went upstairs and talked. Promises to keep in touch. The rest gathered in the back garden, sitting on benches, chairs and empty crates around the wooden table.

All the food had gone.

"What are we going to do?" whispered Niels Peter. "Forget about it?"

"They can always go over to the Chinese takeaway if they're hungry," whispered Gertrud. "Just relax — they're bound to have food at home if they need it."

Ditlev was sitting at the end of the garden table, running a hand through his black hair.

"Do you have any of the college hymn books, Niels Peter?" he called.

Jacob ran in and brought the four they had.

"Let's sing, shall we... ?"

Ditlev led the way:

> Through the night of doubt and sorrow
> Onward goes the pilgrim band,
> Singing songs of expectation,
> Marching to the Promised Land.

After singing all six verses, Elin said: "What about something from Brorson?"

"Yes, 'Here is silence' — that's number one-seven-four."

From behind his thick glasses, Ditlev's gaze flitted from Mette to Simon to Niels Peter.

They nodded at each other.

They knew what they were doing.

Viggo was sitting slightly apart from the others — as he had always done in the old days.

He sat with a child on his lap and sang the first verse. Many of them knew the hymns by heart, certainly the first verse, and usually the last one too. When they sang "Say farewell to the world", they didn't even have to look at the book.

After some lieder by Grundtvig, they went on to mediaeval hymns.

Simon, Mette and Niels Peter sang "A lush and peaceful summer time" in a three-part harmony.

"Don't you have any suggestions, Jacob?"

"Yes. 'I know a lark's nest'. Gran used to sing that one when I was little."

Darkness fell. Blue.

Lights went on in some of the windows.

The guests left one by one.

But one small group remained, unwilling to go. There was wine enough — Viggo had seen to that — so why leave?

"Bett would have loved this," said one of her former pupils. "You know, I cried all weekend when Gertrud told me she'd died. I simply couldn't stop."

"But didn't you know she had cancer?"

"Yes, of course I did. But all the same, I couldn't stop crying."

"Do you think maybe you were crying about something else?"

After a moment's thought, she replied:

"Yes, maybe I was. Maybe I was crying over some of my own problems."

Lajla brought her parents' paraffin lamp. The ashtrays were full, and the ground was a sea of plastic mugs and squashed cigarette ends.

The coffee-maker bubbled away.

Elin passed round the cups.

"Oh no — I haven't done my maths for tomorrow," exclaimed Jacob.

"I'll help you," said Bjarne. "Go and get your maths book, then."

"Where are you going, Simon?" Mette asked her brother.

"To the pub."

Mette tried to stop him, but Hans put a hand on her shoulder and shook his head.

Swaying, Simon left the company without even saying goodbye.

At two in the morning, the last guests left.

Next morning, a feeling of being sewn inside a sack. Hearing the boys shout:
"Wake up, Dad! We'll be late!"
"We've nothing to take for lunch."
He turned to the wall and pulled the quilt over his head. Isia would have to see to them. The small complaining voices disappeared. The boys had left the house, with or without their lunch and their books.

Isia came upstairs. Whistling three tunes at once. Stood beside him in her bathrobe, smelling of melon and sour milk.
A half-full glass of wine stood by the bed. He took a sip and rinsed it round his mouth.
"I'm completely exhausted," he said.
Isia sat down.
"Do you know what I dreamt last night?" she said. "I dreamt I was at Østersø High School. They had a course on 'Being a Good Neighbour'. I found out that there was a translator living in Marstrand Street who couldn't sleep."
"So you decided to help him?"
"Yes. I decided that I'd start helping him to get to sleep. And in that way, I would be doing something useful for the community."
Isia laughed.
"I'll make you a cup of coffee."
Everything was somehow shimmering before his eyes. He went out to the bathroom and threw up.
Then he lay down to sleep again.

It rained. Then there was thunder. Then the sun shone again.
A neighbour was standing in the doorway holding a bunch of flowers.
"For you. Because you sang so nicely for your mother last night."

"Could you hear us?"

"I'll say we could! We could hear you all the way down Marstrand Street. Do you know all those songs by heart, then?"

"We were singing them from the High School song book."

"That's what we thought."

In the evening he wrote in the boys' contact-books: *Dear Teacher: The boys were late today because we overslept. Apologies.*

It is a golden October, always a beautiful month in Denmark. The ploughed fields round Forest House glowing in the afternon sun.

The shadows are long — blue and purple.

The clouds lie low on the horizon like sleeping faces.

Elin and Niels Peter are walking slowly through the birch avenue, up the hill. He turns his head and looks at Elin in surprise.

"Did I hear you right — did you say this *marvellous, lovely summer*? You surely don't mean *this* summer?"

"Yes I do," said Elin, blushing a little. "You mustn't misunderstand me, but... "

"I think it's been a terrible summer."

"But at the same time... how shall I put it... at the same time it was so intense and meaningful."

Niels Peter nods and knocks his pipe out on the wooden sole of his shoe.

"Try to explain how... "

"I think there's been something special about this summer."

"That's probably because she wasn't your mother."

"Yes, I'm sure that's true."

Elin stops and looks at her nephew.

"For me, it was as if we were all wrapped in love and an extraordinary kind of warmth. We could feel that Bett was losing control, but at the same time there was a fantastic tenderness."

"Yes, but wasn't that terrible for you?"

"No," says Elin. "I wouldn't have missed this summer for anything."

He carefully fills his pipe and strikes a match, the flame

invisible in the sunlight.

"So you don't think that society let us down?"

"No," replies Elin calmly. "Definitely not. Quite the opposite. Society actually gave us a great deal. Those two nurses who came every day. They were level-headed and supportive. You got home-helps. You had constant communication with Bett's doctor. And at the hospital — you had a whole team at your disposal."

They start walking slowly on. Niels Peter puts his arm round Elin's shoulders and she puts her arm round his waist.

"Didn't we have all the help you could think of? If you think about it. No, Niels Peter, society was actually extraordinarily generous on this occasion."

He stops and for a moment is lost in thought.

"What are you thinking about?" says Elin.

"I was thinking about the day that we sent her off in the hearse."

"Are you unsure about something?"

"There'll always be something."

"You're very much against funerals, aren't you?"

"Yes. But I was actually brought up that way. By Bett."

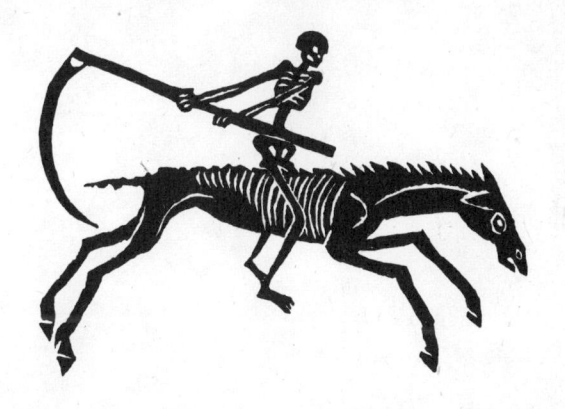

"I've come round to thinking that funerals can be a good thing," says Elin. "A good rounding off. It's a way of gathering together around a person. I don't hold the same view of funerals as Bett did. A funeral isn't just an empty phrase to me. It represents fellowship. I really would have liked to have gone along too when Bett was driven away. It was rather empty. There's some meaning in quietly driving away with the dead. It's sorrow and non-sorrow at the same time."

They walk past the smouldering bonfire.

The house is partially hidden by the copper beech.

Niels turns to Elin.

"Sometimes I feel," he exclaims, "that we're crazy getting rid of Forest House."

"But what on earth would you do with it if you kept it?"

"That's what I don't know."

"You could only keep it by moving here permanently and living here."

"But I want to live in the city. I'm much more a town-dweller than a country person."

"You're looking for something else, aren't you?"

"Yes, my freedom."

"Do you know what you're going to use it for?"

"That's another story. I don't know yet... "

SATURDAY 25 OCTOBER

A roe-deer runs nervously across the ground, past the remains of the bonfire, taking long silent leaps through the twin worlds of life and death.

At that moment, Niels Peter wakes in the attic room and looks at his watch. Soon be seven. A pale early-morning sky. Can't be long before sunrise.

His heart is thumping. We're destroying too much.

In his mind's eye he sees them carrying box after box out of the house and throwing them on to the fire.

Pictures, books, letters, all curling up in the heat — blackening and disintegrating.

He hears the children in the next room, probably reading their comics.

The rest of the house is still asleep.

Today is the last day but one of the autumn holiday. Hans is coming. Mette is due to meet him at the station in an hour or two's time.

Is it an act of violence, the way we're cutting off our roots?

Is it at all possible without violence?

Is it an essential part of the process?

They pick their way between stacks of old newspapers. They pack things into the packing-cases provided by the removal firm — only half-full, because otherwise they would be too heavy.

Niels Peter goes through the things that he's taking back to town with him. It turns out that it's more than he thought. Four chairs with rush seats. A drawing-board and two trestles. An assortment of tools. Books. The boys' summer clothes and their fishing nets. A mirror. The transistor radio bought in Brugsen. A couple of saucepans.

Jacob, Zigzag and Milla are by the table in the barn, cleaning the skeleton of the roe deer with warm water and toothbrushes.
　The gravel in the yard crunches.
　Mette gets out of her car, carrying her shopping.
　Hans gets out on the other side. Milla drops her toothbrush and hurls herself into her father's arms.

Hans is busy clearing out the outhouse, sorting tools and brushes, tins of paint and gardening implements.
　"What about the workbench?" he calls.
　"Did you say something?" Mette shouts back.
　"What about the workbench?"
　"Shall we ask Simon if his collective would like it?"
　"Mummy?" calls Milla.
　"Yes?"
　"I want a thinner jersey."

Niels Peter hears voices coming from all directions. He likes it this way — the sound of voices coming from different parts of the house. It lets him off having to say too much; he can just go about his business or sit working on his own.
　He goes outside with a big bag of rubbish.
　"Can I do the fire?" says Jacob.
　"Yes," says Niels Peter, giving the bag a kick to get the fire going. The bag tears. The contents spill out and the flames crackle.
　Jacob looks on, appalled.
　"You're burning my eighty-eight-piece puzzle."
　Then a little later:
　"Dad?"
　"Yes."
　"Do you think about Gran a lot?"
　"Yes, every day."
　"So do I."

Jacob sticks out his lower lip.

"Sometimes I think about the times when I was nasty to Gran."

Niels Peter drops the pitchfork he's been using, goes down on his knees and grasps the boy by his shoulders.

"When?"

Tears course down Jacob's hot cheeks.

"Well, when we played football, Gran and me... "

"Where?"

"Up in her apartment."

"Did the ball hit something?"

The boy shook his head.

"No, but it was a pity, because she got so tired."

Niels Peter threw his arms round his son with relief.

"Nothing else?"

"No."

The boy was sobbing.

"You're *not* nasty," Niels Peter consoles him. "You must never think that. You're just like any other nine-year-old in the world. Gran was only too happy to play football with you in her apartment."

"The trouble is that Gran was suddenly gone. I couldn't understand it. I can't even remember when I last saw her."

Jacob wipes away his tears, leaving a black streak across his face.

"I wish I'd been with her when she died. Or at least seen her when she was dead."

Niels Peter gets up.

"You know what I think?" he says calmly. "When a person dies, you always feel that something's missing. And what's missing is the dead person. It doesn't matter how it happened — whatever happened, you'd still feel it didn't go the way it should. I think what you're feeling is what we call grief."

Jacob nods. His nose is freckled. He had grown, is slightly broader across the shoulders.

"But I wasn't even allowed to say goodbye."

The nights turned darker at the end of August. The Milky Way appeared and the first birds began to migrate.

They had spent many weekends there, and Niels Peter realized he had forgotten to buy in food. There was none in the house and the refrigerator was empty.

He kept having mental black-outs. Couldn't remember names, places or events. He would go over to the bookcase, stretch out his hand — and then couldn't remember why. Sometimes he had to repeat the movement several times before he remembered what it was he had started doing.

He started putting notes on the floor. Writing messages to himself, in the way that people usually leave messages for one another:

Don't forget to set alarm.

Don't forget to phone publisher.

Don't forget to buy food.

He wrote the notes with different coloured pens, so as to make them easier to remember. One in blue, another in red. When he looked in the mirror, he saw cancer. His lungs hurt. And his handwriting was getting worse and worse.

A bad dream broke through his artificially induced sleep, forced its way up and up through the layers of stone, and roared like a gale across the surface. We should *not* have moved Bett into town! She should have stayed in the country. It had been a crazy idea. Why couldn't she have died in her own house?

When he was younger, he had studied with great interest the photographs of concentration camps in some of the books that Simon had brought back from Poland.
　　He had always felt somehow attracted by the stony, dignified beauty on the victims' faces.
　　But this — this was something different.
　　What did all those photographs mean when set against the reality of what he had seen — her, lying there.

When a child has flown, even once, in an aeroplane, then it knows what it's like. It has got used to it.
　　When a woman has given birth, she knows what it's like.
　　When your parents have died... then you know what that's like, too.

He was to start again at the university in September. He spent the days preparing for his course. He had to stock up on the literature of Yugoslavia's minority cultures. Ordered a number of books.

Gave Lajla the flying case — the black leather case in its velvet cover. About which Bett had said:
　　"Remember, it must never go flying."
　　He always ignored conditions attached to gifts.

Perhaps he should have done everything that his mother had wanted. Encapsulated Bett and himself. Not consulted anyone else. Not listened to other people...

An official looking letter came. He used the handle of a spoon to open it. It was from the Bispebjerg Churchyard and Crematorium. He read it to himself:

> We wish to inform you that the placing of the ashes in the common grave at the above churchyard has now taken place, as requested.

He suggested to the boys that the bed she had used should be taken away.
But Jacob and Zigzag wouldn't hear of it.
Her bed was to be kept.
So he let it stay and did nothing for the time being.

The smell in the house also began to fade. He would not have to scrape off the wallpaper as he had feared, or scrub the woodwork and the floors, or soak the walls with a strong chemical solution to remove the dreadful smell of liver cancer.
None of that was necessary. The house now smelt of children's sleep and feet and breath, all mixed in with the smell of food. A rather greasy, sweetish and quite ordinary smell.
But the dishwasher had begun to make a strange noise. As if someone were throttling a chicken.

He opened his younger son's contact-book:

> Zigzag has recently been some trouble in class. He finds it difficult to get into his work. Once he has started, he finds it hard to maintain his interest. His reading has also become less confident. If he is the same at home, perhaps we should discuss the matter.

Mette and Simon came to the house in Marstrand Street the same day that he started teaching. Together they went through Bett's letters. Those to be kept were put in one heap. Bills and papers to do with Forest House went into another.
They opened her little basketwork case and found the small boxes contaning the coral necklace, the medallion, the little Indian red bean with the tiny elephants inside it. They put things in envelopes and wrote various friends' names on the outside.
"I feel as if I've got a vice clamped round my head," Mette complained. "A kind of nausea. Maybe it's stress. It's been going

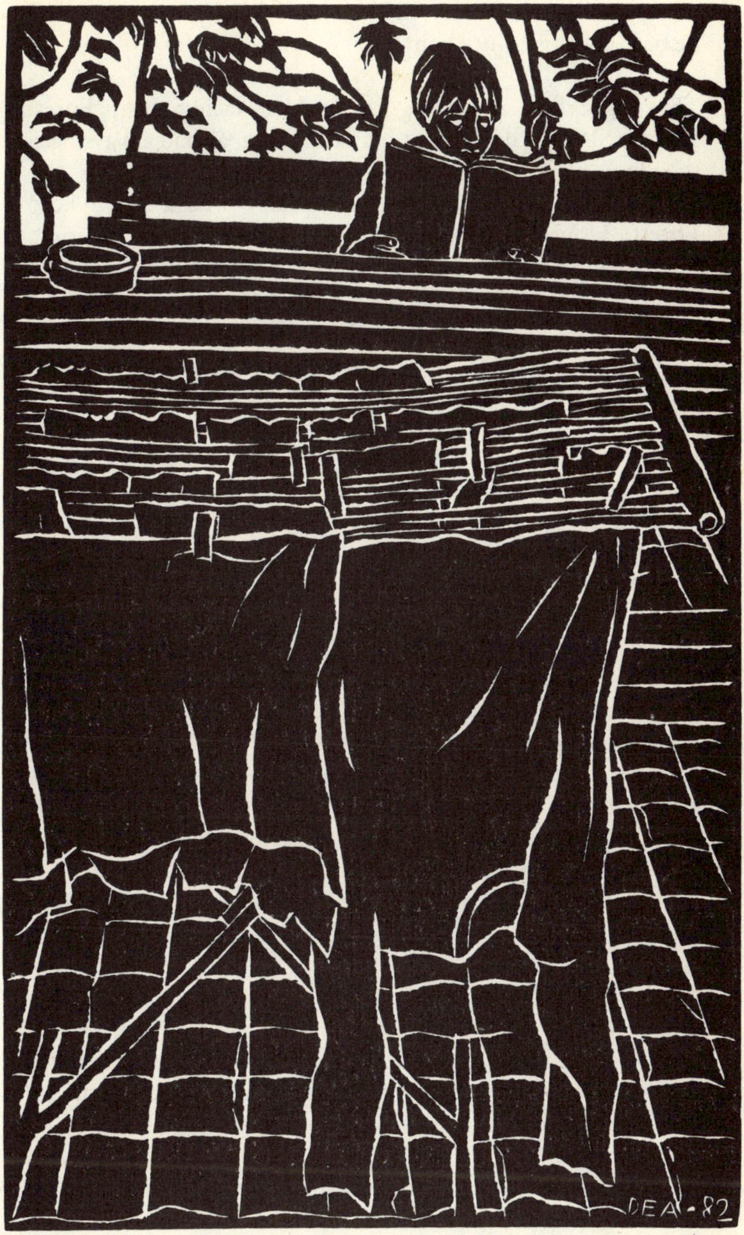
DEA - 82

on for the last two weeks. All I can think about is how long it will be before Hans comes home."

They embarked on the biggest problem facing them: Forest House. Should they keep it between them, as had always been the idea?

Their accountant had calculated what it would cost to keep Forest House. Including paying the mortgage, heating, telephone and maintenance, it came to thirty-five thousand kroner a year.

"How are we going to do it? Share it, or what?" said Simon. "You know I don't earn very much."

Mette frowned.

"Yes, let's share it."

"I don't think I can handle it," said Niels Peter. "I couldn't cope with an arrangement like that. I need to be free."

"But we promised Bett that we'd keep it together," whispered Mette.

Niels Peter glanced from his sister to his brother.

"Instead of having a summer house, I'd much rather travel with Isia and the boys. So I think I'm going to back out."

Simon looked alarmed.

"I can't do without my studio," he said. "Couldn't we rent the house out?"

"Who would maintain it and run it, just from the administrative point of view?"

If Niels Peter backed out, would Mette and Simon then take over the house? Or just one of them? In which case, who?

"I simply can't afford to, Mette," said Simon. "It'll have to be you and Hans."

"We've been talking about it half the night," said Mette. "Hans and I. We've gone through all the possibilities. We know we can't take on any more work. Not now, with Hans writing his thesis. And anyway, we don't even know if we'll be able to get extra work. Times have changed."

"You mean?"

"That we've come to the conclusion, Hans and I, that we can't do it."

"What shall we do, then?" said Simon, uneasily.

"We can sell it. The accountant thinks we could get about nine hundred thousand for it. Of which half is mortgaged."

"What does that mean that we'd each get out of it?" asked Simon.

"The accountant says about thirteen thousand a year for each of us — that's in investment bonds. It's worth considering."

"But is that *all* we inherit from Bett?" exclaimed Simon incredulously.

"Your inheritance is here," said Niels Peter angrily, pointing to his forehead.

"But I don't want your capitalist investment bonds," Simon shouted. "I'd sell mine."

"All right, you can do that," said Mette. "But you'll get very little for them."

"And is there any cash?"

"It'll probably all go on legal expenses," said Niels Peter.

"What would you spend the money on if there were some?" said Simon.

"I'd buy the *Dictionary of the Danish Language*," said Niels Peter. "All twenty-seven volumes."

"What about the children?" said Mette, crying. "It's awful for them not to have this house."

But what were they going to sell?
The house or their freedom?
The house was now dead, after all.

His grant would run out in December.

No job waiting for him. He had been educated for unemployment. Unless he found himself a sideline.

He started thinking about applying to have his grant extended for another six months. Or applying for a temporary teaching job. He would have to talk to Isia about it.

At nine the next morning, a sour-faced electrician came to see to the dishwasher.

The man was irritable because he had been troubled for no good reason. Just drained the machine. A bill for 350 kroner.

Wind. Sudden violent winds, swirling the yellow leaves and pieces of plastic up off the pavement. Bicycles fell over with a clatter. Salt and cold whirled in over the city from the sea. The chestnut trees dropped their fruit, the dull white shells lying gaping.

If you walked under the trees you might be lucky enough to find them. Great shiny mahogany-coloured chestnuts. Heavy. Dense. Good to have some in your pocket.

Schoolchildren collected them in the daytime, adults at night.

Autumn equinox. The vines grew green, yellow and flame-red right up the side of the house.

Gradually he had stopped listening to religious services and had reverted to listening to whatever was on the radio.

The boy slipped his contact-book on to the table:

> Zigzag has found it very difficult to behave himself today, especially before lessons began. He wouldn't come in when I rang the bell. He also fooled about a lot during the fluoride session with the dentist.

Niels Peter talked to Isia about Zigzag and they agreed that he needed more attention. They would also have to go through his homework with him every day.

"I'll help with that," said Isia. "I'd like to."

After dinner, Niels Peter lay on the sofa with his head on Isia's lap.

The boys sat on the floor watching television. They would soon learn about torture in Turkey, the war in El Salvador and the free trade-union movement in Poland.

Isia stroked his hair.

"I'd really like to be fit and healthy and live for a long time," he whispered.

"You are," said Isia. "You will."

He was sitting with his uncle Viggo at a chilly outdoor café underneath the green and brown leaves of the chestnut trees.

Suddenly he imagined seeing Bett in amongst a group of

people. Niels Peter saw himself going straight over to the group and up to his mother. Her face lit up. She was pleased and about to throw her arms round him. Then the vision dissolved.

Viggo was offering to help financially with Forest House.

Maybe they could set up a trust or some kind of housing association?

Niels Peter wouldn't hear of it. He dismissed the thought, on behalf of his brother and sister as well, without feeling the need to consult them.

He cycled home, with a feeling that he was not getting anywhere. The cars were going too slowly.

Everything was coming to a full stop. Even his heart-beat.

In Sølv Street the wind is always against you. An amazing phenomenon. He wondered whether the headwind in Sølv Street had anything to do with the street's architecture.

His bicycle tyres left dark tracks, winding in and out.

His thoughts turned to one dark winter's morning in a snowstorm. It must have been at the end of the war. Bett was cycling along with Mette in a basket on the handlebars and he was on a child's saddle behind her. They were on their way to day-nursery or kindergarten, whatever it was. He couldn't remember. Only... that his mother was crying as she cycled.

The same dream came back to him again. One morning he was sitting on the steps of Forest House, listening to the children's voices coming from various parts of the garden. Bett was busy in the living-room. Then there was that sound of sunshine, that satisfying, dense sound of the sun in May. The day had only just started. Expansive. Brilliant.

He couldn't detach his emotions from that house.

He had never expected it would be so hard.

He tried to explain it to Isia.

"Perhaps it's not Forest House itself that you're so anxious to be rid of," she exclaimed, as if it had only just occurred to her. "It's more likely to be your mother. You haven't allowed yourself to feel — or express — any loss over Bett's death. You've blocked it out completely, Niels Peter."

"I've blocked it out?"
"Yes, surely you must realize that now."
"I don't want to be so dependent on others, though."
"But you are."

Isia had begun to look after him and the children to a much greater extent than before. She often did the shopping, cleared up and helped them with their clothes, although she didn't actually live there.

But then there was that extra little room next to the children's, the room which had first been Karin's, then Bett's.

But it would be far too small. Perhaps they could switch rooms?

At the same time, he began to wonder, uneasily, whether Isia wasn't taking Bett's place.

No one could take Bett's place. That was inconceivable.

He had had one mother. That was enough.

It also worried him that, as he saw it, Isia somehow had such a poor relationship with her own mother.

His life was slipping into a new phase.
 A liberating phase.
 He couldn't tie himself down again.
 He daren't, anyway.
 Instead, he threw himself into his work.
 Love passes — work endures.

It was the beginning of October, the day that *Death and the Dervish* was to be published.
 Niels Peter was very nervous.
 The book was reviewed in one newspaper, and Niels Peter's translation was highly praised.
 And Simon's jacket design was used to illustrate the review.
 Niels Peter bought two more copies of the paper, translated the review into Serbo-Croat and posted it, together with the cutting, to Mesa Selimović.
 He slipped the other cutting in through Ditlev's letter-box.
 Half an hour later Ditlev came down with a bottle of schnapps.
 His publisher phoned and congratulated him.
 They had a new piece of work for him.
 Even he had to admit that he really was *quite* pleased.

He felt quite proud when he saw the novel, fat and crisp, in a bookshop window. I translated that, he thought. And my brother did the jacket, and it's excellent.

Isia made beetroot soup that evening.
 "Do you know why ducks have green heads?" Zigzag asked.
 "No."
 "Because they eat school dinners."
 In the middle of their meal, Niels Peter plucked up his courage and came straight out with it.
 "You know that we've been talking about how Forest House is a very large and difficult place to keep up as a summer house, don't you?" he said. "Well, it turns out that neither Mette nor Simon nor I can cope with it."
 Jacob put down his spoon.
 "So... ?" he said in a firm voice.

"So we'll have to sell it."

"Oh, no, no... "

Without a sound, Jacob hid his face in his hands.

Zigzag started crying, then sobbing, weeping at the end of the table, tears dripping into his beetroot soup.

"That's what life's like," said Niels Peter, bowing his head. "People buy houses. Then they have to sell them. That's what it's like."

"Won't we ever see Forest House again?"

"Yes, we're going to spend the autumn holiday clearing up."

He had a sudden vision of the boys walking along the little avenue of birches at Forest House.

Turning out of the avenue and leaving it behind them.

That is how the avenues of childhood disappear for us all.

At that moment, they disappeared for his two children.

Saturday evening — the last evening of the autumn holiday, everything packed and ready. They had achieved what they had set out to do.

Tomorrow they go back into town.

They are lying on the big bed or sitting on the coconut matting in front of the fire.

"'Why can't we keep Forest House?" asks Zigzag.

"Can't we stay here?" adds Jacob.

"What would you do about school?"

"There's one in Lindebjerg."

"What about friends?" says Niels Peter. "No one lives around here."

"Can't you have the house, then, Elin?"

"But I've got my own apartment in town."

The children try to be reasonable, try to understand.

They understand nearly everything.

"It's strange," says Hans. "A few days ago I had a film developed from last summer. There are lots of good photographs of Bett."

Milla looked at her mother.

"Where's the little rope-ladder that was in the tree?" she says.

Mette frowns.

"We've taken it down."

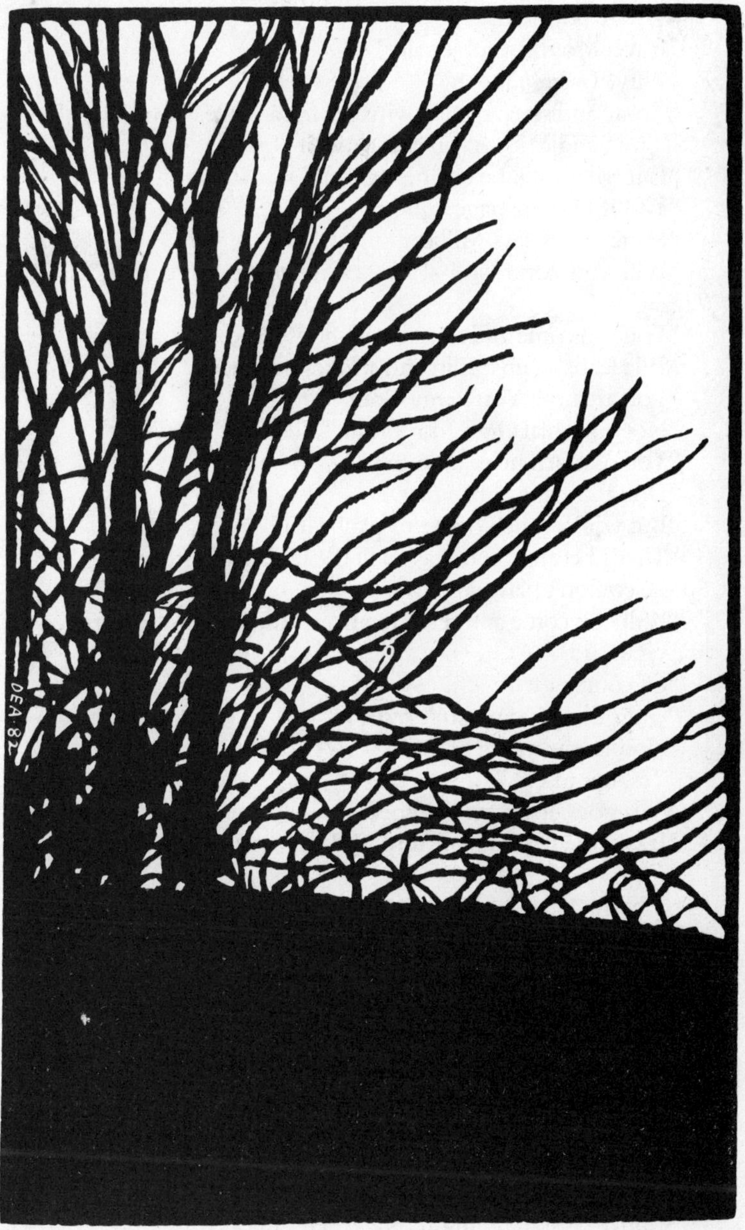
DEA·82

"Where is it then?"

"It went to the jumble sale."

"Why? I wanted that."

"Come and sit over here with me for a while," says Elin.

Zigzag and Milla sit on each side of her.

"Is it true you'll be our new Gran?" says Zigzag.

"Yes, if I can manage."

"Mine, too?" says Milla.

"Will you come and sleep at our house sometimes," said Zigzag.

"You can come and sleep at my house, too."

Milla leans against Elin and strokes her cheek.

"You are nice. You're my Gran."

"Not your real Gran," says Elin. "That was Bett."

"You're much nicer than Bett."

"Don't say things like that."

"But you're much better to play with."

"That's because Bett was so ill the last six months of her life. So she couldn't play with you."

"Will you come and fetch me from kindergarten sometimes, like Gran did?"

"Of course I will."

"Gran Elin, you mustn't *ever* die."

"Not for the moment, no, I won't do that."

"Yes, because... "

Milla goes down on her knees.

"If you die," she says firmly, "I'll cut your head off."

"You know what," Simon mutters. "I went and burnt my best pictures."

"You can say that again," says Mette drily.

"Why did you do it, anyway?" asks Hans.

"I burnt the pictures I wasn't sure about." says Simon. "And kept the others..." Then he added. "But I'm going to miss them, I already do... "

An owl had begun to hoot. Another owl answered in the distance.

Shortly before midnight, Niels Peter phoned Isia:

"Did I wake you?"
"No, I knew you'd phone."
"I don't know what to do. I feel lost."
"Do you miss me?"
Silence.
"Yes."
"When are you coming back to town?"
"We're leaving tomorrow afternoon — by train."
"Wouldn't you rather I fetched you in the car?"
"Would you? Really?"

SUNDAY 26 OCTOBER

Niels Peter wakes in the attic room, and it suddenly becomes quite clear to him: I tried to save her while there was time.

I saw the way that things were going two years ago.

Tried to get her to accept treatment. Tried to spare her, take the burden off her and manage the finances.

But she wouldn't go into hospital in Copenhagen. Only to the small regional hospital. She refused to have an operation. She wanted to manage the whole thing on her own.

She rejected all offers of help — until the moment the diagnosis was made. Then she agreed to whatever was offered.

On the way, we gave up and thought, well, things will have to take their course. We must support her in the choices that she makes — come what may. But we weren't able to. It was impossible to fulfil all her wishes. She expected too much.

It has taken Niels Peter quite a time to come to the realization that it wasn't he who killed his mother.

With a great effort, he will once again find the love that he once felt for her, the love he has felt all his life — but which seemed to have left him during these nine months.

Step by step he will learn to regain her.

He finds himself thinking over and over again about the way that everything can turn into its opposite:

How love can become hatred.

And again become love.

And beauty can become horror.

And again beauty.

A huge removal van, as large as a railway engine, makes its way through the willows and along the birch avenue.

Stops in the yard. It is midday.

Two broad-shouldered men in leather aprons start carrying the packing-cases and the larger pieces of furniture out of the house and the barn. They pack them into the van, carefully and systematically. Their cargo is to be delivered to various places in Copenhagen, so the things that are to be delivered last are packed furthest to the front of the van, and those to be delivered first are packed to the rear.

It is soon done. An hour and a half later, the men jump into the cab, reverse the truck round and drive off up the avenue.

Mette and Elin sweep up and wipe the remaining work-surfaces. They have left a couple of bowls on the window-sills, and two of Simon's drawings are still pinned to the wall. So that it doesn't all seem too cold and empty.

"Can I have the ruler that's in the outhouse?" says Jacob.
"Yes."

"And me?" Milla blinks and points at Bett's sewing-box which is still sitting on a shelf.

"Of course you can."

Zigzag comes in dragging a heavy hammer: "This is Thor's hammer. I want to take it home."

A few hours later, there are several cars parked under the hazel trees. The solicitor — a friend of Hans's. The estate agent. And Isia.

The children have disappeared down into the woods, to their hideout.

The adults walk round and look at the house. They go from the main house to the barn, then on to the studio.

"Well, I suppose it would really be best suited to a collective of some kind, wouldn't it?" says the estate agent.

"Yes, that's what we were thinking."

"Or maybe somebody who wants to set up an organic market garden."

"Yes. Or a married couple with two high incomes."

"What's the access like in winter?" the agent asks, a little while later.

"We-ell," says Mette, looking to her brothers to help her out.

The house usually gets snowed in. Many a time they've had to go up and down the hill with a sledge to get their groceries.

"Not ideal," says Niels Peter.

They walk round the grounds. They see the woods, the

distant blue hills — disappearing one behind the other as if in a Brueghel painting. They see the fields and the fjord, in the distance, twinkling.

"It's an unusually lovely spot," says the solicitor.

It's a terrible thing that they're putting Forest House up for sale. The three of them feel as if somehow they're selling their mother's body.

They have afternoon tea sitting on the white garden benches by the lake, from where the house looks its most beautiful.

"Autumn and winter are not the best times for putting houses up for sale," says the solicitor.

"No, and it's a buyer's market, don't forget that," adds the estate agent. "After the oil crisis, everyone wants to get rid of big houses."

"And lots of people end up having to auction them off," says Niels Peter.

"Should we reckon on it taking many months?" says Mette.

"Yes."

"We'll soon have a credit account," says the solicitor. "That can cover expenses until the house is sold. Who will stand surety for that?"

"I can," says Hans.

"So can I," says Niels Peter.

"Good. Well, best of luck with the book," says the solicitor. "It's had some fine reviews. Can you make a living from translating?"

"No," said Niels Peter. "You need something else."

"What sort of money will you be wanting for the house?" asks the estate agent.

"A million," says Simon jauntily, his silver tooth flashing.

"You'd never get it," says the agent.

"Nine hundred and fifty thousand, then," says Mette, as a concession.

The agent pulls out his lighter and lights a cigarette.

"I wouldn't count on it. How much are you asking as a deposit, by the way?"

"Fifty thousand," Niels Peter suggests.

"If we say forty-five thousand, it'll be easier," says the estate agent. "It doesn't sound so much."

The estate agent was given the keys of the house. He went to his car and drove off.

They stood talking to the solicitor for a while; then he too left.

Mette and Elin swept the yard.

"I'm done for," Niels Peter sighed.

"Well, look on the bright side. We've got a good solicitor," said Hans. "And it's in the estate agent's interest to get as much as he can for the house..."

Simon blinked.

"Now *there's* a good, steady job!"

Isia and Niels Peter went hand-in-hand down to the woods to fetch the children. Stopping now and then to kiss.

The mist lay on the grass and was creeping in under the trees, lying there like a reminder of something.

Niels Peter stood still, closed his eyes and tried to sense whether Bett's presence was still there...

He got no response. Rather, it felt as if she were *not* there.

"Do you know what I dreamt last night," he said to Isia. "I dreamt they were making apartments inside the dome of the Marble Church. The place was being fitted with floors from top to bottom. The apartments were almost triangular — with slightly curved outer walls, and big windows facing out on to the harbour and the Inner City and Langeline Quay. They were quite modern and comfortable."

"Yes?"

"And I wanted the best one of all."

He threw his arms around her.

At that moment, the children appeared from their hideout.

"Hi, Dad."

"Hi, Isia."

"Would you put your shoes on, please, Zigzag. We're going now."

"These are the worst wretched left-wing shoes in the world," complained Zigzag.

"What's so left-wing about them?"

"Their stupid laces."

The boy was sitting on the steps of Forest House wrestling with his shoe-laces, and crying.

Golden clouds.

Walking out slowly on to the grass.

Mette and Hans took Elin with them; she sat in the back seat of the car with her arm round Milla.

Niels Peter sat in the front of Isia's car, with Simon in the back, sandwiched between Jacob and Zigzag.

A variety of last-minute things were packed in the boot — a number of carrier bags, hangers from the porch, a pair of rubber boots, a mirror...

The sun was slanting right through the house — that was the last thing they saw as they left.

They drove through the birch avenue. A red ribbon of fire lay on the horizon and above it the sky was green. Then blue. Getting darker and darker.

Up over the point. The view across the water. The fjord.

Bushes like witches' brooms against the sky. Everything standing out like paper silhouettes.

Stillness. For the last time... that stillness given off by the blue-black earth.

Then someone out shooting, their neighbour, fired a shot.

After that, streaming, flashing lights on the main road.

A roar.

It was Sunday evening.

The autumn holiday was over and everyone was on their way home.

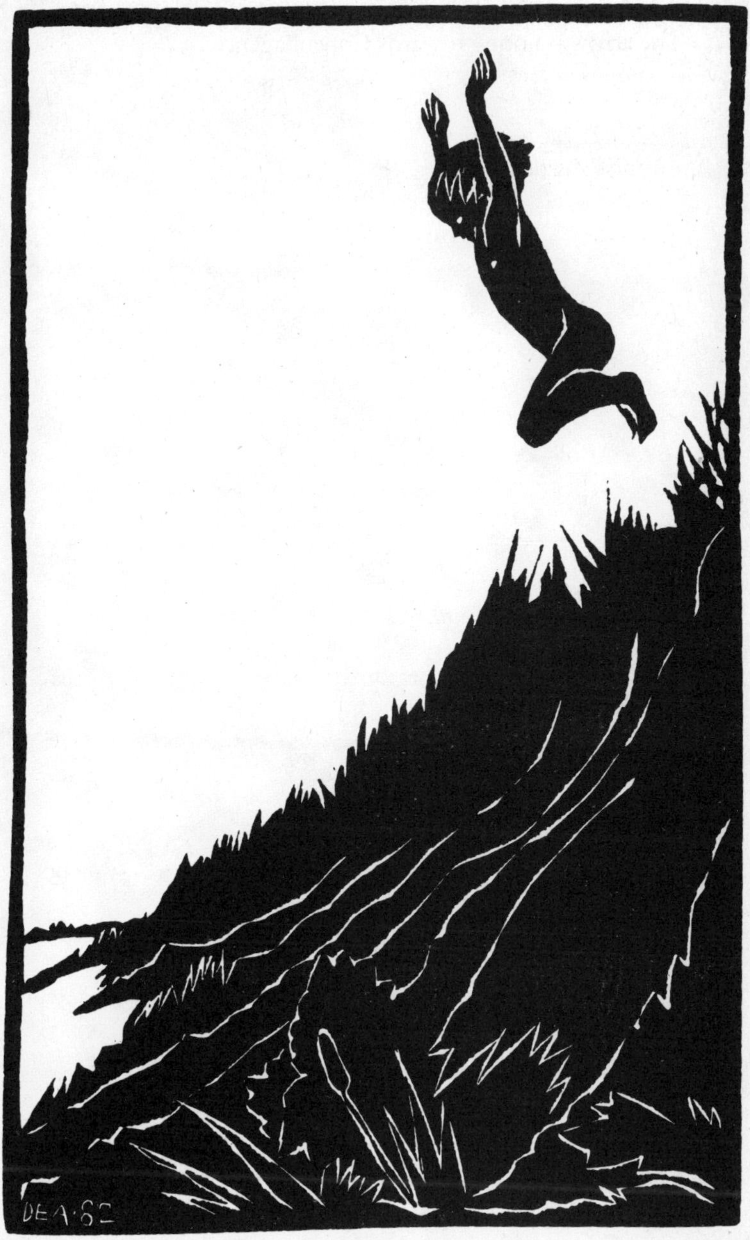
DEA·62

Road signs in the dark.
The arrow pointing towards Copenhagen.

I owe many thanks to friends, members of my family and my publishers. Countless long conversations with them have helped me in understanding and describing the difficult themes of this book.

Dea.

OTHER TITLES
· FROM ·
SERPENT'S TAIL

FICTION

JOHN AGARD *Mangoes and Bullets*
JORGE AMADO *Dona Flor and Her Two Husbands*
DAVID BRADLEY *The Chaneysville Incident*
MICHEL DEL CASTILLO *The Disinherited*
ANDREE CHEDID *From Sleep Unbound*
ANDREE CHEDID *The Sixth Day*
ILYA EHRENBURG *Life of the Automobile*
WAGUIH GHALI *Beer in the Snooker Club*
WILLIAM GOYEN *Had I a Hundred Mouths*
OSCAR HIJUELOS *Our House in the Last World*
LANGSTON HUGHES *Selected Poems*
CHARLES JOHNSON *The Sorcerer's Apprentice*
ISMAIL KADARE *Chronicle in Stone*
CLAUDE MCKAY *Banana Bottom*
DEA TRIER MØRCH *Winter's Child*
DEA TRIER MØRCH *Evening Star*
DANIEL MOYANO *The Devil's Trill*
KENZABURO OE *A Silent Cry*
J. J. PHILLIPS *Mojo Hand*

NON FICTION

IAN BREAKWELL *Ian Breakwell's Diary*
NOAM CHOMSKY *The Chomsky Reader*
LANGSTON HUGHES *The Big Sea*
CLAUDE MCKAY *A Long Way From Home*
KLAUS MANN *The Turning Point*
TOM WAKEFIELD *Forties' Child*

M A S K S

NEIL BARTLETT *Who Was That Man?*
MICHAEL BRACEWELL *The Crypto-Amnesia Club*
IAN BREAKWELL *The Artist's Dream*
LESLIE DICK *Without Falling*
JUAN GOYTISOLO *Landscapes After the Battle*
LUISA VALENZUELA *The Lizard's Tail*

· Winter's Child ·
Dea Trier Mørch

Set in the maternity ward of a Copenhagen hospital, *Winter's Child* chronicles the elation and despair of eighteen women who each face a 'difficult' childbirth.

'You can almost smell the heavy perfume of birth, a mixture of blood and sweet milk. Evocative and powerful writing, it rings true to women's experience.' **SHEILA KITZINGER**

'communicates the very scent of birth' **VERNE MOBERG**

'simply wonderful' **CITY LIMITS**

'How I wish that *Winter's Child* had been written (when I was pregnant) . . . I came away from this book with a clearer perception of my own experience.' **WOMEN'S REVIEW**

Illustrated by the author
272 pages   £4.95 (paper)